To Jefry Singer
C.A. Soto Aguirre

The Guitar Maker

An Exploration of Wisdom Design and Love

C.A. SOTO AGUIRRE

Kavyata books are available at special quantity discounts for bulk purchases for educational, fund raising, premiums, or sales promotions use. Special books, book covers, or book excerpts, can also be created to fit specific needs. For details contact us via the Internet at www.kavyata.com, via email: customerservice@kavyata.com, or via postal mail to: Kavyata Publishing, P.O. Box 7270, Ann Arbor, Michigan 48107, USA.

ISBN-10: 0-9749391-5-3
ISBN-13: 978-9749391-5-5

The Guitar Maker

An Exploration of
Wisdom, Design and Love

C.A. SOTO AGUIRRE

Kavyata

Kavyata Publishing
Ann Arbor, Michigan

www.TheGuitarMakerExploration.com

ISBN-10: 0-9749391-5-3
ISBN-13: 978-9749391-5-5

First Edition, October 2005.
Library of Congress Control Number: 2005904176

Publisher's Cataloging-in-Publication Data:

Aguirre, C.A. Soto
The guitar maker : an exploration of wisdom, design and love / C. A. Soto Aguirre.
p. cm.
ISBN-10: 0-9749391-5-3
ISBN-13: 978-9749391-5-5
1. Guitar–Construction–Fiction. 2. Design–Philosophy–Fiction. 3. Multidisciplinary design optimization–Fiction. 4. Love–Fiction. 5. Self-actualization (Psychology)–Fiction. 6. Conduct of life–Fiction. I. Title.

PS3551.G9 G85 2005
813.4   2005904176

Kavyata Publishing is an imprint of Kavyata Group, LLC. Ann Arbor, Michigan.
www.Kavyata.com

For my family
and
all who dream a better world
C.A.S.A.

Preface

The first few pages of this novel were born in the beautiful city of Copenhagen in January of 2002. It was there, during the long Danish winter nights, with my wife and two children, in the old cozy house of Jonna and Knud on Egetoften street in the Hellerup suburb that I stole many hours from my family and from my sleep in order to write the first chapters about quality, beauty, value, and Nature. Six months later, back in my home in the United States, with only thirty-some pages completed, I began to write the rest of this novel. It was then when I included the subjects of love, fairness and happiness to give a more realistic, and less academic, character to the novel. Put it in a single word, this novel is about living.

The ideas presented in this novel, although not original, came to me as if I had discovered them by myself, which gratified me in a way difficult to explain, but that I hope you'll understand. These ideas are the result of the interaction with great people, the experience of intense moments in my life, the visit to wonderful places in the world, the reading of great books, and the desperate search for answers to life's questions.

The first purpose of this novel was to pass my advice to my children before it was too late in their life, or too late in my own. The first title I had for this novel was then, "If I Die Before You Grow," but later I realized that it was too mournful for a title, so much so, that even my children had told me they wouldn't read the novel if I decided to use such a title. As a result, I changed it to one that is fresh in spirit and explicit in content: "The Guitar Maker: An Exploration of Wisdom, Design and Love." The intention and content remained the same, but the title was broadened for a larger audience.

I don't expect this novel to become a literature classic, especially because the reader may realize after few chapters that my native language is not English. I still remember the first essay I wrote in English —in a class I had to take because I flunked an English writing test, at age thirty. The essay was about a concept I had been maturing for years: *all problems are at the interface*. My English teacher, after reading and correcting the essay, asked me to discuss it with her. She asked: 'And how do you solve these problems?' Even though I had been tossing this idea for years, I still didn't have a good answer. However, she encouraged me to keep writing about it until I had an answer that satisfied my expectations. Now, it is satisfying for me to see the result of that small conversation that took no more than two minutes, but took more than a decade to crystallize. My English is still quite plain, but I hope this will be a benefit for the reader who will be able to concentrate in the concepts presented here rather than in the meaning of fancy words or in the flow of a rhythmic prose.

The Guitar Maker is the fictional story of a regular person, with the same problems that we all have; with the same questions we all ask; with the same pains we all encounter in life; and with the same big challenge we all face: *we learn as we go*. There is no *'rewind'* button that allows us to repeat the same moment in time with the gained experience. However, it is better to think about this as an advantage, rather than as a problem. From thousands of years our DNA has stored precious improvements made by us, but Nature has been clever enough not to store our memories in it. This would have been the worst design mistake of all. I am glad we all start from a *clean sheet of paper* where we write on our lives, day by day, experience by experience.

Life is full of surprises, some of them painful, but most of them joyful. The ones I enjoy the most are those that come with challenging questions; questions that we've never heard before, but that we have or need to answer sooner or later. This novel is about overcoming challenges in life, those that we search for, and those that show in front of us by chance. This novel was written under the premise that all problems in life occur when two entities, separate at the beginning, enter in contact and create an interface in between. It is at this interface where things happen, and where problems may appear. I use the guitar maker, Walker McBride, as the interlocutor that will expose to you such interfaces, but most importantly, he will tell you in simple words how to solve such problems in life.

One last point I want to make is about my name. I am using a pen name, very similar to my real name, but different enough to separate myself from my other identity as a writer of journal papers in the scientific research field of *optimization*. I strongly believe that trust is one of the foundations for human relations. By telling you that I am using a pen name, I hope to build my relationship with you —the reader, who will spend some time understanding my ideas— upon a foundation of trust. Thank you.

All characters are fictional, with the exception of some worldly known personalities that are mentioned in the novel. The same statement applies to places and scenes.

C.A. Soto Aguirre
Ann Arbor, Michigan
March 2005

Note:
Chapters named *Design I, II, III*, and *IV* talk about the engineering subject of design optimization. Readers with no interest in this subject may skip these chapters without missing the continuity of the novel.

The Guitar Maker

An Exploration of
Wisdom, Design, and Love

C.A. SOTO AGUIRRE

From Chelsea to Sigüenza

ALL PROBLEMS ARE AT THE INTERFACE; EACH ONE OF THEM HAS A SOLUTION.

That's what my dad used to say when we had a conflict, or when something went wrong in our house. I never understood what he meant until I was an adult, married, with children. I don't know why I am thinking about this now; it must be the boredom. I am in the Metropolitan airport waiting for my flight to Madrid, delayed two hours already. It is the middle of a very hot summer, and the airport is crowded, noisy and humid as never before. There are some who wander around to kill time, and there are others who look busy, but are probably wandering as well, in their minds. I am glad I decided to keep this book in my carry-on luggage, so I can read it while I wait. I've read this book before and learned a lot from it, but I need it again for the trip to Spain. It is about guitarmaking, my hobby and passion. Actually, it is more than that; it is my business and my profession. Many years ago I took a short course on guitarmaking in Boston, and since then, but not before going through many difficulties, I've been running my own business: a small guitarmaking shop in Chelsea, a town in south-east Michigan.

More people are arriving and the room is becoming hotter and noisier. It is always interesting to see how people say goodbye at airports. Each goodbye is the rupture of a link, the modification of a relationship. A young couple far away, on the other side of the room, is going through that situation. She is leaving, but he is staying. She is crying, but he is not. They are living the same moment in time and space, but under totally different perspectives. What makes the difference is that they are going to pull the link that connects them. Their connecting feeling at the mental and physical interface is going to be altered. This alteration produces pain, and the pain becomes the problem.

My dad's theory was that any problem could be interpreted as an alteration, a change, or a rupture at the interface of any two entities sharing or trying to share something. However, I was frustrated with his theory because he never provided a solution to such problems, even though he always said that all problems had at least one solution. Now that he is gone, I guess it is my duty to finish his inconclusive theory, but it is a difficult task for me. Twenty years have passed since his death, and I've only figured out that when the problem is between two people, a simple solution is to use empathy and compassion towards the other person. It always works. Sincere and profound empathy, the one a mother has for her child, is what it takes to resolve a conflict between two people. When one is empathetic and compassionate, one wears the shoes of the other person, lives his experience, and understands the issues from another point of view.

As I was saying, I make guitars for a living. I am good at it, and sell enough of them to support my family. However, there is something I want to improve; something I could not learn in Boston that I can't explain even to myself. That is why I am going to Spain. I want to spend some time with one of the finest luthiers of classical acoustic guitars. Once there, I hope to discover and fix the problem. It may sound stupid that I can't even understand the problem myself, but that doesn't surprise me. Many people live their entire lives without knowing if something is wrong with them.

I put my suitcase on a table and sit in the waiting room until it is time to board. Everybody stares at me when I handle any kind of weight. Idiots! I simply ignore them; I have learned how to deal with them throughout the years. This is how I am since the day of the accident, that's it. Yes, that's it.

Once I comfortably sit, two pretty women pass by in front of me. I fake reading my book to show indifference, as I watch their well-cared-for feet with sexy red nails, and their tight skirts wrapping their bodies, elegantly and gracefully displayed, with a subliminal message screaming 'look at us' that few women can convey. After they pass, but not before I notice how all men around me were turning their heads towards the pair, I put my book on my lap and see this tall and old guy sitting across from me. He looks at my book with curiosity. I sense his inclination to start a conversation.

"Guitarmaking?" He asks with interest as he grabs his glasses to make sure he can read the cover. "I didn't know we manufacture guitars in Michigan," he says jokingly. "I used to work in manufacturing too, but in a big scale manufacturing company."

The guy is graceful when he talks, and exudes feelings of serenity and wisdom. "What did you make?" I ask quickly while I put my book away and lean towards him.

"Well, I worked in a car company. I didn't make anything by myself, I was a link of the whole chain, but I knew the process very well because I worked for them for 14 years."

"Oh, I see," I respond. His shirt pocket, full of pens and pencils, gives away his profession. "Are you an engineer?"

He takes a look at the wall clock and says, "I used to be."

"Not anymore? Why?"

"I quit after those 14 years, in 1995. I got tired of all that, became a consultant, made even more money, traveled around the world, and here I am, on my summer trip to Denmark."

I realized this man is someone special. His attire is simple, humble, clean and fresh, far from the typical Midwestern style. He wears khaki pants, a white shirt and those small John Lennon type glasses; he's tall, slim and baldheaded. He doesn't use any finger ring, or a watch in his wrist. He's in his late sixties, and an African descendant for sure. I feel intrigued and want to know more about him.

"What do you do in Denmark?" I ask with an eager voice.

He looks at me, ponders my question for a few seconds, and responds, "I go to a small town called Ribe to visit an old friend of mine, Ole Rasmussen. We have been visiting each other for the last 10 years, each summer. Sometimes I go, sometimes he comes. It's a short visit of a couple of weeks. We simply talk about anything that comes to our minds: engineering, philosophy, art, moral values, and of course, about optimization, which pretty much ties all these together."

"My name is Walker, by the way," I interrupt.

He extends his arm, shakes my hand. "Kwame, *born on Saturday*."

"What? What did you say?" I reply.

"Kwame means *born on Saturday*," he explains. "You know, my ancestors are from Africa, so, as with many African names, it has a meaning."

I nod. By looking at his boarding ticket, I notice that he is taking the same flight that I am. This makes me curious, and I ask him why is he going to Spain. He rests back on the chair and explains to me that his flight stops in Madrid, then continues to Amsterdam where he'll change to another airplane to finally get to Copenhagen. He takes a second look at the wall clock and says, "I need to make a call, would you excuse me?"

As he walks away, I think about him. I should find a way to get in contact with him while I am in Europe. I have the feeling that he may help me with my guitars too. But there is a problem; I have to be in Spain for the first eight days taking this intensive workshop on guitarmaking. I planned this trip for two years, and I won't change it for anything in my life now.

I reach for my pad and try to remember the name of the Danish town he mentioned. How do I write that? Reeby? Rybee? Damn! These Danish names are always difficult to spell. Well, at least I know his friend's name, Oly Rasmussen ... I think. I glance up and see him coming back. I put my pad inside the suitcase and wait for him.

"Hi, I'm back. I had to call my wife. She isn't well. She had a heart operation a year ago and she is still recovering from it. My daughter, Alice, is taking care of her while I am away." He pauses for a while as he looks vaguely to the floor perhaps thinking about his wife.

I interrupt the silence to maintain the conversation. "I hope she recovers soon," and I pause for a moment. "I know what it feels like to have a sick person in the family. Some years ago, my daughter, Christina, was diagnosed with leukemia. It was terrible news for my wife and me, not to mention to my younger son, Gabriel, who didn't speak for weeks after he learned about it. We were devastated for a period of two weeks until we received a call from the hospital one afternoon. It had been a mistake in the laboratory results. Someone else's results were given to my daughter, and she actually hadn't had any illness at all."

"What a relief," Kwame sighs.

"Yes, it was," I continue. "But, you know, from bad news something good always comes out. I promised to myself to take care of my children the best I can, day by day, forever. That is what I've been doing ever since.

Kwame smiles. "Thank you for your story; it gives me encouragement."

I change the subject and say, "This friend of yours in Denmark is really special I suppose."

"Yes, he is amazing. When we talk, we talk! It's as if he knows how to get the best out of me, and at the same time, I get the best out of him. It's definitely a mental exercise for both of us." He smiles with a thoughtful expression as if his friend were next to him.

"Did I tell you I was going to Madrid?" I ask. "It is a business trip. Actually, it is more like a training for me. I want to learn some new tricks from one of the great luthiers in Spain. When I come back, I hope to be able to design and make better guitars."

"Oh, that means you have your own business."

"Yes, I do. It's a small acoustic guitar shop with one employee, my apprentice, Manuel, who is becoming quite a fine luthier. I am responsible for the design and construction of the guitars, plus running the business."

"And what kind of guitars do you make? Are they country music guitars, or those guitars that they use in classical concerts?"

"I make both, but I prefer making the classical acoustic guitars. They require more skill and precision to satisfy the more demanding client, the professional guitar soloist of chamber music." I pause to check the schedule board, but the flight is still delayed. "And do you still do consulting? What kind of consulting is it?"

He laughs. "I am an old retired engineer my friend. I don't do it very often now. But what problem can I solve for you, if any?"

What a nice opportunity he is giving me! "Well, I am going to be honest with you. My guitars are not selling well. My clients are not satisfied with the final product, not because of the quality, which I personally make sure is the best, but they say my guitars are not at the level of those built in Spain. I think that the problem has to do, in my opinion, with the design, or maybe with the construction process. I have made quite a few excellent guitars, but I am not consistent and sometimes, as I said, they don't perform or sound like Spanish custom-made guitars."

"Well, if your problem is improving the design, then I think I can help you. Even if the construction process is not consistent, I may be able to help you too. You will have to teach me a lot though, because I don't know anything about guitars, my friend. Actually, I have never had one in my hands." He laughs aloud, and fixes his glasses that were about to fall.

"This is great, Kwame. I appreciate your offer. I may need it."

"However, there is a condition," he replies promptly.

I look directly at his eyes. I wonder what he may say. "What is it?"

"Well, the lessons come with a caveat. What I teach is not only design, but much more. It's the relation between design and nature, and how to create better designs to live in harmony with our environments. To me, *design* is a very big word that we use too lightly nowadays. I cannot talk, or teach about it, without explaining other subjects as well." He looks at me as if waiting for an answer.

"It sounds good to me." I say, "I have no problems in learning more. In fact, I always say we should learn something new every day."

What he doesn't know is that my concerns go beyond design as well, but I sense we both can learn from each other. Life, happiness, love, and trust are as important to me as the perfection of my guitarmaking techniques.

"Then, my friend, we are going to have a fruitful friendship," he says while doing a thumb up sign with both hands, and with a bright smile on his face.

2

Guitarmaking

THE FLIGHT ATTENDANT, A GORGEOUS WOMAN with blue eyes and thick brows, announces that they are going to start boarding. The first class passengers are called first. After a while, I hear, "Rows eleven to twenty two, please aboard." I get ready and as I pass by my new friend, put my hand on his shoulder and say: "I'll tell you everything you need to know about guitars. I'll find you inside the airplane to explain things in more detail."

He smiles, gives me an approval nod, and sits back to wait for his row number to be called. I walk to the door and hand over the boarding pass to the flight attendant; she scans it and gives it back to me. What beautiful hands she has too. "Have a nice flight. Thank you for flying with us," she says sweetly.

I walk the jet way, reach the airplane door and hear, "Good morning, welcome aboard. Good morning, welcome aboard. Good morning, welcome aboard," three times. The flight attendant greets each passenger that enters the plane. He is like a robot, with a forced frozen smile, typical in these cases. I put my suitcase inside the overhead bin and sit anxiously waiting for Kwame to pass by.

Minutes pass, but he is not coming. I pull out my suitcase, and open it. I don't know why I open it. I put it back in the overhead bin. The airplane is almost full. Maybe he is not on this plane. What I am saying? He's got to be on this plane. Finally, there he is, slowly walking down the aisle.

"Hi, Kwame."

"Hi, Walker. I don't know what happened here. People were so slow."

"You are right. I guess they are in no hurry. Tell me, what is your seat number?"

"38D. I'll talk to you later, I am holding up the line."

I sit and wait for all the formality of the take-off: seat belts on, instructions, no cigarettes, no this, no that. Minutes seem like hours. We take off and after 20 minutes the seat belt light is off. Great! '38D, 38D, 38D' I say to myself while walking to his seat straight down the left aisle of the airplane

"Kwame! Hi, I'm back."

"Hi, Walker. You look anxious. What's the matter?"

"Good morning, sir," I say to the man next to him who is already with his eyes closed, armed crossed, and immutable. He doesn't respond to my question.

"Excuse me, sir," I say louder, "I need to talk to this gentleman about something very important. Do you mind if we exchange seats?" I pause for a second to see his reaction.

He opens his left eye, glances at me, opens the other eye, and says, "If your seat is next to the window I have no problem in swapping."

"Yes, my seat is a window seat. Here is my ticket. Thank you very much."

He grabs my ticket, his pillow, his bag, and say, "Just in case the flight attendant asks, what's your name?"

"My name is Walker McBride, but they shouldn't care."

As we watch the man go to my old seat, Kwame says, "You have a problem. Did you go through all these troubles to talk to me? You must have a big problem."

"Well, who doesn't have a problem in this life? But I have the feeling that you can help me with it."

He waits patiently as I try to organize my thoughts before starting. Suddenly, the flight attendant passes next to me and offers peanuts. I don't like peanuts.

"No, thanks," I say.

"Yes, please," Kwame says, "I love peanuts." He grabs a bag, opens it, takes a couple of peanuts and says, "Well, teach me something about guitars. How do you design and build a guitar?"

"That is a short question with a long answer, but I'll try. Guitars are very complex instruments. A professional guitarist demands the highest quality in terms of sound, materials, construction and style. Now, I'll give you a very short version of the process of fabricating a custom-made guitar. These are the steps."

He seems puzzled by something, so I pause to let him talk.

"You know, all the attributes you just mentioned sound very much like the requirements for building a car, which is my area of expertise, but I notice you did not mention the price or the cost of the guitar. Why?"

"Simple, because a professional guitarist will pay anything as long as the guitar meets the quality he or she is looking for." He smiles. I feel he knows something I don't know.

"Are you sure about that? What if you ask for ten million dollars for one of your guitars? Would you find a buyer?"

He got me. "Well, ten million dollars is out of the range. Nobody pays that much for a custom-made guitar."

"Then ... *price* is important too." He insists with a convincing voice.

"Okay, you are right. Price should be considered too, but let's assume for a moment that it is not important."

"Perfect, but eventually we'll have to consider it," he insists. "Otherwise, we'll be just doing a mental exercise, not engineering."

"Well, as I was saying, the steps to build a guitar are like this: first, I select the wood. This is a step that only a well-trained luthier can do right. The direction of the wood grain, the direction of the cuts, and the kind and age of the tree the wood is cut from are the primary aspects to consider. But I also smell it, touch it, and feel it before making a decision."

He is feeling tired, I notice, but he is still alert and asks, "Is there any objective way to identify the good wood from the bad one? You know, if we want to apply any engineering method to improve your guitars, you need to have more objective ways to measure and differentiate between the good and the bad wood. If there is no metric, there is no engineering. This is the essence of my profession —the ability to measure."

"I know, I know, but it is not easy. For instance, how can we measure the smell? Also, the fact that the wood has or has not been aged should be considered. I could make a list of all the issues in the wood selection, including the selection of other materials like hardware, strings, lacquer, and the rest.

"Good," he says, "we need to have that list. Now, once you choose materials, what do you do?"

"What comes next is the construction process. I usually start with the neck of the guitar. All my guitars are made with the exact same template, that is, I make them all with the same dimensions."

"Stop it right there!" He interrupts. "Are you telling me that there is no need for a shape improvement? You went from material selection to construction without considering the objective of your design. I think you are going too fast. Let me tell you this, my friend. In guitar making, as well as in life, you need to define your objectives, your purpose, before you begin the construction. Otherwise you are going without direction."

He is right. This guy is sharp. I have to be more precise when I talk. "Well, yes, I agree. But I know the objective already. A guitar is a guitar, Kwame, and the external shape has to look like a guitar."

"Oh, yes. You sound like engineers in the manufacturing industry. They don't take risks, and repeat what works until something goes wrong."

I don't like that comment. I consider myself a fine artist and he is comparing me to engineers.

"Kwame, a classical guitar is exactly that... classical, and I can't change the world."

"Well, you are partially right. The exterior has to look like a classical guitar, but boy you have a world of freedom to make changes in the inside, don't you think?" Kwame asks.

"That is what I do every time I make a guitar. I make changes in the interior and in the construction process to accommodate new materials, innovations, and any requests from guitarists. However, I do it as I go along with the fabrication. I cannot plan the design much in advance because it depends on the material I get and on the variations I make during the construction."

"You really sound like a manufacturing engineer to me."

There he goes again. I don't like his comparisons.

He notices my discomfort and says, "Okay, I won't interrupt anymore, please continue."

"As I was telling you, I use the same external dimensions for all my guitars. I start with the neck, you know, the long slender piece of the guitar. Once the neck is done, I make the headpiece. This is the part where the strings are wound with the hardware to tension them. Next comes an important step: joining the headpiece and the neck," I explain enthusiastically.

"Now, let me tell you something my father used to say: *all problems always emerge at the interface of two things.* I have come to the conclusion that he was right. Unfortunately, he never told me how to solve interface problems."

He closes his eyes, seems to be contemplating my description, and says: "It sounds like an interesting idea, but what is the relation between your father's idea and your guitars?"

"Well, anytime I need to glue two pieces, I am creating an interface between them. The joint between the neck and the headpiece is important. It is subjected to high forces from the strings. A bad joint is a potential problem in a guitar. Just as my father used to say: *the problem is at the interface.* So, I make sure that the interface between these two pieces remains strong throughout the guitar's life. For that I use a v-type joint, a very secure and firm joint."

Kwame keeps listening with interest although his eyelids look heavier. I continue anyway. "Gluing is the essence of guitarmaking. We don't use nails but glue to fix and connect different components. Once the neck and headpiece are glued, I proceed to carve the bottom of the neck, the heel, where the neck joins the sound box. Again, this connection is carefully made since it is probably the most critical of all joints. I love to make the heel because it requires some artistic talent to make it look beautiful. The next step is to prepare the top and bottom plates for the sound box. Since I use templates they always come out the same size and shape."

Turbulence shakes the airplane violently. We, terrified, grab our chairs and look at each other with frightening eyes. The seat belt light turns on. Some children start screaming, but a few seconds later the plane finally settles and the tension and screams disappear. What a relief!

"Scary," Kwame says.

"Yes, it was. I hope it doesn't happen again."

"Don't worry, Walker. Let's forget about it and continue our conversation. Tell me: is the thickness of these plates the same everywhere?"

I am still in shock because of the shake, but I follow the conversation to distract myself. "It should be, but in practice, because the construction is done manually, the plate is a little uneven. The process goes like this: I thin the plate with my hand plane very methodically to avoid gaps between passes. After the first pass, I tap the sound board, listen to the sound and keep planing it until the sound is uniform, solid, and firm all over the plate."

"But what is the purpose?" He asks. "Remember, in every design there must be an objective, a goal, a purpose, a target. So far, you haven't mentioned one."

He seems frustrated. I really don't know how to describe it in words. I know the exact thickness I need for each plate by just listening to the taps, but I don't know how to explain it. I keep trying anyway.

"The objective is to get to the right thickness and the right sound."

"That is still too vague, Walker. What do you mean by the right sound? There is much more engineering that can be put into that process. You could set some goals for vibration, for stiffness, for sound levels, and many other quantities that we can *measure*."

"I like that," I say. "I was right about you; you really can help me. Let me tell you more. Once the plates are thinned, I take the top one and make the sound-hole, you know, the circular hole that every acoustic guitar has. Then comes a long process of gluing several bracing ribs to the inside of the plates. Braces are there to increase the stiffness of the plate; otherwise, it would break with the tension of the strings. Then I install the bridge, where the strings are tied to the sound box, and finish the art design for the hole. With both plates already braced, I make the sides of the guitar by a sequence of heating and bending long strips of thin wood until I get the right curvature and shape that matches the sound box plates."

"I guess it is very difficult to make the sides," Kwame says. "You could overheat and ruin the piece, or over bend and break it."

"You are right, but by experience, by hearing, by feeling, by seeing, one develops a method that quickly gives the perfect shape for the sides. It sounds difficult, but it is not so, really. When I finish both sides, I am ready to make the assembly. Again, glue and more glue is the way to assemble everything. Finally, after all parts are glued together, the last and perhaps most important step, the polish of the guitar, begins. Professional players demand a perfect finish for their guitars. A single scratch can spoil the entire product."

"This was," I continue, "a short description of the fabrication steps, Kwame. I can show you more details if you visit my shop or my home."

He is quietly thinking, pondering something. His hand rubs his short gray beard. "Interesting process. I would not have imagined the similarities between guitars and cars from a designer's point of view. How long does it take to make one guitar?"

"How are you doing over here?" It's the voice of the flight attendant, the one with beautiful hands and blue eyes. I'm tempted to make a provocative comment to her, but it would be inappropriate.

"We are doing just fine, thank you," I reply reflecting her smile. She walks away and I follow her with my eyes until I feel the heavy glance of Kwame waiting for my answer.

"Sorry for the interruption. I was going to say that I make several guitars at the same time, but on average, one guitar takes about sixty hours of work. One thing I really do is making sure that my guitars are of the highest quality. I don't think twice if I have to scrap a defective piece. However, I want to know why such high quality guitars are not as good as the Spanish ones that use the same wood and construction process. I am looking for an answer."

He smiles, takes off his glasses, puts them back on, "And do you think I can help?"

"Yes, I am almost sure you can."

He smiles again. I don't understand. Why does he smile?

"Okay, we'll do it. I'll work with you. I think I can learn and have fun at the same time. Remember, having fun is a very important part of life.

3

Minimize, Maximize

FTER A WHILE, MY STOMACH BEGINS complaining and asking for food. I can smell it from the carts already rolling on the aisles. A flight attendant stops next to me and offers me a choice of chicken or beef. I try to decide, but I can't. Kwame asks for the chicken plate since I don't say anything. The flight attendant grabs the plate, and passes it to him. She asks me again which one I want. I am still undecided and say nothing. Kwame saves me again and asks for a glass of orange juice. She serves the juice and passes it to Kwame. Then she looks at me now with some impatience and says, "The chicken is warmer than the beef," and I quickly say, "Chicken please ... and a glass of water, please." The tension disappears. The chicken is served, and I feel relaxed.

Kwame smiles and says, "That was an optimization problem you solved right there."

"What?"

"Nothing, nothing," he says. "Going back to your problem, I think I have enough information for now. I guess we can go into details later. Since I am trained as an engineer, I learned to solve problems using more mathematics than your luthier instructors in Spain. I think we can build a good team and fix your problems. I will provide my knowledge in design optimization techniques, and they will teach you the art of guitarmaking."

"Design optimization techniques?" I say with an ignorant tone as I scratch my head.

"I know, you have no training in engineering," he replies, "and much less any training in optimization. But don't worry, you will learn. It is simple common sense in most cases."

I feel uneasy now. His comments sound offensive. I had gone through college and didn't hear anything called *design optimization*. I ask what optimization means for him and he replies:

"Walker, anything you do in life is solving optimization problems one after another. Some are large, and some are small. Some have solutions, and some don't."

I don't understand what he is talking about, and he notices my perplexed expression.

He then says, "Let me tell you this: any sane person looks for the maximization of happiness, right?"

I nod, but I also make an inquisitive wince, asking for more explanation.

"Well, maximization of happiness is an optimization problem. That simple! Let me give you another, more concrete, example. When you walked from your original seat to here you did it in the most straight way you could find."

"Yes, of course. I took the left aisle all the way to get to the 38D seat. Where is the optimization in there?" I ask, gesturing with my hands.

"Well, very simple," he replies. "Can you imagine if you had gone all around the plane, zigzagging from aisle to aisle in order to get here?"

"That would be silly," I respond.

"Not only that, it wouldn't be optimum. You would have taken a long time and wasted energy for no reason. This means that unconsciously you took the *shortest path* to come to this seat. In other words, you minimized the travel time, that is, you solved an optimization problem inadvertently."

I ponder his explanation, as he waits for me to understand the concept. "Interesting," I say. "What happens if there is no straight route between point A and point B?"

"Oh! You are a clever person, Walker. You are asking for more complex optimization problems where there are constraints."

"But is it not true that we all have constraints in life?" I ask.

"You are right. I didn't say you couldn't solve such problems, but that they are more complex. Let me give you another example. Moments ago you could not decide which meal to choose. Do you know why?"

"Well, I was equally inclined to eat chicken or beef. That's all."

"Correct. However, that was until the waitress gave you more information and you made a decision. Right?"

"And ..."

"Well, you solved an optimization problem again. Don't you see? Your goal was to maximize your satisfaction with a good meal. With the initial information you had, both plates were equally satisfactory to you. Your decision was constrained by the amount of information you had. When she gave you more information —the chicken is warm— you made the decision. The less constrained the problem is, the easier it is to solve. Logical, don't you think? Your meal problem reminds me of managers in big corporations. They think that their employees are giving them all the information, and with that, they have to make a decision, otherwise they look stupid. At the end of the day, they cannot make a decision for lack of information, and the project is delayed one more day. Employees complain that the downstream information is bad, but the upstream information is sometimes worse."

Now I realize this old fellow is worth his weight in gold, and with more knowledge than I thought.

"Managers," he continues, "need to ask for more and more information until they are in a position to make the best decision, the optimum decision."

"But sometimes, gathering more information takes more time or more money. And some other times, there is no more information at all," I reply forcefully.

"Great! You are thinking. I like that. Then you need to solve a different optimization problem: maximize the benefit of your decision with a fixed amount of information."

I am confused and he notices it. He is too scientific for me. He keeps using this word *maximize* that seem to have a special meaning for him. I don't get it.

"Kwame, you are right, I am not an engineer. I studied liberal arts and business. However, I am smart enough to understand your lectures if you go slowly. If you go step by step, I can follow."

He laughs. I also laugh. I feel better now. He looks less condescending too.

"Let me understand this about *information*," I say. "If I have employees who can provide all the information I need. Why should I limit their output?"

"Okay, let's start from the beginning. First, let me tell you that when I say optimization, I mean the process of minimizing or maximizing something. This *something* is anything you can count or measure. Clear?"

"Yes... I think."

"Good. It turns out that anything in life can be resolved as an optimization problem, as long as you know what you want and how to measure it. There are plenty of examples: investors try to maximize the return of their investment. Men and women maximize their chances to reproduce, which gives a mathematical setting to Darwinian evolution. Your employees, like most employees, solve a daily optimization problem: minimize their workload. I could give you thousands of examples, but the one you have in your guitarmaking business is a design optimization problem, and a manufacturing optimization problem as well. These are problems engineers are trained to solve. I can help you, if you want to learn."

He rests back, closes his eyes and ends his rhetoric with, "Think about it, and wake me up when you have more questions. I need some rest now."

The Guitar Maker

I keep thinking about what he said. He said my employee minimizes his workload. Why? I pay him well. Why? I think about it for a while, and then I realize that by minimizing the workload, he is maximizing the benefit of their fixed salary. He is maximizing their per hour pay rate. But... that doesn't explain my case. I work so much! Every day! Maybe my optimization problem is different and I haven't noticed it. I'll ask him later. He seems very tired now.

His ideas keep going around in my head. He said 'everything in life can be resolved as an optimization problem.' How about love, trust and fairness... how can we solve problems where feelings are present? I think he is wrong, definitely wrong. I'll ask him when he wakes up. For now, I'd better sleep too. This is a long trip.

The flight attendant passes down the aisle offering blankets. I take one, but this time I search for her blue eyes trying to steal a smile before going to sleep. She looks at me, holds my gaze with grace and finally smiles. It feels nice to go to sleep with a beautiful image in your mind. She leaves, and everything starts looking blurry. My eyelids feel heavy. I think I should. I think I should...

4

Bad, Ugly and Cheap

AFTER A COUPLE OF HOURS I WAKE UP bothered
by the cold air coming from the nozzle in the ceiling.
My back is in pain and my neck is stiff like wood. There is a screen
up front showing where the airplane is flying over: we are in the
middle of the Atlantic now. I wonder what is happening back
home. We live in Chelsea, a small mid-western town in Michigan
near Detroit. Emily is one of the many soccer moms in town,
and drives Christina and Gabriel everywhere for their practices
and games. They both have been playing soccer for the town team
since they were little. I feel nostalgic every time I travel for more
than a day. I miss going to the games and watching them play,
watching their smiles and listening to their screams. Christina is
fourteen and plays defense very well, according to her coach. She
argues that defensive players can play the entire game without
getting dirty, but that the offensive players always get tripped and
fall, and at the end of the game they have muddy socks and pants.
She really cares about staying clean and pretty.

I can bet Christina adorned the table for dinner last night. She always does that. No matter how simple the food is, no matter how many are eating, she insists on a table beautifully decorated, matching colors and shapes. Sometimes I think she is obsessed with that. I wonder if Kwame can find an explanation for that. He says everything in life is an optimization problem. Can he explain my daughter's behavior with his theories?

Anyway, I think Christina may have a problem. Beauty is her priority no matter what, where, how or when. I close my eyes, and try to remember that day when the school tennis coach asked each player to buy new shoes for the season. She liked the idea of new shoes, and I saw the opportunity to give her a lesson on how to buy good quality shoes. So, next day I decided to take her to the shopping mall near our town. The coach, Mr. Johnson, a well seasoned trainer with years in the school, advised the players to spend their money on a good pair that would last the entire season, a good quality pair of shoes that would provide comfort and durability for at least four months of hard training and many intercollegiate games.

The very next day I woke up early, prepared some toast for us, and then we went to the mall. We were among the first in the store, around 9:00 AM, I remember. There were two big shoe stores where I was sure she could find the right tennis shoes. In the first one she liked a pair with the worst quality I had ever seen. They wouldn't last two weeks. They were made of fabric on the top, like those shoes one buys in emergencies. Of course, they were pretty shoes, according to Christina. That's what she was concerned about: they were blue and pink, with glittering stars on each side and white soles.

"Aren't they pretty, dad?" She asked with her head tilted to one side, eyes wide open, and sweet smile trying to convince me. That's her typical trick; I know her well.

"Yes honey, they are pretty, but you need quality shoes to play four months on asphalt courts. These won't last two weeks." She dropped her shoulders, put down her head, turned around and walked away. That is her typical second strategy. She tries to make me feel guilty. I followed her and say: "Christy, this is not the best pair of shoes to play tennis in. You really need durable shoes to last the whole season."

"I know dad, I know." Her face is melancholic now.

We left the store, disappointed and sad, and went to the next one. That second store was big, really big. She tried on several models, but nothing convinced us. Quality was difficult to find. Some had bad seams while others had bad soles. There was one pair that looked perfect, but inside they were hard, like Swedish clogs; she could not play for a minute with them. As expected, she kept picking the pretty ones, but I was determined to find a pair of tennis shoes that would last. We dug and dug in different places inside the store until, after one hour, I found a pair that would be perfect for the task.

"Here Christina, try these."

She took them, examined them, and even before trying them on she said, "Dad, these are for men."

"I know, but we have been looking for a good pair for so long, and we can't find them." Her eyes were wet by then. She suggested going to another store, but since she couldn't find them in this one, I was sure she wouldn't find them in any other.

"Dad, I can't. These are ugly, thick, bulky, not for me."

"There you go again. Stop looking for beauty. Quality is more important. Try them, please."

She started to cry, but tried them on any way.

"Do you see? They are fine, Christina. We don't have to look for shoes any more."

She was not convinced at all, but accepted my decision with resignation saying, "It's okay dad, it's okay."

"Christina, you'll get used to them, and they will do the job, as coach Johnson wanted," I said to cheer her up.

Before going home we stopped by an ice cream store to ease the sadness and have a little talk. She was fine by then. She even smiled when finishing her ice cream. When we got home, Emily was outside taking care of the garden, feeding the roses. It was June, the peak month of the flowering season. I tried to avoid talking about Christina's shoes, but I knew Emily would ask for the price.

She always does. As soon as we stepped out of the car, barely after saying hello, Emily asked:

"How much did you pay for your new shoes, honey?"

"One hundred and twenty five! And they are men's shoes, mom." She responded with sadness mixed with anger and impotence.

As expected, Emily did not pay attention to Christina's complaints. I knew she only wanted to know about the money. Her face changed tones, going from pink, to pale red, to almost orange and finally to fire red.

"Walker!" She screamed. "A hundred and twenty five is, is..." and she could not complete the sentence. She threw all garden utensils on the grass and ran inside the house, banging her arms against her thighs, cursing to herself.

She always does that. No matter what I buy, as soon it is more than ten dollars she starts questioning whether I shopped around, or if I used the store coupons, or whatever. I can't understand her. We are well off, I make enough money to live in a big house, take vacations, buy cars, and much more, but she always complains.

I turned around and saw Christina waiting inside the car. "What are you waiting for?" I asked.

"I know mom is coming out to take me back to the shoe store."

"Why are you so sure?"

She didn't have to answer. Emily was already back with her purse, her car keys and her 'don't-talk-to-me' face, walking with long steps and her heels almost braking the pavement. She opened the car door, got inside, turned the ignition, and pulled back. Christina waved to me and said, "See you Dad," with a big smile that read 'I told you!'

Once more Emily went to return what I bought. It's frustrating. She doesn't respect my decisions. It's as if she does not care what I think or do. She is in control of the house like an army general. I hate this feeling.

I went inside the house, to the basement, my favorite place in the house. It is my private guitar shop. As I went down the stairs the bad memories of the incident that had just happened were disappearing with the smell of the new wood that had arrived. I had bought a very good wood from Colombia called 'Honduras mahogany' that I was going to use for the guitar necks. For the plates I had bought Alpine spruce, imported from Germany, the wood I prefer for the sound boards. The smell, filling the whole basement, was as always, very pleasant, woody and fresh. The half-finished guitars hanging on the walls looked like growing babies to me.

I always feel relaxed when I am in my workshop, with guitars, wood, strings, and the entire environment down here. I wish I was a famous master luthier and my guitars were all around the world playing in the great music halls. For now, I have to accept that my guitars are not even top class. I've been making guitars for fifteen years now, and somehow I still cannot make them as good as the great luthiers do.

Time had flown, and I heard the car coming back. I saw my watch and realized I had been in the basement thinking and dreaming for two hours. I stopped what I was doing, and took a deep breath to gain some courage before going upstairs.

Christina did not look happy. She handed the box to me and said, "This is what mom bought me."

"Well, let me see," I said as I grabbed the box with my right hand. I felt the tension in the air, as if we all three were waiting for the bomb to explode. I could feel the heavy gaze of Emily from a distance saying 'don't even dare to say a word.'

Emily started to talk before I said anything. "They cost fourteen dollars and ninety nine cents, and the manager of the store told me that if they fall apart within four weeks I can return them, and pick another pair. Do you see? That's what I call a good deal."

I said nothing. It's a waste of time to refute. Those were the ugliest shoes I've ever seen, not to mention the poor quality. I knew right away that Christina didn't like them.

Christina ran upstairs crying and shouting: "You don't care about me. *You* dad, you think I am a boy; and *you* mom, you just think about saving every single penny. I hate you both." And she ran up to her bedroom. The bomb had been finally dropped.

I went back to my guitars, the basement, the only place where I can think clearly. Emily, with a tough face and tight teeth, went back to the front yard, as if nothing had happened.

As I sat in front of the Honduras mahogany I realized that Christina was right. My only concern was the quality of the shoes, the durability. But for Emily, the only concern was the money she had to spend. At the end we both failed Christina; we didn't care about her needs, only our own satisfaction.

However, things were not so clear in my mind. Something didn't fit. I kept thinking and thinking, and then I came to the conclusion that Christina was not being rational either. I started to go upstairs, and as I walked, my steps were purposely loud to let her know I was coming. She set a higher volume on the radio so I couldn't hear the sobs. I stopped just before the door, tried to smile, and finally opened the door. She was fake-reading a book, covering her face with it.

"Hi honey. Can we talk?" I said with a father-like attitude, the one I never saw as a child, but learned by myself with time.

She dropped the book to see me, but no words came out of her mouth.

"You know what?" I said, "Tomorrow, I am going to give you one hundred dollars, we'll go back to the mall, and you'll pick the shoes you want. I won't pick for you, as long as you spend most of the money." My bet was that one pair of expensive shoes would be durable, with more quality than what her mother had bought. Her face changed immediately, with lustrous eyes, and the sweet smile that always makes my heart content. She accepted the conditions and ran to tell Gabriel about it. I didn't realize the mistake I had made until seconds later when Gabriel came to the room and said, "Why can Christina get that deal, dad? That is not fair."

I fell victim of my own teachings. I had taught them fairness to each other at every level of life. So, I had no choice but to treat him the same way. "Okay Gabriel, you'll come with us tomorrow. You can also pick your own shoes." They looked at each other, smiled, and ran out of the room to the backyard.

The next day, after I came home from the shop, both Christina and Gabriel were waiting on the porch for me. My car was not even turned off before they were opening the doors. They could not wait.

"Dad," Christina said, "you promised yesterday to take us to the shoe store. Mom is not home, so she won't complain if we go now." We saw each other's eyes through the rear view mirror inside the car. We both understood, so there was no need for more explanation or discussion. Gabriel's laugh was muted by his hands on his mouth.

We headed to the mall, the same one we had gone to the day before, and once inside the shoe store, I simply distracted myself buying some new socks while they were buying their shoes. After about half an hour Christina had picked what she liked. I grabbed the box, but when I opened it I was disappointed. Her choice was still of bad quality. I was about to say something, but decided not to make any comment that would hurt her. I kept my promise and said nothing at all. That was my part of the deal.

Gabriel, on the other hand, had picked the better shoes. They were really good, with a nice design, at a good price as well. I didn't know why Christina couldn't pick something like that for herself. I smiled to Gabriel and said "Good job, son, good job," and I patted him on his back.

The story did not end there. I knew we had to face Emily when we got home. We had spent almost two hundred dollars by now, and she would scream again when she found out. When we got home I asked Christina and Gabriel not to talk about the money spent because I was going to handle it directly with mom later. They agreed. We got out of the car, and once inside, I saw Emily kneeling in front of the fireplace cleaning the ashes from last winter.

"Hi, Emily."

No response.

I had to be careful with what I was about to say. The first sentence is always the most important. "We went back to the shoe store and got a better deal, Emily, you won't believe it."

"Oh yes? How is it?" She asked with demanding voice.

"Well, I'll tell you tonight. I have to go downstairs to finish something." I knew that she knew I was lying, but she did not say anything. Besides, I knew she would bring it up again sometime later in the week.

Before I went downstairs Christina hugged and thanked me for the new shoes. Gabriel was already playing basketball with his new shoes in the front yard. I went downstairs looking for a relaxing time for the rest of the afternoon. I found it. I picked a #120-grit garnet sandpaper and started smoothing the neck of a classical guitar for a local guitarist in Ann Arbor. I've made many guitars, and I still feel I've learned something with each one I've made. This one, for instance, turned out beautifully with the Brazilian rose-wood I had bought for the first time last summer.

I suddenly felt a touch in my shoulder, a tapping feeling. I thought it was Emily. I turned around to see who was there but I couldn't see anybody. It was scary. Then I felt a push on my shoulder, much harder than before, but I still didn't see anybody pushing. Suddenly, I woke up. I was still on the airplane to Madrid. I was sleeping again, and Kwame was trying to wake me up. He wanted to go to the restroom and I was in his way. It felt weird. I mixed a past reality, with a present event, all while I was sleeping. For a minute I though I was going crazy in the basement of my house.

"Sure Kwame," I say and stand to let him pass. I sit back, still confused, and start to think about the next question for Kwame. If dreams express our concerns of reality, I could try to ask Kwame about this dream I just had, I said to myself.

When he comes back I notice he is still sleepy, but I go ahead with a question. "Kwame how do you explain that some people are obsessed with saving money?"

"I don't know, I just want to sleep a bit more," he replies gently, smiling.

"Okay, I understand. But before you go back to sleep, let me tell you this. When you woke me up I was dreaming of my family: my wife has always been obsessed with saving money and my daughter obsessed with beauty. They can't see that quality is the most important aspect of anything you do, buy or build. That's all I wanted to tell you."

"Well, now I can't go to sleep without saying a few words about that," he replies. "First, I could write a whole book just talking about your wife, your daughter and you. Each of you has a piece of the puzzle of life. What you all three have together is what your employee should learn to make good guitars. Second, and more important, I want to go to sleep if you allow me."

He doesn't look upset, but is very firm. This is a hard way to learn optimization. What can my wife, my daughter and I have that my employee should know?

I am sleepy too. I'd better go to sleep and find out tomorrow. The flight attendant passes by, and I ask for a second blanket. She brings it, and I drape it about my torso. My thoughts begin to wander again ... Emily, Christina, Gabriel, Manuel, ...

The Middle East Connection

UDDENLY, I FEEL A BIG SHAKE, SO HARD, that my head hits the window. It is the plane landing on the runway, Madrid. Kwame wakes up too, and his tiredness is evident. The sagging skin below each eye tells how little he slept, that is, as little as I did too. We look at each other the same way two friends do when finishing a marathon: we did it.

"What time is it?" He asks while covering his mouth with his long fingers.

"It's 9:00 AM, Madrid time."

"Did you dream again?"

"Not this time, but you left me puzzled with your last comments about me, my wife and my daughter."

He stretches his legs and seems to ignore my comments, but then he faces me, closes his eyes for an instant as though getting inspiration, and says with his grave but smooth voice:

"Let me tell you this short story that my friend Carlos told me some time ago. When he was a little kid, in Bogotá, Colombia, there were street merchants that would knock on the door of his house to sell blankets, towels, shoes, cloth, and many other things for the house. These people were Middle Eastern immigrants with little knowledge of Spanish. They and their ancestors had been merchants in their native countries for centuries. They were now in Colombia trying to use their traditional selling techniques as if they were in the Middle East. They carried boxes all around the neighborhood, tireless, convincing housewives to buy their products. They even used to finance their clients to engage them in a never-ending relationship that guaranteed a next visit for payments and for selling more merchandise. They were masters of the trade."

He pauses for a short time. He seems to be meditating, but then continues:

"Sorry, I was trying to remember three words in Spanish and finally I got them. Well, as I was saying, these fellows were going from door to door selling merchandise all day long. But this is the important part of the story, the part that connects with your dream: in order to start their business, the first thing they learned to say in Spanish was *bueno, bonito, barato*. Do you know what that means?"

I shake my head side to side.

"Literally it means good, pretty, and inexpensive, but the real meaning is much deeper than that. These salesmen had used these three words from centuries to convince people to buy their merchandise. This century-long tradition had allowed them to refine their sale strategy. In other words, they had used time as the optimization method."

"I did not get that last part. What do you mean by optimization method?"

"Don't worry, you will understand later. Let's go back to the Spanish lesson. These merchants only knew how to count, how to wave their hands, and how to say the three magical words: *bueno, bonito, barato*. When Carlos told me this story, he did it because he wanted to show me how these people became very rich within a few years. These fellows were very clear in what they wanted. Most of them ended with a nice store in downtown, with one or two employees and a nice place to live nearby. They saved all they could and sent it back to their families in the Middle East. That was a long time ago, now things have changed."

"Oh! I see. Your story is about goals in life. About saving money like my wife. This mean you agree with her."

"No, I don't. I have not finished my story. The three words are probably better translated as quality, beauty, and value, but in order to keep the same initials as in Spanish, I've decided to use betterment, beauty, and bargain, that is, BBB. In their broken Spanish these merchants tried to convince the customer that their products had, according to their ancestral tradition, the three most important characteristics that a product should have, otherwise, it wouldn't sell."

Our conversation had gone on for a while, and we did not notice how late it was. A flight attendant approaches us and asks whether either of us is staying in Madrid, because this was the last chance to leave the airplane.

"Sorry, we were distracted," I say. "He continues to Copenhagen, but I stay in Madrid. I'll leave in a few seconds."

She accepts the explanation but tells me that she can't wait much time for me. I will have to leave now.

"Well, Kwame, it was a nice story. We will meet again. We'll have to cut it off here."

"I will finish the story next time we meet. But before you leave, let me tell you that there is one more letter to add to the three Bs."

I ask him for his phone number in Michigan and promise to call him. He writes it down along with the number of his friend, where he'll stay in Denmark, in case I come up with another burning question.

"See you soon," he says. "Have a good trip. I'll be waiting for your call so I can finish telling you the story."

"Yes, I'll call you in two weeks."

I take my jacket, run, and quickly get off the plane.

What a rush and what very bad timing to land! The story seemed to be interesting. It's a pity he could not tell me the end. Well, I suppose I can ask him again when we meet in Michigan. For now, I am on another mission. I need to take advantage of this visit to Spain.

6

Spain

THIS IS MY THIRD TIME IN MADRID. I love this city, its majestic buildings, its people, but most of all, its food and night life. Unfortunately, my final destination is not Madrid; I wish it was. I still have to go to a small town called Sigüenza where I will be taking a short intensive workshop in a nearby monastery. This is going to be exciting for me. I will be coached by a great Spanish luthier, Don Rodrigo Ibarra de Castilla. What a name! And what a reputation he has.

I pick up my luggage and wander for a moment before I find the exit doors. Once outside the airport I ask for directions and find out that Sigüenza is about 80 miles from here. It will cost me a fortune to get there in taxi. A man, with a fast walk approaches me and asks where I am going. He wears a black overcoat, old shoes, dark glasses and a white hat. I tell him my plans to go to Sigüenza, but that I was looking for an affordable way to get there.

"Wait here, I'll find you someone who can take you to Sigüenza very cheap," he says as he walks to the next street intersection, turns left and disappears for a few minutes. He then comes back with another man and says:

"He will take you to Sigüenza for 50 American dollars, is that good for you?" It seems reasonable for such a long distance, and I accept the deal. The first man asks me for the 50 dollars in advance. By now I understand his job; he is just a taxi broker. He takes a 10 dollar bill, takes off his white hat, opens a small pocket inside, rolls the bill, puts it in the pocket, and wears his hat again. The other 40 dollars are for the taxi driver, who has been patiently waiting for the ceremonial broker.

We walk down the street to the intersection where the car is parked. It is a small, very old, nicely kept car. We get inside and head towards the highway. The silence is consuming me, and I try to start a conversation with the young man. He looks to be from the Middle East: short hair, beard, crooked long nose, and thick eyebrows. He's wearing a tee-shirt with the Real Madrid logo, the local and very famous soccer team.

"It is a nice day. How long has it been this way?" I ask.

He smiles and in broken English says, "last month."

He doesn't seem willing to have a long conversation, but I continue. "Nice car. Do you like it?"

He smiles again and replies: "Yes, yes."

"What do you like the best about this old car?"

A third smile and an answer I was not expecting:

"It is good, it is beautiful and because it is old, it was cheap."

I was astonished, just 20 minutes ago Kwame was telling me about the same three words. It is incredible.

"What do you mean?" I insist in finding out exactly what he has in mind. He tries to explain and says:

"I've had this car for three years, and no problems with it. So, it is good car. All passengers like the leather seats, so it is beautiful car too. And because it is used car, it is also cheap to me. My mother always says to me: if good, beautiful and cheap buy it with no doubt."

That is a one-minute lecture taken from a centuries-old tradition. Marvelous! I stay quiet and thoughtful the rest of the trip. He doesn't seem to mind.

We arrive at Sigüenza, a medieval city. A friend of mine told me that this is a wonderful town with more history than many other places in Spain. The main attraction is the castle, which has been transformed into a beautiful hotel called *Parador de Sigüenza*. *Parador* means "a place to stop," according to my tourist guide, and this is definitely a place to stop, stay and admire. The castle is from the fourteenth century, although the successors to the Romans rebuilt it many times after its foundation was laid in the tenth century. The castle is on a hill overlooking the town that surrounds the castle. Most streets are still in their original stone finish, which makes them very romantic and medieval.

We get to the entrance of the hotel. He stops his car, and I give him an extra tip for the little chat we had. After checking in the hotel and unpacking my luggage, I drop myself on the bed and start thinking about the three words Kwame was telling me: betterment, beauty and bargain; betterment, beauty and bargain. I am so tired that I can barely stay awake to think. My biological clock is confused, and I couldn't sleep very much on the plane. The bed is puffy and the fragrance in the room is delicious. I rest my head on the pillow full of soft feathers. Oh, so nice! But before even closing my eyes, suddenly, in a flash of light, everything clicks in place in my head. Yes! I got it!

I am always worried about quality, my daughter about beauty, and my wife about prices. This is exactly the same meaning of the three words Kwame and the taxi driver were talking about. Oh, this is great! I can't wait two weeks to talk to Kwame. I'll call him now.

I find his phone number, and make the call to Denmark, but the phone is busy. I feel anxious to talk to him. What should I do? Ah, I know. I'll take a shower to spend some time, and I should trim my beard too, it's getting too long.

Once inside the shower I will feel less anxious. The hot shower will relax me for sure. From the window of the bathroom I see the town. I see the people in the streets and a long line of merchants selling souvenirs to the tourists. Trading, trading, that's what the world is about. After I finish showering, I regain some energy and enthusiasm. I call again, and this time I get a tone. As the phone is ringing I begin to imagine Kwame's surprise.

"Ole Rasmussen," I hear from the other side of the line. It's the thick voice of an old man.

"Hi, my name is Walker McBride, I don't speak Danish."

"It is okay, how can I help you?" He gently replies.

"I understand you are a friend of Kwame, aren't you?"

"Yes, I know him very well. Is there any problem with him? I am expecting him today."

"Everything is fine with him. He should be arriving soon. We took the same airplane from Detroit and had a long conversation. Actually, he talked about you very fondly."

"Oh, yes. We have been friends for a long while."

"Well, I am in Sigüenza, Spain, and would like to talk to him when he gets to your home. It's nothing important, just a quick question. It's about a three-word concept he taught me today: betterment, beauty and bargain. I found..."

Before I finish my sentence, he interrupts and says, "Yes, I know what you are talking about. They are the characteristics of the objective function of all problems, but I thought that Kwame and I had agreed on four words to describe it, not three."

"Function? He did not mentioned that to me," I say.

"I think I will ask Kwame to call you when he arrives. Do you agree?" He replies.

"Yes, sure. Please tell him I am in the hotel *Parador de Sigüenza*. I gave him the telephone number. It was nice to talk to you."

"Thank you. We'll call you later."

Nice guy. Now I have no choice but to rest in this marvelous hotel and wait for Kwame's call. This hotel is beautifully decorated, the service is great and the price is even better. Oh, I can't believe what I just said. I used the three concepts that Kwame was talking about. I guess I've been using them all my life without realizing how important they are. Mmm, this bed is so comfortable that I'm going to take a nap for a moment.

7

God

HOURS LATER THE PHONE RINGS. I wake up elated knowing it must be Kwame.

I rush to the phone, trip over my shoes, and finally get to it, "Hello, this is Walker."

"Walker, it's me, Kwame."

"Kwame! Thank you for calling back. I needed to talk to you. It's a quick question. It won't take long."

"Go ahead," he serenely says.

"Remember when we talked about the relation between BBB and my family? Well, I was thinking about it, also about the story of your friend from Colombia, and now it all seems so clear and obvious to me: betterment is about the quality I always search for; bargain refers to the savings my wife Emily is so worried about; and beauty is exactly my daughter Christina's obsession. And when you asked me about the goal I should have when making guitars, well, I also figured it out. My objective must be to maximize all three Bs in order to build the best guitars."

The Guitar Maker

"Yes, you've got it, Walker. I am glad to hear that. In optimization theory, the goal has a name; it is called the objective function; but, as you can imagine, I prefer the engineering name: *the design objective*. It is more explicit, less mathematical, more purposely driven, when we say *design*, instead of function. But remember this: there is more than the three Bs. There is one more concept that must be included along with quality, beauty and value. I did not have the time to explain it to you in the plane, and if I try over the phone it will be more difficult. For now, just keep in mind that *Nature* has to be counted in the design objective. I will explain it to you in more detail later. So, the complete set of letters, so far, is B-B-B-N, or Q-B-V-N, however you want to say it."

"So far? Why do you say so far?"

"Walker, life is a never-ending learning journey. We may find later on that there is more than just four letter to explain our problems in life."

I can't refute what he just said, so I comply with a "Yes, I agree." Suspecting he is as tired as I am, I decide to quit the conversation: "Well, I will keep in mind the fourth concept and will wait eagerly for your explanation. I don't want to bother you any more today, Kwame. Thank you again for your call, and enjoy your stay in Denmark."

"Not a problem. I'll talk to you later. By the way, if you want to meet with us next week in Copenhagen, let me know; we're planning to visit the big city for a couple of days this time."

"Great! I will let you know if I can make it, but, don't make plans with me, yet. I have so much to do here in the monastery."

"Monastery?" Kwame quickly asks.

"Oh, I forgot to tell you that the workshop takes place in a monastery in Sigüenza, not in Madrid," I reply.

"Mmm, I see. Well, I'll talk to you later. Good bye."

I feel good now. Concepts are in place, and there are no more puzzling questions bugging my mind. I look around the room trying to decide what to do. I'll take a walk and visit the monastery. I step out of the hotel, but instead of taking a taxi, I decide to walk. The workshop will be held the day after tomorrow in the monastery of *Los Hermanos Maristas*, but I decided to come one day earlier to get to know the town and get used to the six hour time difference between here and Michigan. Tomorrow morning I'll move my luggage to the monastery, where they promised to have a comfortable bed and three good meals per day. The interesting thing is that the cooks are the monks. I hope they know what they are doing.

I am on the *Calle Mayor* —Main Street— from where the castle looks like a fortress. It is majestic, tall and as stiff as the stones it's made of. In the street, people are friendly and smile as I pass by. Few speak English, but who needs it here!

After about forty-five minutes through the green pastures outside the town I get to the monastery: a white building with a long entrance escorted by green pines, the same color of the building's roof. Outside, on the front patio, a monk is planting some flowers. His concentration is such that I get very close to him, but he still doesn't notice my presence.

"Hi! Good afternoon. Do you speak English?" I ask.

He turns towards me, and with a smile on his face, radiating tranquility and happiness, says, "Yes, son, I do. How can I help you?"

He is an old monk with white beard and bald head. His hands, dirty, tough, but skillfully handling his tools, show his age by the number, depth, and length of wrinkles in his skin. He cleans his hands with the water from the bucket he carries, and dries them with a white towel hanging on his back.

"My name is Walker McBride. Nice meeting you," I say smiling.

He says nothing while showing a bit of surprise when looking at me more carefully. He extends his hand to shake mine.

"I will be attending the workshop on guitarmaking here in the monastery."

He tells me that he knows about it, since he'll be cooking for us during our training. He asks me if I want to join him in the garden. I agree, so we both kneel down and start working together while we have a conversation.

"Do you do this every day?" I ask.

"In the spring and summer," he says with a smile.

"What do you do in fall and winter?"

"When it gets cold, I go inside the monastery. My arthritis doesn't let me garden in cold weather. I stay inside the monastery and pray. I pray to our Lord. Do you believe in God, son?"

Living in the United States this question is rarely asked. The practice of being politically correct eliminates such deep subjects from our repertoire of questions to start a conversation. Here, however, it is as natural as asking for a banana. I am not prepared for a question like this, but I try. The worst I can do is to say nothing.

"Of course I believe in God," I say. "Who doesn't? We all need God. It represents all our ideals and everything that we want to achieve. But I have another question that I haven't found the answer to, yet. It may sound offensive to you, but since you started this subject, I have to continue. The question is one that my uncle asked me when I was fifteen years old. He asked me whether God was our creator or our creation."

The monk stays quiet and attentive to my question. He doesn't seemed disturbed and then, with the same smile he showed when I came, he says, "That is a mystery that only God can answer. I would pose the question as whether one has faith in God or not. If you do, he is the creator; if you don't, he is our creation." He smiles again, and seems to know that his answer, and maybe the question itself, is somehow illogical.

I try to show that his answer is ambiguous. "I suppose nobody can answer my question. I feel happy enough by knowing the existence of the concept of God, and that people use it in many positive ways to reach happiness. Whether *he* is or is not the creator, is more philosophical, a matter of faith as you say, and may be impossible to answer. I guess I am more pragmatic. We should care more about being happier by reducing our suffering. Existence of God is at a higher level for me."

"I prefer to think that God is the creator," he replies. "This way I don't have to deal with so much power. Humility is easier to administer than power. Besides, you cannot explain all around you with logic alone. Nobody can. We all need to believe, to have faith in order to accept or at least explain what logic can't explain."

He sounds very authoritative, and may be right. Power is not only more difficult to handle, but it also corrupts your thoughts with time, and eventually, often degenerates into tyranny and despotism. That is what history has shown. I wonder if God, the one we humans have defined, has degenerated lately. There are so many things going wrong in the world.

He pauses with his already typical smile, waiting for my reaction, but then continues with "You, however, have touched on a very important subject already. You mentioned *happiness* as one goal in life. I have to concede that happiness is among the most important concerns in life, and that it is precisely God, and his infinite, immeasurable spirit, the only one who can guarantee that. Spirituality may sound to you as an empty concept, but without it, without paying attention to the needs of our soul, we are unable to put together ourselves, we are unable to fix our mind for a mission in life, or a goal as you call it. Even more, I must say, once you accept the soft part of our life, that is, not only the fleshy and touchable things around us, but the malleable and metaphysical entities that explain the inexplicable, then you'll realize your happiness, eternal and unbreakable, infinite and immeasurable as the one our Lord provides."

I gaze away, fixing my eyes on a red leaf laying on the grass, quiet, still, inert, but full of meaning in this simple instant of thought.

"What are you thinking, son?" He asks.

"Nothing. I was just doubting the perfection of God. But if I do, then it wouldn't be the God that I am thinking about, right? I would be contradicting the very concept of God. Besides, that red leaf," as I point to it with my right index finger, "tiny and lonely, is also so full of life just because I am looking at it, or touching it. I am confused, I guess."

He laughs quietly and while posing his arm on my shoulder, he says, "That is exactly what I was talking about. If you define God, then you will have doubts, but if God defines us, then we don't have to worry about it."

I look directly at his old eyes, framed by white brows, tilted by time, and I nod with gratitude.

"Thank you for your time, Father. I learned something new today, and I always enjoy learning something different each day. Thank you. By the way, I do not know your name yet."

"I'm Father Mauricio. I hope to see you tomorrow, and also hope you like my food ... and my blessings."

"Thank you Father. I'll see you tomorrow."

"Be with God," he says, as he lifts his tired arm, bows his head and makes a cross sign with his hand.

8

The Timeless Time

THERE ARE SIXTEEN PARTICIPANTS IN THE workshop. All of them are taking the complete two-week training except me. I don't need to be here that long. What I want to know from the master luthier is whether I can fix my technique and construct better guitars. I don't need to make a guitar in fourteen days like the rest of the students; I can do that in my shop, with more time, more inspiration, and no rush.

The master luthier, along with his three assistants, just entered the room, and all students stand up in recognition to such a prominent figure in the guitarmaking field. Don Rodrigo Ibarra de Castilla is considered the best ever, and probably the best that will be. His 50 years of experience have been solidly dedicated to build the most exquisite guitars for the great guitarists of flamenco and classical music. He is going around the room, shaking hands with each one of us. I feel the tension inside me as he approaches.

"Good morning," he says in a very accented English, but carefully pronounced.

"Good morning. It is my pleasure. I've been waiting for this moment for two years, and I am very glad to be here."

He nods and smiles, and squeezes my hand even harder in recognition of my flattering salute. As he continues with the rest of the students, I sit and prepare the material for my first day of class. The room is big and full of sunlight coming from a huge window facing south. The smell of fresh wood combined with the wood polish is the typical one found in guitar shops. It is so pleasant to smell what you are used to. I pick a piece of wood from the floor and feel it. It's soft and cold. I don't know what the name of this wood is. Let me see how it tastes. Mmm, I see. It's bitter like, like, like what? I guess I'll have to ask the instructor what kind of wood this is. For the time being, I'll sit in one of these tall, green chairs.

After four days of classes things are going pretty flat for me. The teachers are polite, trying to do their best with their English. The first day was very interesting to me. I had the opportunity to see many different techniques being used by the masters, and by a few students as well. I have picked up a couple of good tricks to improve my assemblies. It is always possible to learn, even after years of doing it hundreds of times. What I really came to find out has not been revealed to me yet. Teachers have been very busy with the more novice students, while I watch the days pass. Today, however, seems to be a better day. Three of the students, two from Europe and one from Asia, have food poisoning after going out for dinner last night, and decided to take the day off. I hope to get more attention from the teacher.

I am working on a sound board, trying to plane it to the prescribed thickness. One of the instructors has been watching me for half an hour without saying anything, but then he approaches me.

"Hi, how are you doing?" He asks.

"Fine, just fine."

"I've been watching you while you work on the sound board. You are really meticulous, much more than anyone here in the shop."

"Thank you. I try my best on each guitar I make."

"Great! That is a good attitude. But ..."

And before he finishes his sentence I quickly utter "But what?"

"Well," he continues, "I see a problem."

This is the moment I have been waiting for. I wanted to find a problem in my technique. I finally will get what I came for.

"Great!" I say. "I really want to hear what you are going to say."

"Well, don't get so excited. You are a fine luthier, for sure the finest in this group of students, very meticulous, and it is hard to find a significant problem in your technique. Yesterday, Don Rodrigo asked me to pay attention to you and also told me to give you the advice we always give to people with the same problem as yours."

"What is the problem you are talking about?"

"Well, it is like this. When you are a luthier, you are also an artist. Any artist will tell you that the technique is not enough to create good art. The technique is the mechanical part, the one you can learn by example, by demonstration. However, you need a bit more; you need to understand the non-mechanical part of guitarmaking. It is difficult to describe what I mean, but it is an essential component in many professions. For example, when you see a painter working in a masterpiece, you see a hand with a brush moving on the canvas. That is what a person can see from outside, but what is really happening, from the painter's perspective, is a fusion of the painter and the masterpiece as if they were a single entity. Some athletes call this stage 'being in the zone,' and it is also described as being unaware of your environment. You and your art are one, and only one thing. You get to this level after concentration on your work, plus a de-concentration of the environment."

"Oh, I think I understand what you mean."

"Let me give you one more analogy that I am sure you won't forget. There is a difference between having sex and making love. When you are having sex, you are doing the mechanical part. You can learn it in books, in classes, in videos. They tell you what to do, how to do it, when to do it, etcetera. On the other hand, if you love a person, then things are different. All your feelings come into play in such a way that everything is transformed. Life is brighter, easier, more secure, and hope is unlimited. Then if you put both things together, I mean, having sex and loving, you get what we know as *making love*. And this, Walker, is the most intense and sublime experience that a person can have in life. When you are making love your being and hers are one thing, one entity, with no environment, no boundaries between you both."

"Even more," he continues, "the real sign of being in this stage is the lack of biological time. When you are in the zone, your body does not register time at all. You may be hours, even days, doing a work of art, but for your mind it is just an instant, a blink of an eye. It is at this stage that our minds are in the best condition to create any art, any poem, any guitar, any new life from our soul and heart. Do you now understand what I mean by being in the zone?"

"Yes, I understand. It was an interesting description. Thank you. Then my next question is..."

"I know, I know," he interrupts, "you want to know how to learn to be *in the zone*, right? Well, this is the sad ending: we cannot teach you that in a two-week workshop. This is a matter of personality and passion for your profession. You have to cultivate your inner being using your own methods. It is not teachable; it is not a procedure to follow. But don't worry, you are not the first to encounter and also overcome this problem. Famous luthiers that have passed through this workshop have had that same problem. The first step is to realize the existence of a problem in order to solve it. I would only recommend a moment of meditation before starting a job in your shop. Relax your mind. Think of nothing if you can. This has helped others, and may be helpful for you as well."

As frustrating as it sounds, I don't feel disappointed. I now know what the problem is, and I am glad knowing that my technique is good. Now that I think more about his words, I realize that what he said is exactly what dad described as the interface problem. In this case, as long as there is an interface between me and the guitar, that is, between me and my art, then I will not be *in the zone*, at unison with my art. Yes, dad's theory still applies here too.

Dinner is approaching. I'd better go to my bedroom to take a shower before it is too late.

9

Hope, Love and Meditation

ON THE WAY TO MY ROOM, ALONG THE DARK and humid hallways of the monastery, I find Father Mauricio. "I thought you were cooking, Father"

"No, not today," he says while walking towards the kitchen. "Are you having dinner in the monastery tonight? Because I would like to talk to you."

"Yes, I am. I will be there in twenty minutes." I wonder what he wants to talk about. I get to my room and take a hot shower. I feel fresh again. As I walk to the dining room, I keep thinking about the advice I got today. It's going to be hard to fix something intangible, something I can't see while I am making the guitar.

I get to the table where Father Mauricio is calmly waiting for me. He is not like other priests who keep preaching every time they have a chance; instead, he waits for my questions, and engages me in an open exchange of ideas and concepts.

"Hi, Father Mauricio. How have you been?"

"Today is my resting day, which means, I don't have to cook. It is always nice to take a rest from your routine work to re-concentrate and do it better next time."

"This trip has been full of coincidences for me," I say. "Today I was told that my techniques are good, but that I was lacking in the spiritual part of my work, the part that makes things flow smoothly and effortlessly. Now you say that resting from cooking allows you to improve your work next time around. I wonder if what I need is some rest to be able to enter the mystical side of my work."

He smiles, takes a piece of warm bread, and while holding it with both hands says, "Walker, I don't know what religion you profess, but in Catholicism resting is presented for the first time in the Bible, in the book of Genesis. God created the world in seven days, but in the last day, the seventh, he didn't do anything; he just rested and contemplated. I can tell you that if I don't rest, my duties become unbearable and my cooking gets worse and worse. But more than resting, what I need is the meditation time, the contemplation period. That period allows me to put my mind in order and to admire the expressions of God around me, and to start with a fresh spirit the next day. Do you understand? Do you rest, Walker?"

"Yes, I do." I quickly answer, but a second later I realize I never rest in the same way he is talking about. "What do you mean by meditation?" I ask.

"Just a second," he says before taking a bite of the bread, already spread with butter. "Your question has to do with what I wanted to talk to you about. There are three important concepts in life: hope, love and meditation. Hope is the fountain of strength and the fountain of many fundamental feelings. If you loose hope, you can't function, you can't even move."

He takes another bite of bread, and continues, "Then there is love. Love is the most important of all feelings. It is like fuel to our soul and energy for everything. It moves the mountains and rivers if necessary. Love is to give, to spread, and to provide in its maximum amount. Love is multiplicative, while hatred is divisive."

He grabs the last piece of bread, and eats it with gusto. "Finally, there is meditation. Meditation is to explore with admiration everything that is around us and within us. It is to admire the beauty of your children, your wife, your friends, your parents, your backyard, the countryside, the wind and the flowers. Also to admire your body as it is, your hands, you wrinkles, your hair, and any part of you. Through meditation you realize how fortunate you are in having them. It is in this period when you reach a unison state with no disturbances from the surroundings, no boundaries with any external object or person. When you meditate, you rest and recharge yourself for another round of hope and love."

Father Mauricio is very eloquent, and now seems to be in the middle of a sermon. I could describe it as *being in the zone,* the zone of preaching without realizing he is in a dining table in front of me. But it is interesting that he is basically saying what the guitarmaking instructor told me before. I guess he is saying that meditation is the preamble of concentration, which in turn allows us to be one with our task.

"I see your point, Father. Your description is very inspirational and complements very well my dad's theory of all problems in life. If meditation is the moment of unison, which will recharge you with hope and love, then what each of us needs is to pass through this regularly in order to remain united with the rest. Well, my dad approached the same problem from a different angle. He used to say that all problems in life are at the interface of things, at the boundary level. Therefore, if we practice meditation, we will feel always as one, in unison, and there will be no problems because there will be no interfaces or boundaries. Does it make sense to you?"

"Indeed son, indeed. It seems to me that your father was a good thinker."

"Let me tell you this," I say, "I have never practiced meditation, so I don't know its effects on solving problems. However, I have found that when there are problems between two persons, the most effective way to resolve them is by asking each person to see themselves with the eyes of the other person. For example, if you and I were in disagreement, I can easily resolve it by imagining I am you, so that I see myself from your perspective. This helps me to understand your position much better and allows me to resolve the problem quicker."

Father Mauricio accepts my explanation and tells me that the same can be achieved with meditation if I do it right. We continue eating and don't talk any more for the rest of the dinner. We say goodbye and retreat to our rooms.

I am resting on my bed when the phone rings. It's Kwame. He sounds excited and happy.

"Hi Walker. How are you?"

"I'm fine, Kwame. How about you?"

"I'm in Copenhagen with Ole visiting his friend. Guess what! Ole's friend plays classical guitar in concert halls around the world. Well, it turns out that he is shopping for a new guitar and since I had just talked to you, I proposed to him to meet you to see what you can offer. I know you always wanted to sell a guitar to someone who travels around giving concerts. Well, this is your opportunity. How does it sound to you?"

"Great!" But internally I was hesitant. My guitars are not good enough for a world class guitarist. I like challenges though.

"Good. He is leaving in two days for St. Petersburg, but if you come tomorrow I can arrange the meeting."

"That sounds fine to me. Is Ole going to be at the meeting?"

"Yes, he will," he replies.

That is good, because I'd like to meet Ole as well. I have the impression that Ole is as interesting as Kwame. "I'll book the first flight in the morning. Which hotel should I stay at in Copenhagen?"

"I'll make a reservation for you in the Hotel D'Angleterre in Kongens Nytorv. Tell the taxi driver the name of the hotel and he will know how to get there for sure. I'll wait for your call."

We say good bye to each other and I hang up the phone. This is going to be exciting for me. I have to prove to myself and to the guitarist that I can do it right. This may be the way to gain a bit of fame within professional guitarists, which I need badly to bring my business to the next level.

10

Fun

HIS IS MY SECOND TIME IN COPENHAGEN. When I was young we visited this country during a two-week vacation around Europe. I was thirteen and remember how small this airport was. It might have been another building. Now, it is a very elegant structure with a sleek, modern atmosphere. The wooden floor, nicely done, has a mosaic pattern that enhances the grain texture. The famous Danish style is shown in every detail: the furniture is simple and functional; the tables are small but comfortable; the walls have the right number of pictures and art work that attracts your attention, but doesn't overwhelm the visitor. Danish style has two qualities: elegance and simplicity. I like it.

I take my luggage and go out of the building to take a taxi. The weather is perfect. The temperature is twenty-two degrees Celsius, about seventy degrees Fahrenheit; it's cloudy and breezy. Taxis are waiting in line. All of them are black luxury sedans. I take one with a Danish driver named Niels Rasmussen, according to the identification card on the dash panel. Taxi drivers are good thermometers of society; they go all around the city, take different passengers with different backgrounds, concerns, and a vast amount of fresh information.

"Hello, I am going to the Hotel D'Angleterre in Kongens Nytorv." The driver nods and turns on the meter. Just after leaving the airport I see the large windmills in the sea. This country is full of them. They are like white swans in a blue lake, swimming together, synchronized with the wind. It creates a feeling of cleanness and prosperity, two things that rarely go hand in hand.

"How are things in Copenhagen these days?" I ask, looking for a candid explanation of the city's environment.

His face, very expressive, shows an unusual seriousness. "Good enough. Lot of taxes as always, too many refugees, politicians making more promises and cloudy days for the last five weeks." He pauses and turns pensive, but then asks, "Where are you from? From America?"

"Yes, I am from Michigan." I pause to see his reaction, but he says nothing. "You sound upset."

"I am," he says very sparingly.

Trying to lift his enthusiasm I begin talking about me and my family: "You know, I've been days away from my family, and I am also feeling kind of upset too. It's always painful to leave them alone while I enjoy the beauty of the old continent. My daughter and my son are probably feeling the same way because we are very close to each other. Do you have children?"

He is quiet, thinking. His face goes from a sweet smile to an angry wince that could intimidate anybody. "What really bothers me," he says, "is my twelve year old son. He is becoming very aggressive verbally, and does not listen as he used to. I just left home and was talking to him about it. He did not care what I said. He is only thinking of music, clothes, shoes, and now girls. Can you imagine? He is only twelve! If I say anything not related to those subjects, he simply becomes defiant. I really don't care about the weather, or politicians, or anything else as long as I have a job and a family that behaves civilized. My son is not giving me any alternative but to punish him."

I see the man is basically talking to himself. If I interrupt, he will loose the *groove* in his monologue. I better stay quiet and wait until he vents his concerns.

"Just yesterday," he continues, "we were playing this game of dreaming of being a millionaire. I was asking him what he would do if he wins the lottery or if he married a rich woman. You know, I just wanted to see what his priorities were. Do you know what he said? Well, he said he would buy a couple of cars, all the shoes he wanted, all the clothes he wanted, and on, and on."

He squeezes the steering wheel with such strength that the muscles in his arms show the tension. He is about to explode. "I was disappointed," he says, "I have been driving this car for fourteen years building a family and giving him the care and moral support he needs. I have shown him my values by example, not by words, and he knows very well that my priorities are not material possessions, but moral values and human relations."

We are already downtown and I make a gesture pointing to one beautiful equestrian statue in the middle of a plaza. He looses his concentration and gets back to his driving.

"Sorry for the long story, but you asked me what was really bothering me, and I just replied."

"Don't worry, I understand very well. I also have a son about the same age as yours. He is okay, but I guess it is just luck."

He turns to look at me, and with a smile and brilliant eyes asks me with such needy tone, "What would you do in my case?"

I didn't expect this question, but he looks quite desperate for an answer, and is almost begging for help. "You know what I recommend to you? Keep talking to him. Sometimes the examples you give are not so evident to him. Spend some time alone with him, with nobody else around, and most importantly, make sure the time is time for fun, just fun. After a while you will learn about his concerns, he will learn about yours, and once the communication is open, there is no stop to it. He will associate fun and sharing feelings with your presence, and that is more important than any answer to any hypothetical what-if-you-were-millionaire question. He smiles at me as if accepting my suggestion, and I feel better for what I came up with.

11

A Beautiful Guitar

THE TAXI DRIVER, PATIENTLY AND PROUDLY, takes me for an extra lap around the Nytorv Plaza and makes some comments about the wonderful buildings. There is the beautiful Royal Theater with a majestic facade, and the new harbor –Nyhavn– with cafés and tables outside on the sidewalk, a very popular site for tourists. There is the Hotel D'Angleterre, the most prestigious in downtown. No matter where I turn my head, the most common transportation system is the bike, the old fashioned, city-efficient, non-polluting, and trusted bike. Yes, biking is very popular in Denmark, not only for the casual dressed worker, but for even the well-dressed men and women. Men with suits and women with high heels, all go to work by bike, pedaling and signaling, following the bike transit rules.

"They are going to work," the driver explains to me to make sure I understand why we need to wait two minutes for so many bikes crossing the street.

Again, I notice the same combination as in the airport: elegance in the attire, and simplicity in the transportation. There must be something inherent in the Danish culture that drives them to be like that. We stop in front of the hotel, and when I pay the taxi driver, he thanks me once more for my advice.

I stand still in front of the hotel, admiring the hotel building. There are lots of people in the street, men and women, all going at the business pace, walking fast, concentrated in their own thoughts. But one thing is well-known in Copenhagen, and it is how beautiful women are. They definitely catch the attention of any foreigner in the city. My travel guide was right: there is no place like Denmark to find beautiful women.

I decide to enter the hotel, and as soon as I step in, I see luxury everywhere. My reservation was all set and the room paid for already. I go upstairs and after a quick nap to restore my energies I call Kwame. We agree to meet in a restaurant in a suburb called Lyngby, north of downtown, at 2:00 PM.

I am feeling nervous. I have to impress the guitarist with my skills as a craftsman, and be sure he feels confident in giving me the job. Kwame told me he was a Danish guitarist, with a bright future, according to the critics. The clerk in the hotel says that I can take a train to Lyngby, if I want to experience something different. I decide to do so and start walking to the main train station. This is a long walk on a pedestrian street full of stores and old buildings. This is a good opportunity to make some purchases for the kids.

I stop at a music store and buy some compact discs for Gabriel and Christina and continue my walk. I get to the main station after passing by the City Hall, an impressive red brick building with golden statues in the facade. Minutes later I get to the main station, an old building with a high ceiling, lots of shops and people. After a couple of questions to find out which train to take, I finally get to the right platform, and very punctually the train arrives.

Once inside the car I sit on an empty bench, put my suitcase on my lap, take one of the free newspapers that were left on the bench, and start looking at the pictures. I can't read Danish, but pictures need no words. The train stops in one of the stations, and then a woman, a gorgeous woman I must say, enters the wagon and sits next to me. I felt the energy of her body when she passed by me. She's wearing a black leather jacket, black pants, a light cream blouse and a red silk scarf. What a delicate touch of color she has. A pair of black sandals that expose her incredible feet, with manicured nails, and a thin line of red polish on each one of them, give the final touch of elegance to this princess. She really knows how to dress. She is so attractive that it is hard for me to maintain my gaze straight without turning to her. She is simply beauty in the most pristine form. I try to distract myself by opening the suitcase and taking out my guitarmaking book. But she is following my moves making me feel even more uncomfortable.

After a while, I notice, through the corner of my eye, that she is looking at my book with special interest, beyond normal curiosity. I let her do it, but when she realizes that I notice her reading my book, she says:

"Are you Mr. McBride?"

She caught me by surprise, big surprise. How can she know my name? I sigh mutely when I see her eyes, sky blue eyes. How can a woman be so beautiful? She is waiting for my answer, but I can't take away my eyes from hers.

"Yes, I am, but how do you know my name?"

"I am just putting together a puzzle. My brother called me yesterday to meet him and an American luthier —Walker McBride— in Lyngby today. I know all Danish luthiers in Copenhagen and you are not one of them. Then I saw you carrying a guitarmaking book, so I guessed you should be Mr. McBride. That's all. No magic. I am Laura Jacobsen, Frederik's sister. Nice to meet you."

Her lips are pink, soft, fleshy, and shiny wet. I scan her entire face, from forehead to chin, no defects at all.

"Nice to meet you, too. Very nice to meet you, indeed." I extend my hand in search of a good handshake. She extends hers, and slides it inside mine with such grace and sweetness. What a warm handshake it is. It is like embracing her whole body with a sensual squeeze and leaves me inspired the rest of the trip. I don't know if she noticed the pleasure I had in holding her hand, but I tried to disguise it with a quick talk about the weather.

"Nice day, isn't it?"

But I feel I made it worse and try to recover with: "This is good luck for me. I won't have to look for the place because you will guide me to the hotel. Sorry! I meant ... to the restaurant." I make things worse when I open my mouth.

She smiles, and says, "The restaurant is a nice place, you will see."

She crosses her legs, fixes her light brown hair and reveals a beautiful, delicate ear. No earrings. She moves her hands with such grace that I am feeling seduced. Her eyebrows are darker than her hair, and perfectly symmetric. Her fingernails are nicely done, enhancing her long, thin, pianist fingers.

"Well," I continue, "How long do you think the meeting with your brother is going to take?"

"It depends on Frederik. Sometimes he is very meticulous when he buys guitars; other times he is very quick to the point. Also, it may depend on how much time you want to spend with me, I mean, with us."

Now I wonder if her words have a double meaning, or it is my imagination. With the very purpose of finding out her real intentions, I test her with, "I am very interested in you ... both. I came all the way from the U.S. to meet you ... both."

She looks at me eye to eye for a fraction of a second. Enough time to let me know that she understands the second meaning of my assertion.

Suddenly she blurts out, "Oh, this is our stop. We have to get out of the train here."

12

The Deal

HERE IS NO MORE CONVERSATION IN OUR WALK from the train station to the restaurant, but she makes coquettish eye contact with me every time there is a turn in the way. Cordiality never does harm, so I move faster as we approach the restaurant to open the door before she does. One more smile to her, and a shy gaze to the floor is my reward.

Kwame is inside sitting with two more people. They must be Frederik and Ole. We all introduce each other, and Laura and I sit side by side. This is an unfortunate position where a covert look at her won't be possible, which I very much would have liked to have. The restaurant is nicely decorated with mahogany wood, carved and polished by an expert, without doubt. The ambiance is sort of romantic and cozy, but the music is far from desirable.

The waitress stops by the table and asks what we want to drink. We all agree to have draft Danish beer —the best one— according to the natives at the table.

"How was your trip?" Ole asks looking at me.

"It was very good, especially the last leg of the trip, which, unexpectedly, Laura was part of. We met inside the train in our way here."

Even though I can't see her face directly, I notice her smile with the corner of my eye. Her brother, Frederik, realizes that there is more than just a coincidence, and asks, "How is your family in America?"

It is time to be realistic, professional, and to start doing business. "They are fine, thank you. My two children and my wife are eagerly waiting my return home. We live in Chelsea, Michigan."

Breaking European traditions of socializing before business matters, maybe because of the urgency of his problem, Frederik follows with a direct question to me, "And how long have you been in the guitarmaking business?"

I fix my glance to him, very firmly, without blinking, showing confidence I say, "I have been making guitars for about fifteen years. It's been a real passion of mine. I started this profession just when my wife got pregnant with my daughter Christina." I glanced at Laura to check her body language. She winces a forced smile and combs her hair with her hand.

When I turn back to see Frederik again, I caught him staring at my arm, like checking out something. As usual, I ignore it.

"I just finished a visit to Sigüenza, Spain," I say, "where I spent several days with several great luthiers. It was very inspiring for me. They told me they were impressed and pleased with my skills as a luthier. I brought with me a portfolio of pictures of guitars I have made, if you want to see the quality of my work."

Laura takes the portfolio while Frederik starts explaining his problem. He is telling me that he dropped his favorite guitar a year ago on a trip to Paris, and that it is badly damaged, irreparable. He seems very sorry about it because he is forced to use his second guitar, which is not of the same quality, plus the size and shape are not the same either. So what he wants is to order a custom-made guitar that must be a replica of his broken, favorite guitar.

Kwame is listening carefully, and nods often. He seems to pay as much attention as I do.

"Well, Frederik," I reply, "you know very well that it is impossible to make two identical guitars because the wood will always be different from one guitar to another. However, I have no problems in attempting to duplicate your favorite guitar as long as I can take it home with me to use it as a template."

Frederik looks at Laura with a questioning gesture on his face. She nods and consents as if she were the owner of the guitar. I don't understand why she has to approve it.

"Not a problem," he says, "but I want you to know something, Walker. I gave the guitar to Laura as a gift last Christmas, but I am sure she can lend it to you for the time you will need it. Right Laura?"

She smiles as a way to accept his proposition. Now the only thing left is to agree on a price for the job. I don't know how to approach the subject.

Fortunately, Ole senses my discomfort and very cleverly interrupts our conversation. "I think we should take a look at the menu first, and continue with the business later," he says. We all agree.

While we are concentrating on reading the menu, Laura approaches me smoothly, and with her lips almost touching my ears, softly says: "We'll have to meet in another place after the meal."

I am not sure what she is thinking, but it sounds very inviting and ... stimulating.

Once we all order our food, Ole interrupts. "We are witnessing a great event at this moment. Two people who had never met each other are about to engage in one of the most ancient rituals in the history of the world."

Ole talks like he is preaching. He makes eye contact with each of us at the table, uses his hand very expressively, and has a peculiar grave voice. His long white beard and his Santa Claus glasses make him look quite an erudite. He continues: "Frederik and Walker, from two different continents, from two different cultures, are about to make a trade, a commercial transaction that will produce a point of contact between two individuals with separate histories. We will witness the negotiation of an exchange of a product with its equivalent in monetary representation; in other words, Walker will offer a product, a guitar to be more specific, and Frederik will provide the currency compensation for such product. Let the negotiation begin."

Laura is totally confused. I can see in her face that she is almost laughing and at the same time, completely lost about Ole's rhetoric.

"Thank you Ole," I say. "Thank you for the introduction; I needed it."

"Let me say one more thing," Ole interrupts again. "Whenever there is a product to be designed, there is always an objective that needs to be maximized to entice the customer and to make the transaction possible. The objective is divided in three components: *quality, beauty and value,* all three of them under an umbrella of a *naturalistic* design. From the conversation we witnessed between Frederik and Walker, we can conclude with certainty that quality will be guaranteed by the master skills of Walker; and that beauty will be matched to the original art piece currently broken. Since the guitar is made of wood, it cannot be more natural, hence, the only thing left is the *value* component, which for fixed quality and beauty, translates directly into the amount of money to be exchanged in this trade."

I know he is talking about the BBBN concept; he is just using other words to say the same thing Kwame told me during the flight to Spain. Frederik, a very smart man, understands Ole's point and asks me what would be the price for his guitar's replica. The question is very difficult, very much. My reputation and my new friendship with Kwame make this decision a hard one. Also, Laura is watching carefully, and I don't want to disappoint her either. So I am going to propose an idea that I hope Frederik will like.

"I will do this, Frederik. I'll make two replicas as identical as I can. And if you like them both, I will charge you ten thousand dollars, but if you are not satisfied with them, you can keep them at no cost." I stop. I want to wait a few seconds to give him time to think. "Is that a fair deal for you?"

He makes eye contact with Laura. She nods. "Well, I did not want to get two replicas, but the offer sounds very attractive. What do you think Laura?"

Laura smiles, and I do too. We all toast saying *skahll* —or something like that— as a symbol of agreement. The waitress comes with the food. Five different dishes are served. Here I am with exquisitely prepared food, good drinks, a good deal that may launch my career, and a strikingly beautiful woman next to me. I can't ask for more.

We are in the middle of the meal when Frederik shakes his head, and says, "The more I think about the two replicas, the more I like it. I am really glad to meet you, Walker. I am confident we will be good partners from now on."

And Laura promptly says, "So am I."

I am glad they liked the idea of two guitars. It was a way to cover my back. I know I can make mistakes some times, but I never do the same mistake twice.

Kwame has been quiet during most of the lunch. I wonder if he has a problem. I ask him about his wife and he says that she is fine. But then, as if his engineering heart wanted to talk, he says, "Walker, you missed the opportunity to play the bargaining game that usually takes place when a product is being sold. You skipped it with your clever proposition. You and Frederik did not go through the process of offer and counter-offer that would have given you an optimization lesson."

"You are right Kwame," Ole seconds, "it would have been a good optimization lesson for Walker to experience that."

I don't understand why they want to talk about optimization here but, I really don't have an interest in finding out. For the time being I am enjoying the company and this delicious salmon that I ordered.

"Walker seems to be an excellent luthier craftsmanship," Kwame says, "and he also have excellent business skills with his proposition. Where I come from, this is hard to find. You find lots of engineers, self-centered, proud of their creativity, trying to sell new products without knowing the needs of the customer. Walker showed us that if you read the customer carefully, you provide immediate satisfaction, even before the product is delivered."

"Thank you Kwame, thank you for your words," I say.

At the end of the meeting we all exchange phone numbers for future contact. Laura takes a napkin, writes down her address and gives it to me.

"I'll be here the rest of the day. Call me any time to pick up the broken guitar." She places her hand on mine and we both experience a warmth pass through our fingers.

"I ... will," I say while nodding my head.

We say goodbye, and I renew my promise to Frederik to provide the two replicas within few months.

We all take different paths from the restaurant, and I call a taxi to go to the hotel rather than using the train. I want to get ready and call Laura as soon as I can.

13

A Flirt

GET TO THE HOTEL, TAKE A SHOWER, change clothes, comb what is left of my long hair, all that in record time for my standards. I am feeling nervous already, my hand is sweating, my lips are dry. I walk around the room trying to decide what to say first. I pick up the phone, hesitate, grab the napkin with the number, and finally dial it and wait. The phone is ringing one ... two ... three times, and someone picks it up.

"Hi, Laura?" I say before any voice is heard.

"Hi, Walker. What took you so long?" She sounds anxious too.

My heart is pumping like a baby's; my hand is now trembling; the room temperature seems higher. "It is just that... well, it doesn't matter. I am sort of free now. Do you have time to meet with me?"

"Yes, I do. Here is how to get here. Coming from downtown you need to take the train from the Norreport station. Make sure you are going North and stop at the Hellerup station. I'll be waiting for you there, then we can walk to my place."

I heard what she said, but if I go by taxi we'll spend more time together. "I think I am going to take a taxi instead, I will meet you at your apartment if you don't mind."

There is a pause in the other side of the line. It seems an eternity to me, but then I hear her voice: "Not a problem, Walker, I'll be in my apartment."

After we finish our conversation, many thoughts cross my mind; many feelings of sadness mixed with enthusiasm are coming from inside me. I've never felt this before. I feel disloyal towards Emily but, at the same time, the desire to be with Laura is so strong, so powerful. She is so sweet and feminine, and so attractive that I can't resist the temptation to be with her.

It takes me twenty minutes to get to the street where she lives: a nice area of old buildings with large front gardens, green lawns and roses. I pay the driver and step out of the car slowly, thinking what am I doing, thinking *why* am I doing it. This is crazy. I know I love my wife, my kids; but, this impulse is taking over me and I can't stop it. It's been so long since I have felt attraction for a woman.

I keep walking, even though my legs are getting stiffer with each step. Finally, after a few blocks, I find it. I enter the main gate, where a wooden door, probably more than a hundred years old, is half open. I push it, enter into a dark hall, find the stairs, go up two stories, and finally get to her apartment's door. I hesitate for a second, trying to clear my mind, trying to think, trying to convince myself that what I am doing is correct, fair, proper; but, my thoughts bounce from one place to another inside my head. I am confused. I knock on the door and hear her steps rushing and approaching the door. I wipe my face with a handkerchief just before the door opens, and when she is in front of me, with her sweet big smile, looking better than before, my heart begins pumping faster and my jaw is almost frozen. She also has a handkerchief in her hand, which probably was used just before opening the door as well.

"Hi, Laura. I am glad to see you again," I say with my most sincere smile.

"Hi, Walker." She gets closer to me, places her hand on my shoulder and kisses my left and right cheeks, following to the European tradition.

"Please come in and have a seat," she says while pointing to the sofa.

She walks towards the window giving me a view of her beautiful figure. Only the silhouette is visible because the bright light that comes from the window doesn't let me see details. She has the body of a slender guitar. I take a quick look at the rest of the apartment. I can feel music all around: in the little ornaments of musicians playing guitars; in the music sheets laying on the table; in the pictures of concert halls hanging on the walls; I breathe music everywhere. There is a nice dinner table covered with a purple tablecloth, Danish candles on top, already lit. The sofa is made of black leather and the walls are painted light blue in combination with the blinds in the window.

After she closes the blinds, which she did with her innate grace, she turns towards me and sits on the sofa, only a few inches away from me. Silence invades the room: we stare at each other, with poise and calm, with tenderness and a subtle hidden desire. She starts talking about her brother's broken guitar and how she keeps it as a family treasure. I look at her from head to toe when she is not looking at me. She is wearing a red dress with a very low cut in front that makes her look even better than when I first met her.

I contend with my desire to say something to flatter her, and I give in: "I see you changed to a beautiful red dress."

"What? Oh, yes, I spilled orange juice before you came. You are very observant, Walker."

"Well, it is hard not to see the changes; the red looks better on you."

"Thank you," she says with a dry and short tone. I guess I am going too fast, because now, all of a sudden, her gestures become rude. She goes to her bedroom and comes back with the guitar. No words, no smile, nothing, only the guitar is in her mind now.

I take the guitar from her. "Did I say something you didn't like?"

"No, it's all right. I am having a bad day and feel tired."

It sounds like an excuse. I think she wants to talk about something, so I take the risk and decide to invite her for a drink downtown.

She looks at my eyes very intently, silent for a moment; but smiling and straightening her back, with her chest high, and a twist in her neck, she says, "That sounds wonderful. Let's do it." She picks up her purse and opens the door.

Once downtown we start walking on the pedestrian street, in front of the City Hall. We start looking for a place to have a drink. She is from town, so I ask her to pick the place. She says there is a bar around the corner where we can go, then grabs my hand and start walking with a sense of happiness that can be felt by just looking at her. We get to the place, but the door is locked.

"It's okay," she says. "She knocks and the owner comes, then greets her with a big hug and a couple of kisses.

"Walker, this is Michael, my cousin," she says.

After the formal handshake we sit and order a couple of beers. Michael brings them and goes back to the kitchen. I have the feeling that he knows what to do in this situation, as if I were not the first to come with her. Then I look at Laura's eyes very firmly waiting for a word, any gesture, any thing.

She evades my glance, but then says: "Do you have any hobby?"

I don't know why she is asking this, but I tell her that I am very fortunate since my profession is my hobby. I explain to her how the techniques and the art are merged in my profession, which is an excellent combination for my personality. I tell her how many hours I spend in the guitar shop with no regrets at all. She stays quiet, listening with interest, resting her head in her hands, the left one first, and the right one next.

"Well, that is interesting. I can see you spend most of your time in your shop. How about your wife and kids?" She asks.

"Why do you ask?"

"Because, the way you look at me makes me think you are a married man looking for trouble."

"Trouble? Do you call that trouble? I can also see the way you looked at me when I passed through the door of your apartment.

The Guitar Maker

I call it attraction, pure and simple attraction between a man and a woman."

She is smiling, accepting —conceding— would be a better word. She then tells the story of her life. She married a man who was in the Air Force and rarely saw him while they were married. They only were together for one year, ending in a divorce. She has been a flight attendant for several years, which made things worse for her marriage. She's traveled all around the world and speaks five languages very fluently, something that, she says, is a good skill to find interesting men, but not enough to retain them. The way she talks about her job makes me doubt she really likes being a flight attendant. I ask which part of her job she likes best, and she quickly answers "the travel itself, not the places." I get a bit confused with the answer and ask for an explanation.

"After being in this job for seven years," she says, "I came to the conclusion that the best part of a trip is the 'going there.' When you are traveling, you are making an effort, spending energy, making plans, imagining the scenario, predicting the pleasure of being there. That is the best part. But when you get there, all of that is gone. The unknown disappears, and you have nothing else to hope for. It is like when you are climbing a mountain: when you get to the top, you are done; there is no more mystery. The fun is gone and the only thing left is to go down."

It is an interesting viewpoint. I like the way she speaks, her facial gestures, her manners, and the flow of her hands. She really is exquisite. I notice she realizes that I am staring at her, and suddenly she stops talking.

"Walker, are you listening to me?"

"Yes, I am." I answer automatically, without thinking.

"Anyway, I wonder how do you manage to spend so much time at your work. A wife and kids probably need a lot of your attention."

This is strange. The more I know her, the less interest I feel now. It is similar to what she was saying about traveling. It is as if the unknown hints at beauty and hope. Yet, as I peel the layers of her character, that beauty is less prominent and is transformed into a more concrete image that is more real and less idyllic. Now I realize I am getting old. If I were twenty years younger, I would be inviting her to a more intimate place instead of being here, talking about our past. My priorities have changed since the last time I was after a woman.

She notices I am deeply lost in my own thoughts. She makes a gesture to get my attention. Her pupils are big and looking for mine.

"I think we should go back to my apartment," she sensually suggests.

But now I don't want to go. I am feeling deflated after so much enthusiasm. It must have been that reality hit me after hearing her story. I am married, with two children, and even though my marriage is not going as well as I would like to, I should play fair, honestly and trustfully.

"Why?" I ask.

"Well, you left the broken guitar in my apartment."

"Oh, I forgot about the guitar altogether."

We finish our beers, say goodbye to her cousin and leave the bar. The sky is now cloudy and the wind is strong. Once inside the taxi I sit straight, looking to the front of the vehicle. She is facing me, with her right leg delicately crossed over her left one. I cannot resist looking at them. She knows what she is doing. I try to keep my eye sight straight ahead. Then she gets closer to me and touches my knees with hers. I close my eyes for an instant to gain strength.

"Laura, I..., I..."

She notices that I am not in the mood and retreats to her side. No words are exchanged thereafter. Once in the apartment, the one that I was so impressed with just an hour ago, I start feeling different. The colors I loved when I first saw them look pale and monotone. The musical environment has become silent in a way.

She sits on the couch and waits for me, but I, instead, grab the guitar and say, "Laura, it was nice to chat with you. I feel I should not let my impulses overcome my values... this time. Do you mind if I leave now?"

She looks confused and disappointed. I don't blame her. I came on so forcefully at the beginning, and now I am running away like a scared chicken. She breaks her posture with such disdain. But after a moment, she regains her strength, as if she has been through this situation before, and says, "Walker, we both need to organize our priorities. Life is not easy, and we make it more difficult when we act without thinking. I want to say one last thing: you are the type of man I enjoy being with. Can we keep in contact while you make the replicas for Frederik?"

"For sure. I will call you and tell you how things are going in the shop. I promise. Thank you for understanding."

We have a little hug, a soothing kiss on the cheek and a lasting handshake that seems to never end. It's nice. I like what she said: life is difficult, but we should keep trying to do our best, prioritizing and thinking before acting.

14

The Quartet

IT IS EIGHT BY THE TIME I AM BACK in the hotel. I drop on my bed and stare at the white ceiling trying to understand what has happened. I feel emptiness, a feeling of nothingness that leaves me confused, sad, disoriented. I should have been more sensitive, I think. I don't know why I behaved like I did. I don't know.

The phone rings. I hope it is Laura. This may be my second chance to repair the damage. But no, it is Kwame calling from the lobby, asking me to meet him in the hotel's restaurant where he and Ole are having a drink. This will set my mind in another place for a while, which may be good for my mood at this moment. I go downstairs.

As soon as I enter the restaurant I see them. They are sitting next to the windows, watching the people pass by in the Nytorv Plaza. I am happy to meet them again, and they show the same feeling towards me. "Walker!" Kwame says when I arrive to the table.

"What a nice surprise. I thought you guys were heading to Ribe."

"Yes, we were planning to, but we decided to stop by and have a little conversation with you." Kwame replies.

"Actually it was my idea," Ole interrupts. "I think I couldn't complete my argument during lunch time. There were too many interruptions and other interests. I was trying to tell you about the beauty of duality in optimization. It is a simple but powerful concept that you should know. Let me explain it with the seller-buyer situation."

I don't feel like listening to this anymore, but they came all the way here to teach me something, so I'd better pretend to be attentive.

"When a person is selling a product," Ole begins, "he or she tries to maximize the transaction price. That's the goal for the seller, to obtain the maximum amount of benefit —money— from the selling of the product. However, simultaneously, the buyer is trying to minimize the amount to pay for the product. In other words, the buyer wants to minimize the price paid. Therefore, if there is a price at which both agree to make the transaction, this price is the simultaneous solution of the seller's maximization problem and buyer's minimization problem. You see? In mathematics, these two problems are called *primal and dual,* and they play an important role in some methods to solve optimization problems."

I understand his explanation, but I don't know how to use it in my problems. "And how do I use this concept of duality?"

"It is used in many situations during the problem formulation, or during the solution process," Ole responds. "But you don't have to worry about it. It is a very difficult concept that can be learned later. You only need to realize that there are two ways to solve any optimization problem you face. The primal and dual ways are indeed like the two sides of a coin, both belong to the same token and provide equal value."

"Wait a minute, I see an analogy here," I say abruptly. "If we take the seller-buyer example you mentioned, we can think of them as two people going in opposite directions, but at the end both meet at the same point, the solution point. This reminds me of the situation of personal conflicts. Yes, this is a good analogy. For example, when two people are in conflict, they are each solving an optimization problem, aren't they? Both problems are probably the primal and dual problems. Don't you think Ole?"

"I don't know Walker," Kwame responds. Personal conflicts are not within my area of expertise. You may be right, but I don't know."

I feel I'm in the right path. I should think more about this later. More people gather in the plaza across the street. The waitress comes to the table and asks me what I want to drink. I order a glass of French red wine. I can't miss the opportunity to drink good wine in Europe.

"Any particular brand, sir?" She asks with perfect British accent.

"You may bring the one you like most."

"Walker," Kwame says, "there is another reason we came to talk to you. We have not mentioned the last attribute of a good design. I am talking about the N in the BBBN quartet. It refers to Nature, and I am going to explain it in more detail before you go back to Michigan."

"I am glad you bring it up, Kwame. This way I can go home with all concepts clear and understood."

"Let me start from the very beginning," Kwame says. "Hundreds of years ago, when the Betterment-Beauty-Bargain concept was first taught, Nature was not threatened by our civilization. Natural resources were plenty for the few million people living on earth. This is why the original version was made of just three items: B-B-B. However, since the industrial revolution things are quite different. The population has grown so much and our polluted style of living is so intense that the planet is feeling the impact of our human activities. Cars, trains, airplanes, nuclear plants, dams, all pollute or disturb the environment in one way or another. People are generating tons of garbage each day in the modern throw-away lifestyle, wasting water to green their lawns, driving wildlife to extinction, and even worse things are happening. Therefore, the best design cannot be one with only quality, beauty and value. We need to consider an additional measure to leave a living planet —a nurturing planet— to our children. In other words, we need to add one more measure in the design process, that is, a measure of friendliness with nature, or a *Naturalistic* metric. So our quartet is finally: Betterment, Beauty, Bargain and Naturalistic.

"What we mean by Naturalistic," Ole interrupts, "is more than just the use of natural materials. It means to create products in the same way Nature does it. A Naturalistic design is adaptable to the environment, it is not static, but evolutionary. A Naturalistic design uses the waste of other natural processes and produces the input for another natural process. It uses the minimum of energy and simultaneously cleans the surroundings. It adapts, and cohabits with, even dissimilar, designs."

The waitress returns with an open wine bottle and a glass of wine. In her soothing and sweet voice, she says, "I'll pour it for you." I like her eyes, green and bright. She smiles at me as she place the glass on the table and waits for my response. I pick up the glass, and tilt it back and forth to check the consistency. It is good. The red is intense and it smells of vanilla and berries. I take a sip. "It's good," I say, "really good." She gestures with gratitude and leaves. We all three look at her back as she walks to the kitchen. What a figure! I say to myself.

Kwame notices my distraction so, with a graver voice than usual, he says: "For millions of years Nature has brought to us all kinds of BBB designs, with the perfect balance of each B for every situation. But most importantly, Nature has done it for free. Now that we are creating a society that consumes and wastes so much, we need to reverse gears by avoiding depletion of resources, and making sure that the waste from our activities does not deplete, but rather feeds another entity or process. Eventually, all must return to Nature to complete the cycle of life in harmony with it. Put in simple words, every design we create must have a natural purpose, one that Nature would have chosen."

"But coming up with such designs seems almost impossible to achieve," I complain.

"I know," Kwame replies, "but we, as a civilization, are running out of time before the damage to Nature is irreversible. As an engineer I feel responsible to stop this nonsense. Let me give you an example of a bad design. Let's talk about computers. As you know, computers become obsolete very quickly, and piles and piles of personal computers are thrown away every year. That waste is a cost to us, society. This cost is not factored in when you pay for the computer in the store, though. The costs of cleaning the waste, of eliminating toxins from the disposed materials, are not mentioned in the advertising of the product. However if we could build computers out of materials that can be recycled, the disposal cost would be very low and Nature would bring back its source of resources each time. So, when you think of new designs, keep in your mind that whatever you build must consider the entire cost, including the cost to nature to take care of the waste your product generates."

"But Kwame," I reply, "when we use Nature's resources, we transform them in a way that sometimes is impossible to reverse. For instance, you can't make Natural rocks from cement."

Ole smiles. "You are right. Entropy, as physicists call it, imposes an extra problem on us. The laws of physics indicate that Nature tends to equilibrium, but on the way to reach equilibrium, energy is transformed, and a portion of that energy is not recoverable. Our job is then to make that irreversible energy as small as possible, in a way that it is possible to sustain a world where Nature and business thrive and humanity enjoys a happier life."

"Besides," Kwame continues, "I think it is not a matter of choice. There is only one possible thing to do. We need to change one by one, with the power of each person, one at a time. Each of us can influence companies by using and buying products that are Naturalistic in the way we described before. And you Walker, you are a manufacturer; you can even be part of the solution from the business side. Build your guitars with the right materials, with the right manufacturing processes that pollute the least, so that you become a responsible manufacturer."

"Keep in mind that every time you make a guitar," Ole says, "you are transforming energy from raw materials to structured, usable materials. This transformation is not one hundred percent perfect since, as I said before, some energy is lost in the process. For instance, the electric power you use in your shop is already the end result of oil or coal burning; hence, it is a polluting energy to begin with. How about the glue you use in the guitar joints? Is it a natural product or a pollutant chemical? But don't misunderstand me with regard to materials. It's not that we have to use rocks, leather and wood to build everything we need. Technology has created excellent materials and solutions to solve real problems in our society. The issue is about sustainability of the planet, either with synthetic or natural materials. There are many hidden sources of non-sustainable materials and processes that we don't know. The tons of chemicals that the industrial society is pumping to rivers, lakes and to the atmosphere every day will bite us back some day. When that happens the B of *bargain* will become E of *expensive*, because it will be extremely expensive to clean the environment to maintain healthy breathable air, for instance; So Nature will not be able to provide us with bargain resources, but with very expensive ones."

"I still think it is very difficult. Where do we start?" I ask with a desperate tone.

Ole smiles and says: "That is the question I was waiting for. What we need to do is to use the same methods used by Nature. We need to imitate its approaches."

"But what are they?"

Kwame and Ole look at each other as if they know what they have to say. Ole nods indicating to Kwame to continue.

"We need to pose every problem using the BBB concept, but then, evolve intensively."

"Evolve? What do you mean?" I am getting confused now.

"We are talking about evolution," he says. "We are talking about making mistake after mistake. This way we will accommodate and find a better solution with each small mistake. I told you before that time is the best optimization algorithm. This is the reason for that. The more time passes, the more small mistakes you make, the more you learn, and the closer to the optimum you get. This is evolution in its simplest form. Darwinian evolution can be, and has been, applied to design problems for centuries. But the key ingredient is to make small mistakes and learn lessons as fast as you can, so there is constant improvement."

The waitress comes to the table, gives me another smile and takes the empty bottles of beer. Ole speaks in Danish to her, and from the movement of his hands I understand that he is asking for another beer.

"How about you, sir, do you want more wine?" She asks as she shines my face with her smile.

"Thank you, but I am fine with this. Thank you."

"As I was saying," Kwame interrupts, "that is why the injection of new ideas is so important for society. New ideas are like mutations of the DNA. New ideas bring fresh approaches to solve problems and are combined with the old ideas to improve designs and products. Alternatively, old ideas are slightly modified to generate better methods and solutions. As you see, now I am talking about mating, crossing and mutation. I am talking about pure evolution. It is survival of the fittest design."

"Let me see if I understand," I say. "You say that BBBN is not enough. We need to mess around and make small mistakes and adaptations very quickly, and so generate new solutions that are continuously better."

"You got it right," Kwame says with a big smile on his face. "The more error-proof your solutions are, the more robust the design is. Naturalistic designs have several features that we need to imitate. They are robust, reliable, multipurpose, durable, adaptable, and persistent. But in order to get to such designs, you have to make small mistakes very quickly, don't forget that. If you do it slowly, you will look dumb and your product will be out-paced by another one in the market."

"Market? I thought we were talking about society's well being," I complain.

The waitress brings the beer for Ole. It is getting dark outside, and the city lights are already on. It is such a nice view from this restaurant.

"You are right," Kwame says. "I jumped ahead too fast. Let me be clear. You may have noticed that Ole is fascinated with the mathematics of optimization. Well, it happens that he is a mathematician. When we first met, I told him about the BBBN story and he translated it to the field of optimization very nicely. However,

I was always reluctant to accept that everything was so mathematically designed. I knew something was missing in his optimization model. My years in the manufacturing industry taught me that we engineers have a different and very important job in society. We are responsible for *creating products and services that change the world to make it a better place to live.* That is my definition of engineering in a nutshell.

"If we just apply the mathematics to a problem, we don't get the product out. We need more than that. So comes the need for evolution, for mistakes, for judgment and experience from a human perspective. Engineers deal with all that imprecise mathematics to make it work. This is called the science of statistics, where things are not one hundred percent predictable but *probable* up to a certain degree, and very complex at the same time. Once we engineers sort out all this imprecise and complex world of problems, we have one last step to take. Can you guess what it is?"

"Well, once you solve the problem and manufacture the product, the only thing left is to sell it to the public," I respond matter-of-factly.

"Close, but not the answer. Unfortunately, there is always a middle person. Our last step is to communicate to the manager, or salesperson, what we have created, and convince them that the product is the optimum solution of the problem. Since words are not as precise as numbers, this last step introduces even more fuzziness to the already fuzzy design problem. But we have to live with that."

"Oh, I hate that!" I say. "That is why I keep my company small. I deal directly with my customers. No middlemen!"

Kwame lifts his hand and calls the waitress. She comes, like a graceful swimmer through the tables in the restaurant. "Do you want one more beer?" She asks.

"Yes, please," Kwame responds. After she leaves, he continues. "Well, you have not gotten rid of the manager though. The difference is that you are both, the engineer and the manager as well. My point is that we do need the salesperson because if our BBBN product does not reach the market, we are not fulfilling our mission as engineers, which is *to change the world to make it a better place to live.* If we keep the product on the drawing table, or in the computer model, we are doing nothing but a simple mathematical optimization exercise."

I am starting to understand his argument. We stay quiet for a moment, as if we all agree on the issue. But there is something I can't do with my guitars. "Kwame, I have a problem with the idea of making small mistakes. You see, I can't go to my shop and start making guitar after guitar, mistake after mistake, in order to get to the *optimum* design. I would be out of business in a few weeks."

"I understand, Walker. I have the solution for that. What you need is modern engineering and more mathematics. You need a virtual laboratory, a virtual model of your guitar where you can test your ideas, make mistakes, without spending much of your money. I can help you with that. It is not a problem for me."

"Well, it sounds interesting," I reply. "I like that idea. But tell me, how does Nature do its experiments? Nature has no computer!"

Ole smiles, and Kwame too. "Now we are entering the difficult part of the subject," Ole says. "We could argue that the entire earth, that is, its rivers, mountains, animals, humans, plants, everything, is a fully virtual experiment of a supreme being."

He stops there, waiting for my reaction. What an interesting concept. It combines God's existence and science. "I smile, and then nod to both of them."

While we were talking Ole was drawing a pyramidal figure of four corners on the restaurant's napkin. I ask him what is on the napkin.

"It is the quartet of optimal designs," he replies. "This shows the three main attributes of a design: Betterment, Beauty and Bargain, which when combined produce a Naturalistic design. You can see that if a design is focused on one of the corners, it is far from optimum. A design near the Betterment corner is usually a product of pure mathematics where the beauty and the cost are not considered. A design near the Beauty corner is usually a product of pure artistic talent where the benefit and the cost are not considered. A design near the Bargain corner is usually a product of a salesperson where the benefit and the beauty are not considered. It is only the Naturalistic design that is perfectly in equilibrium with all three

Bs in harmony. It is the Naturalistic design that will provide the true global optimum with a Natural purpose for society."

Ole passes the napkin with the drawing. It is so understandable once I see it.

It's been a nice chat, but it is late now. I have to excuse myself to go upstairs to get prepared for the flight tomorrow. "My friends, please accept my apologies, but I need to go upstairs now. It has been an excellent experience to meet you both. I am sure we will see each other again."

Ole and Kwame stand and we stretch and shake hands with a sincere feeling. I get to my room and start preparing the suitcase. Christina and Gabriel are going to like these presents. They always expect my gifts when I go away for long trips. I can't wait to see their faces.

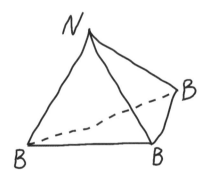

15

So is Life

AM BACK IN MICHIGAN AFTER MY wonderful trip to Europe. I am happy to see the kids and Emily after so many days. There is nothing better than to spend an afternoon with family. Gabriel is sitting next to me, jumping up and down with a big smile on his face. Emily is sitting on the couch folding some shirts she just took out of the dryer, and Christina my dear daughter, is next to me, hugging me as if I was gone for years. We are talking about my trip, sharing anecdotes, and talking about some of the characters I met during my days away from home —like Kwame, Ole and Father Mauricio. Emily is fascinated and intrigued about Kwame, who I have praised several times already.

I am about to open the bag with the music CDs I bought for the kids when I realize that I didn't buy anything for Emily —a big mistake. I should've remembered. Damn it! It happened again! I act as if I am looking for other things inside the bag, but then I close it. "I can't find a postcard of Sigüenza I wanted to show you kids," I say to trick and mislead Emily, but in her face, with her very expressive green eyes, and pointed brows, I see that she notices my false move, but purposely ignores it to save me, I believe, from an embarrassment in front of the kids.

We continue talking for some time, until I realize how late it is, and how tired I am. I send the kids to bed and I begin a soft walk to my room, thinking on what this night may bring to us. Emily went upstairs before me. I hope she is still awake. I get to the bed and contemplate for a few seconds the silhouette of the woman I have adored for most in my life. I wait and wait, then finally and quietly slide under the blanket looking for some action. However, to my surprise, after so many days without seeing each other, without touching each other, she is deeply asleep. I guess she didn't miss me much while I was gone.

It is Monday morning. I wake up early to get to the shop before Manuel, my diligent young apprentice. The shop is a few blocks away, on Park street, next to the farmer's market where Emily and I used to shop each Sunday until the tragic day when Gabriel was born.

Once in the shop, Manuel shows up and I call him to my office to talk about what I learned in Sigüenza. I also want to tell him what Kwame taught me during the trip. We sit on either side of my drawing desk, and I start a conversation with the intention of convincing him about the benefits of doing BBBN designs. He is sharp and grasps the important points quickly. However, with the same speed as he understands, he starts asking questions that I am not prepared to answer.

"I am not sure we can do what your new friend wants," Manuel argues. "You want a design that will give us a product with quality, beauty, low cost and at the same time be naturalistic? I don't see how you can do that. You are asking too much."

"Well Manuel, let's take one thing at a time. The first B is for betterment which not only means quality in our case, but also consistency of quality. You know fully well that some of our clients return their guitars because of unexpected defects. We must avoid that. Similarly, other clients are so impressed with the quality of our guitars that they even send letters of congratulations. We need to keep repeating that. Consistent quality is vital; it is a requirement in a well designed product. Do you think that we can find a way to repeat our good designs and avoid the costly mistakes?"

"Yes, I do," he says with excited but agitated voice. "But, we need to repeat the design and manufacturing process for every guitar we make. We cannot improvise depending on our mood or our desire to experiment with new methods."

He doesn't like my style of management. He is right. Each time I get a new wood, I give him different instructions on how to make guitars. It is hard not to. I love to experiment with new ideas.

"Okay Manuel, I know what you mean by that. We have to be more consistent, too. I promise I'll change; I promise."

"But let me finish my explanation. The second B, beauty, is also an important characteristic in our product. You know very well that when a guitar has a beautiful design —good ornamentation, fine wood, stylish hardware— it is easier to sell than others. I am not worried about beauty in our case because we are very consistent in that, don't you think?"

"Yes, I agree. Actually, I would say that nine out of ten guitars are sold just because of the way they look."

"The third letter, B, for bargain, cost or value," I continue, "is the one that affects the bottom line of our business. We need to reduce the design time for customized guitars, reduce the construction time for all guitars we make, and reduce the material waste. If we concentrate in these three areas, we will be more profitable."

He nods in agreement because we have talked about this before. It seems simple, but it is really hard to resolve all three issues effectively.

"The last characteristic is to create Naturalistic designs and products. This is a complex issue that I could not understand fully from Kwame, but I will try to elaborate once more. A naturalistic design, or product, has all the three attributes mentioned before. The best way I can put it is that each step to create a guitar, starting from the harvest of the wood, involves the use of natural resources. If we minimize that use, or misuse, we will be doing our best for Nature and for the generations to come, do you follow?"

"But when you say *Nature*," he replies, "are you including us, humans?"

"Good question," I say. "The way I see it is like this. Nature has its methods to evolve that follow some principles that we don't know very well. On the other hand, humans have other methods and objectives that often are in conflict with Nature's, so even though we are part of Nature, I would put us outside for a moment, in order to be able to examine ourselves, to see how we affect the rest of the environment, and to try to be able to evolve without jeopardizing the future of our children. If I think of humans as part of Nature, then we have no need to re-examine our behavior, because Nature's principles would take care of that."

"Mmm, I see your point," he says with a pondering expression in his face. He then shakes his head and looks down. He walks back and forth a couple of times and says very convincingly, "You know what happens when you reduce cost: quality goes down along with it. How do you expect to have a good quality product at a bargain price?"

As I said, he is sharp. He's got me now. This young man is going to be someone some day. He is just 20 years old, born in Texas from a poor Nicaraguan family, and here he is, learning the trade of a luthier, studying for a computer science degree at the Community College, and never complains. What a hard worker he is! That is why I decided to hire him a year ago —he deserves it. I pay his tuition as a fringe benefit because I know he will be a great man.

"Let me think more about it, Manuel. I'll give you an answer soon. For the moment, keep in mind what I said: *increase quality, increase beauty, reduce cost, and make it in harmony with Nature.*"

We stop our conversation, stand and continue with our duties for the day. He goes to the back of the shop to bend some guitar sides, and I start thinking about how to be prepared for Kwame when he comes back from Europe. I think I am going to monitor my procedures to see how to reproduce them with more precision. This is probably the best way to gather information for him.

I spent most of the day collecting information, taking notes, making some drawing, all that for Kwame. At the end of the day, soon after six, I head home.

The next day I wake up earlier than usual because of the jet lag that is still changing my internal clock. I take a shower, dress, and go to the shop when the sky is still dark. I begin with the neck of a guitar that needs sanding. I count the passes of sand paper per minute, just in case Kwame asks me for that. He insisted many times on having measurable quantities in order to apply optimization techniques. I devised a caliper to measure the thickness at any point of the guitar plate. I rented some electronic equipment that Kwame asked me to have for him. I am sure he knows how to use the instrument to improve the guitar tones. I use the rest of the day to write a detailed manual of how a guitar is made and try to relate each step to the quality, beauty and cost of the guitar. I am sure this will be helpful information for Kwame when he visits the shop. I hope all this translates into better guitars.

The week has gone by very fast, and I am still taking notes for the manual. I may be exaggerating the whole thing with the one hundred and fifty pages I have written in few days. But as my mom used to say —*write, write, write, and preserve your memories for future generations.* The worst that can happen is that I finish with a nice book for luthiers.

When I get home, Emily tells me that Kwame called and proposed to meet with me next Monday at the shop. But I'd prefer to invite him to dinner here at home to introduce him to Emily and the kids. This coming Friday is a good time. Emily also likes the idea because she is now intrigued about my new friend that I've talked about so much since I came back from my trip. When I call Kwame he sounds very enthusiastic about the dinner, and quickly accepts the invitation.

It is Friday afternoon; I'm exhausted. It's been a hard working week. Fortunately, it is just about the time to leave and get prepared for the dinner. Manuel, who has been going around and around in the shop, enters my office. He seems concerned, but says nothing about what is disturbing him. "Hi, Walker. How is everything?"

"Just fine. I am about to leave for the dinner with Kwame."

"Oh, I see. You like that guy, don't you."

"He is a nice guy, I told you already," I reply. Manuel stays quiet, but he stares at me.

"Okay Manuel, what is the problem? You did not come to ask me about Kwame. What do you need?"

With an unusual hesitant voice, he says, "I don't know how to say it but... I need some money. My grandmother is sick in Nicaragua and my cousins told me she may not live more than a week. I am thinking of going."

"No problem Manuel. How much do you need?"

"It is just for the airplane ticket, I am guessing about 450 dollars."

I write a check and give it to him. I need no more explanation. "Now go home, and say hi to your grandma for me."

"Thank you Walker, thank you. I'll pay you back."

It is hard enough to be away from home, even harder when you want to help and you can't. I feel so pleased to be able to help him because he is such a good person and worker.

When I get home, Emily is busy preparing dinner, and the kids are in their rooms. The food smells good. I enter the kitchen to see what she prepared. It is salmon in mustard sauce. Emily knows I love it. She has also prepared onion soup that tastes delicious, especially with Parmesan cheese on top. I am sure Kwame will like it too. I then go upstairs and find Christina laying on bed and crying.

"What is the problem, honey?" I ask, but she doesn't answer. I comb her hair with my fingers and ask again.

This time she says, "It is about this boy..."

She catches me by surprise! I guess I have not spent enough time with her to realize that she is already dealing with boys.

"Is he your boyfriend? I ask calmly, hoping that nothing bad already happened between them.

"Yes... well... no, not really. He is just a friend, but I like him."

"And he likes another girl." I try to complete her sentence.

"No, no... well... yes; he does... I think."

She looks very sad and confused. When I was her age I had no interest in girls yet; so, I cannot place myself in her position. This is the first time I have no answer for her problems, and I feel like a novice on this subject. I tell her not to worry too much, and start thinking of the dinner we will have tonight with Kwame. She looks at me and nods, but I know it won't last long. She has been a very nice daughter all these years —no problems at schools, no problems with boys, very easygoing personality.

The doorbell rings. Christina hugs me and lets me go. I go downstairs, slowly, thinking about all problems I've encountered since I came from Europe: my wife prefers to be sleeping instead of with me; my apprentice is having family problems; my daughter is becoming an adult; and my guitars are still not selling as well as I would like to. So is life, I guess: full of problems to solve.

I open the front door, and see Kwame with roses in his hand. "Kwame! Please come in."

"Hi, Walker. I am glad to see you again."

Emily, Gabriel and Christina come to the door to greet him. I feel as if I saw him yesterday. He is wearing a black leather jacket, blue jeans and a white shirt. He brought some candies for the kids too. He presents the roses to Emily who takes them with a smile, but I can tell she is surprised about Kwame. The kids, curious as always, don't take their eyes off Kwame's hands. He has long, slender fingers like a piano player. This is going to be an interesting dinner.

"Emily, we will be downstairs for just a moment," I say. "I want Kwame to see my private shop in the basement." This will give Emily some time to do the final touches for the dinner.

16

Design I*

AS WE TAKE THE STEPS I START describing what I have and what I am working on. "Kwame, this is my shop and my passion. I have my business on Park street, but this is my private place, at home in Garfield street. I've been making acoustic guitars here in my basement and in my shop downtown for fifteen years. I enjoy it so much that sometimes I stay in my shop without interruptions for long hours just making guitars."

Kwame looks around with interest and starts asking questions. "This is wonderful, Walker. You are a real artist. Do you create your own designs?"

I show him pictures of different guitars I've built over the years. "Yes, I create my own designs, plus the ornamental details in the head-piece and sound-hole rosette. The external shape of the guitar is kept pretty much the same for all of them, except for some customized designs. You won't find two guitars alike because the

---

*This chapter may be skipped if you have no interest in the design optimization subject.

wood varies, the customer's requests are different, and the artistic details we put on them are never the same."

"What is the sound-hole rosette?" He asks, prompted by innate curiosity.

I pick up one of the guitars and explain to him. "The ornamental circular strip around the hole of the guitar is called the sound-hole rosette. It is wood inlay, you know, a lengthy process that needs patience and requires skills to make. When you make a guitar for a customer, the sound-hole rosette will be unique and the guitarist will feel a personal attachment to it. It is a feeling that only guitarists experience."

"Oh, I see. Well, all that sounds neat, but what do you do to guarantee the right sound and tone of the guitar?" Kwame asks.

"The rosette has nothing to do with that," I reply. "It is just a cosmetic touch that gives identity and personality to the guitar. An experienced luthier can change many things in the design in order to produce the right notes with the right intensity. For instance, we can change the sound board plate, the one with the hole, by thinning the plate in different spots in order to get the right sound. The sound plate is by far the most important component in terms of sound quality. Similarly, there are other things that can be changed, like the pattern of braces inside the guitar, the type of wood, the direction of the wood grain, the stiffness of the neck, and many more things."

Kwame then enters one of his mute, meditative lapses. I just stand next to him, waiting. After about ten seconds he is back.

"Interesting, Walker. I have to confess that after our conversations in Europe, I had the impression that you had no idea what optimization was, but now I realize that you know many things about it already."

"I don't understand. What do you mean? I haven't received any training in optimization in my life."

"You don't know formal design optimization methods, like I do, but you know it by experience. Your job has taught you design optimization without you knowing it."

I grab his arm and invite him to sit and talk in more detail.

Emily calls from upstairs. "Dinner is almost ready!" she says. I yell back and tell her we'll be there in a couple of minutes. Kwame takes a piece of paper and pencil from his pocket.

"For instance, when doing design optimization, you must be able to change *something* in order to improve the design."

"That sounds obvious," I say.

He ignores my arrogant response and continues. "In the design optimization jargon that something is called *design variable*. It is the variable you have control over, and that you are able to change. By experience, you have learned that the thickness of the sound board is an important design variable. You've learned that when you change the thickness in the entire plate, or only at specific spots, the sound quality can improve or worsen."

He pauses to see my reaction although he hasn't said anything really new to me yet. I nod to show agreement, but stay quiet waiting for more.

"You also found that your guitars will change their sound quality when you change the internal braces, right? Then there are many ways to improve the quality of sound, depending on what we change."

"I see what you are getting to. That means there are many design variables and the design can be improved by changing one at a time until you get the best design. Is that right?"

"No. Unfortunately things are not that simple. If that were the case, design optimization would be an easy science. The problem is that design variables interact among themselves. If you find the optimum value of one design variable while keeping the others constant, you won't get, necessarily, the best guitar. You need to account for the interaction between the design variables in order to find the BBBN design of any product. You need to address the whole system at once.

"Could you be more specific? I can't follow you."

"An example will help. Let's say we are building a bird feeder with a plastic pipe. When you go to the hardware store you find pipes of different diameter and length, so, the problem at hand is to find the *optimum* diameter and length for the bird house.

If we want to maximize the area of the pipe —in order to have more room to drill holes for the birds to be fed— but at the same time you want the bird house to have a limit in the volume —in order to make it not so heavy when filled with seeds— then you can formulate an optimization problem with two metrics: area and volume. But it should be clear to you, now, that the length and the diameter are now dependent on each other. We cannot choose them independently because we may build a too heavy bird house, or one with a too small diameter."

"This is interesting and new for me. Then, how do you go about it? Do you buy different pipes with different length and diameter? I can't do that with guitars. I don't have the resources to test all possible combinations of variables."

"I know Walker, I know. That's why there is a whole theory on how to solve design problems: techniques, methods, mathematical theorems, computer simulations and more. Using design optimization methods will help you find a better design without manufacturing all combinations."

I am confused and Kwame notices it. He continues, but not before grabbing one of my sound plates and a piece of sand paper. As he speaks, he begins sanding the plate with such calm pace, as if he knew how to do it. With his long hands, he makes a pass to the right, and another to the left, back and forth, with precise rhythm.

"Another good thing you have learned while making acoustic guitars," he says, "is the concept of sensitivity. It is a simple concept that you have already mastered. For instance, just a moment ago you mentioned that the sound-hole rosette was just a cosmetic item and that the thickness of the sound board was a critical variable. Well, in engineering terms this means that the sound quality is more sensitive to the sound board thickness than to the rosette design. In other words, a small change in the thickness will make a big change in sound quality, while a small change in the rosette design will make a small change, or none at all, to the sound quality."

"Interesting... I always knew that, but I never thought there was a mathematical way to describe it."

"Oh yes. In design optimization theory there is a whole sub-field called design sensitivity analysis that takes care of this. For now you only need to know that for a given guitar design, every performance characteristic of the design has a sensitivity for each design variable. This is called the *sensitivity coefficient*. Notice that I said *every* performance characteristic because there are many things that can be used to measure the performance of a guitar, right?"

I think for a moment and I begin seeing the entire picture of what he is describing.

"Then," I say, "it is like a large table of numbers, with performance characteristics in the rows, and design variables in the columns. Every entry in the table could be filled with the sensitivity coefficient. Right?"

"Good, very good. I am impressed Walker. Such tables have names too; they are called *sensitivity matrices*. They are the key information for optimization methods."

Matrices? I ask myself. Oh no, I hated matrices when I was in high school. "Let's say," I continue, "that I want to fill that table, or matrix as you called it, for my guitars. This will be useful; don't you think?"

He starts laughing. "No, no, no; it is not like that. The table is not constant; it changes as you change the design. As I said, for every design, for any minor change, there will be another sensitivity matrix. You can't go and compute *the* sensitivity matrix for all your guitars and do design optimization. The sensitivity matrix is different for every new design you produce."

"Okay," I insist, "let me ask you a different question, then. How do you compute the sensitivity matrix for a given design?"

"To answer that question, we need to talk about mathematics, calculus, and probably I will draw some pictures to illustrate the concept. But I prefer to quit now and go upstairs for dinner. You won't understand the concept if I keep pounding you with more information."

He puts the sand paper and the sound board on top of the desk. His suggestion was timely. I hear the summons from the kitchen calling for dinner again.

"I have one last question, Kwame."

"Go ahead."

"Well, it is about the BBBN concept you taught me. I explained it to Manuel, my apprentice, and he came back with a question I couldn't answer. He asked me: 'How can we improve quality and lower the cost at the same time?' "

Kwame starts laughing, big and loud laughs.

"I guess I missed something. Why are you laughing so much?"

"Walker, that is the most common complaint from design and manufacturing engineers. They think that quality can only be achieved with expensive budgets, and that pumping money to the product will always increase the quality of it. They are wrong, simply wrong."

"So, what should I tell Manuel?"

"Walker, let me tell you one little trick. When you are asked a question and you don't know the answer, look at Nature, and find out the way Nature has reached the optimum. You will always find the answer that way. Nature has the highest quality, the richest beauty, and the lowest cost when compared with all man made designs. Always remember that."

"That sounds good, but Nature does not make guitars," I reply.

"I know, but a guitar is a device to produce sounds, sweet and harmonious sounds, and Nature has plenty of them in different forms. But you are missing my point. We don't need to imitate the Nature's devices, but Nature's *ways* to get to the optimum. In other words, what we need is to emulate the process to achieve such optimum designs. So, the answer for your apprentice is simply this: use the best processes with the best materials and best tools, and the BBBN product will come out if the optimization problem is set up properly. But keep in mind, when I say *best*, I don't mean, expensive, but simple the best for the situation."

"What do you mean by 'if it is set up properly?' I don't think Manuel will be satisfied with this answer."

"You may be right, but if you want to know a more scientific answer, the dinner will be cold by the end of my answer. This has to do with the simultaneous optimization of two conflicting performance characteristics, that requires more optimization theory and some knowledge of Pareto sets. You will need concepts that require more explanation. I think we shouldn't discuss it today. But if you still want an answer for Manuel, then you can tell him to use *time and mistakes,* small mistakes that allow him to build knowledge slowly and methodically. Remember what we talked about in Copenhagen, with Ole?"

"Oh, yes, I remember."

"Great. Remember that time is also an optimization strategy, but you need to be a clever user of time, otherwise you are simply wasting resources. That is what Nature has done. It has used millions of years to improve and improve every process, every living creature on earth, in order to get to the present optimum point of life now. You see? Time and small mistakes. Clever mistakes."

I am getting desperate for a direct answer to my question. "I see your point Kwame, but I really want to give Manuel an answer he can use."

He swing his head side to side, and says, "You are really persistent, Walker. I will be short, because I am sure you are not going to remember all that we have discussed today. If there are only two objectives in conflict, like in this case are quality and cost, you could set an optimization problem with one single objective that combines both. For instance, you could try to minimize the ratio of cost/quality. This way the people that may potentially buy your guitars will receive more quality for the money they pay. This means they get more *value* attached to the product."

"That is very intuitive and helpful, but that does not guarantee a low cost, does it?"

"You are right. It does not guarantee that you will get a low cost guitar, but then you need to add a constraint to the problem."

A constraint? ... I ask myself. He sees my ignorant expression and says, "Why don't we go and eat? You are not going to get so much information in such a short time. I will explain it to you more formally in another occasion."

He is right. We'd better quit now. I stand up, and he does too.

17

Finding a Partner

WHEN KWAME AND I GET UPSTAIRS, we walk to the dining table. As expected, it is beautifully decorated, something that Christina has done for sure. The napkins are folded in such a way that they look like origami hearts. The silverware is symmetrically placed and shining. There is a bouquet of red roses in the center of the table, and the smell that fills the room is delicious. She also added two small candles I brought from Denmark that introduce a romantic accent with the dim lights.

Emily brings the food to the table. I go to the kitchen and bring the bread. Gabriel, always talkative and curious, starts asking indiscreet questions: "Kwame, how old are you?"

Kwame smiles and very politely replies, "Why do you want to know, son?"

Gabriel, with his baby face, explains, "My dad said he could not figure out how old you were, so I just wanted to know."

"Well, I'll tell you this. I am as old as ten times the fourth prime number." Gabriel's face shows his ignorance about prime numbers. Emily interrupts the conversation and passes the bowl of rice to Gabriel to distract him. Christina is smiling and I give Gabriel a wide-eyed look. He knows what I mean.

"Kwame," Emily says, "I guess consulting is a tough field to be in these days."

"Well, yes and no. Some clients pay well, some don't, but I do it for fun. I retired some time ago, and all my current clients are old friends with technical problems. I enjoy solving their problems; that's my reward. By the way, this salmon is delicious. I had never tried it with mustard. I love it."

"Thank you," Emily acknowledges. I know she is still uncomfortable with Kwame, but he is doing a good job in gaining her confidence.

In the middle of my first bite of salmon, I realize that I've been using Kwame as a consultant but forgot to ask him about his fees. I interrupt immediately before Emily makes things worse. "Honey, Kwame and I need to talk about his consulting fees. We can talk about that later. Could you pass me the salad, please?"

She understands my signal, and passes the dish. Gabriel remains mostly quiet for the rest of the dinner figuring out what a prime number is. Christina seems very far from the conversation; she must be probably thinking about her boyfriend.

The dinner ends nicely with good ice cream and coffee. Kwame leaves soon after. I send the kids to bed, while Emily and I take care of the dirty plates in the kitchen.

"Nice guy," Emily says, trying to start a conversation that we probably left pending since I went to Europe.

I approach her from behind, put my arms around her waist —something she's never liked it— but this time, surprisingly, she doesn't complain and turns around to face me. Her gaze is penetrating and sensual. I say nothing for a moment, while the water runs freely from the faucet left open. I lean forward and kiss her with care and tenderness, and then with fire and passion. A loud silence fills the room from wall to wall. She is almost melting in my arms because we —even though we love each other so much— we rarely kiss.

No words come from either of us, maybe because of the sadness of remembering so many years of not being close, maybe because of the fear of hurting each other again. She turns her face away and continues working in the kitchen while I take a piece of cloth to clean the table.

The kitchen is now shiny, as if nobody had eaten here. I go upstairs to take a shower before it is too late, but as I pass in front of Christina's room, I remember what I had promised. I need to talk to her about her boyfriend. I enter the room trying to see her before she sees me. She is in her bed, staring at the ceiling, thinking about him, I guess.

"Hi honey, can we talk?" She doesn't say anything, but the language of her eyes tells me the answer.

"How did you like Kwame?"

"He is okay. A bit funny and weird sometimes, but he is okay."

I don't know how to start the real conversation I am supposed to begin. She also knows that I'm not here to talk about Kwame; it's her boyfriend who fills all her thoughts. We see each other and without a single word, simply by gazing at each other's eyes, I know, and she knows, what we want to talk about, so we smile to release our tension, and smile again before we start.

She sits on the bed, crosses her legs, faces me, and asks, "Okay dad, if you were me, how would you choose a boyfriend?"

That is a very direct question, very difficult to answer, but I'll try. "Well, I am not a girl, but I can tell you this: girls are always in control of the situation. You decide where and when to do things, while we, boys, in most of the cases, always want to go for it. In other words, boys only have the forward gear, but girls have forward, reverse and neutral. Actually, I think you girls also have the side gear, one that cars don't have. Do you get what I am trying to say?"

She looks at me disappointed. "Dad, I am old enough to know what you are talking about."

"Good, because when I was your age, I had no idea of such things. Well, then, since you ladies are in control, you don't have to worry much about him. It's him who has to worry about you."

"Dad, that is not what I want to hear," she says moving her hands up and down, making the bed bounce with her. "It is too easy for you to say that. That is not advice. What I want to know is what I should look for in a boyfriend."

She always hits the nail on the head. I keep trying. "Well, I learned a long time ago that women are way more intelligent than men when dealing with relationships. Women don't look for what men are or what they offer in the present, but for what they will be and my offer in the future. Have you heard that men fall in love with their stomach, and women with their ears?"

"No, you never told me that. How is it?"

"Well, it is an old saying I learned from Manuel. It means men *look for* the present and for the corporal satisfactions while women *listen* to know what we have in mind, and what our plans for the future are."

"So... what you are telling me is that I should listen more?"

"Yes, listen and ask. The more information you gather, the easier your decision will be. For example, how does he treat his friends, his family and strangers? How good are his grades? What after-school activities does he enjoy doing?"

"I don't know any of that yet, I haven't asked him."

"Too bad. Grandpa used to say *'the one who asks is the one in control.'* You have to ask him. Use your intelligence and the advantage of being in control of the situation in order to figure out his plans. That's all you need to know, and the rest will fall into place."

She stays quiet for a moment, considers my argument, and continues. "How about beauty, dad. Does it count? Should I look for a handsome man?"

I smile, because I knew she would ask. "It counts at your age, honey, but it doesn't last forever, you know. I'd say that humor and a caring personality are more important than beauty. A humorous person is most likely to be intelligent and happy. A person that cares for others will also care for you. None of these two things are related to a pretty face."

Again, she says nothing for seconds, as if she was really thinking about my answers. "How about health? I don't want a sick person to be my boyfriend. Do you?"

"Well, that is more difficult to answer." I pause for a second, trying to come up with a good answer. I remember what Kwame said: *watch Nature and you'll find answers you don't know.*

"It is natural to avoid the ill. You see this behavior in Nature where sick animals won't reproduce and they die without offspring. It is not quite the same in humans since we are able to think and have feelings, and we can consider other parameters, but in general terms, yes, it is better to share your life with a healthy person. But let me be clear; health is not only about a good body. A drug addicted athlete is not healthier than a drug-free crippled person."

She looks thoughtful for a while, and then comes back with, "Where did you learn all this, dad?"

"I am older, that's all. Time makes you wiser. Let me tell you one last thing. Above all, pick a person that makes you happy when you are with him. The rest is just the spice of life that can be changed and improved with love, experience and with a lot of communication. If you are happy in his company, if you both are having fun and play fair with each other, and as long as nobody is sacrificing its happiness for the partner, then you have found the right companion for the rest of your life."

"Is mom your right companion?"

A chilly rush of blood runs through my back when I here the question. I can't let her know. "Yes, of course," I say as quick as I can.

She smiles. "I'll remember your advice. Thank you, dad."

Still confused by her unexpected question, I say, "Good night, honey, good night."

I give her a kiss and a fond hug. As I leave the room I hear Gabriel's steps, running to his room. I wonder what he is after and follow him to find out.

"Hi, Gabriel."

He's on bed, faking being asleep. I wait a few seconds until he responds, "Hi, dad."

I stand quiet looking at him. He can't keep a secret; I know him well. I'll be here until he tells me what he was doing.

"Dad, what are you waiting for?"

"For you."

His eyes are evasive, and I know he is up to something. "Okay dad, I was there, listening."

"Listening to what? Where?" I demand.

"I heard the last part of your conversation with Christina," he says while lowering his gaze.

"Oh, I see. You know that you shouldn't do that, Gabriel. You know better." He doesn't say a word, and then he seems suddenly sad.

"You never give advice like that to me," he complains. "I also have a girlfriend, and you don't say anything to me."

No, not again! Now it is Gabriel with the same complaint. How could I know he had a girlfriend? I have no alternative but to take a deep breath and start over.

"Sorry, Gabriel. I didn't know you had a girlfriend."

"Yes, you did. I told you once."

I don't know what he is talking about. "Who? Since when?"

"Adriana, the daughter of the Sullivans across the street." His face is as read as a tomato when he says her name.

"Adriana? But she has been your friend since kindergarten." I shake my head demanding explanation.

"So what? She can't be my girlfriend because of that?"

He is right. Now where should I start? I am tired and want to sleep, but I have to be fair. He needs attention, too.

"If you can give advice to Christina, you sure can give advice to me," he says with his face still looking down.

"Yes, I can, and I will, now. Any burning questions?" I lift his chin and fix my gaze on his eyes looking for an expression or a question.

"Nothing in particular, just give me some advice."

I think he is just jealous, but I will play along. "Well, let me tell you a couple of things. First, be polite and courteous with any girl, but always firm in your position and opinion. Don't let them force you to do anything you don't want to do. Be fair, with her and with yourself as well."

"Dad, that is not advice. That is common sense. I want to know what to do to get her attention."

He makes me laugh. I see how much he needs to know about girls. "Well, there are a couple of things girls like about boys. They look for boys who make them laugh. If you are humorous, you have an advantage."

"I can do that. I'm good at that," he says with confidence and pride.

"Second, girls like to be surprised once is a while with little things."

"Like what?" he quickly asks.

"Like a gift, or a trip, or a wacky thing she may like to hear." He stays quiet and thoughtful.

"But one thing they sure like the most," I say as he opens his eyes waiting for what he may be thinking will be the best advice of all, "is to be listened to with real attention. If you sincerely listen to what they say, they will notice it and will love to be with you."

"And what was that about future plans you were telling to Christina?"

"Oh! You heard that too? Well, this is for older boys and girls, but you can use it too. As girls get older, they also care about your aspirations in life. They want to find out what you have on your mind; what you want to be; what places you want to go to; what your goals are. They want a man with potential and a bright future."

"But how can they know what I want to be, if I don't know?" he asks with ingenuity.

"Good question Gabriel. They have something special. Some people call it intuition. They can figure it out, even when you don't know. It is like the sculptor in front of the marble boulder: he knows the sculpture that is hidden inside eventhough he cannot see it at first. Girls, or women I should say, are like sculptors in that sense. They can tell what a man can be by just listening to him. Women have that trait in their genes, I think."

"Dad, I don't understand what you are talking about."

Oh, I forgot I was talking to a boy. I needed to give him some examples. "Sorry, Gabriel. It is simple: keep talking about your plans, your future. That's all you need to know for now. When you get older, I can tell you more things."

"And how about my clothes, my hair cut, and my shoes? My friends at school are always talking about that kinda stuff."

"Oh, Gabriel. If a girl goes after you because of your shoes or your hair cut, then she is not the girl for you. She probably has nothing inside her head. Don't worry about her. But don't get me wrong either, you have to take care of your appearance, especially your hygiene."

He brought up a good point. He doesn't like to shower, but to attract a girl he may want to stay clean and fresh. "One last thing, Gabriel. A loving relationship, or any relationship between two persons is the art of giving and taking. You give your time, your thoughts, you care for her, but then you must also take what she gives you, her time, her thoughts, and her care for you. I tell you this because in many cases there is one giver and one taker. Then, as time passes, the giver becomes empty, and the taker gets full, creating an uneven situation. When the relationship gets to this point, it is likely to die soon. It's like keeping the balance while skating, you put weight on one foot to take away from the other."

He is again confused by my comments. I try again. "Well, imagine that there is a girl you like. Then you buy her gifts; you call her every night; you always think about her; you invite her out for treats, and so on. So you are the giver. But imagine that she rarely thinks about you; she doesn't give you gifts; she never calls you; she always asks you for favors, and so on. So she is the taker in the relationship. Sooner or later, you will get tired of giving, and the relationship will end.

"But dad, that is the way most boys treat their girlfriend at school. How can they be all wrong?"

"Let me ask you this: how long do they stay as boyfriend and girlfriend?"

He doesn't say anything. He knows that I know the answer, and smiles.

"When you are older," I continue, "you will see how important this give-and-take advice is. You will apply it to your girlfriend, to your friends, to me, to your children. It is the way relationships should be. You give, you take; you give more, you take more. But don't get me wrong; you must never stop giving first. You must be pro-active in the relationship, not reactive."

He yawns. It's getting late. I kiss his forehead and wish him a good night.

"Good night, dad. Thank you."

I turn out the lights and leave the room. I feel tired, physically and mentally. I walk to the main bedroom, take my pajamas from the closet, put them on, and walk to the bed. As soon as I rest my head on the pillow, Emily says: "What is all that conversation with the kids?"

Now I have to explain to her everything all over again. When am I going to sleep? I sigh.

"Now what?" she says. "Can't you tell me what is going on?"

And she is in a bad mood too. Where should I start? "Can we talk tomorrow? I am feeling tired and have no energy to start a conversation."

She turns away violently and mumbles some words.

"Emily, I promise I will tell you tomorrow. Besides, it is nothing important."

More mumbling.

"Okay, I'll tell you this: Christina has a boyfriend, and Gabriel a girlfriend. They had some questions about it. That's all."

With the same speed she turned away, she now turns back to me. "What? Christina has a boyfriend? How come she asks you, and not me? I am her mother. Walker, you are kidding me, aren't you."

My patience is ebbing away. I am too tired to have a discussion now. "Emily, I want to sleep. Please."

She turns away again, but this time the mumble is louder although still unintelligible. I can't sleep with such noise either. I sit up. "Okay, honey, let's talk. What do you want to know?"

"Nothing. Go to sleep. I'll talk to her tomorrow," she replies with a voice of anger and frustration.

I grab the sheet, turn around, and say, "Well, don't tell me later that I didn't try. Good night."

"Whatever."

18

Preparation

HE NEXT DAY, AS SOON AS I WAKE UP, even before my morning coffee, I pick up the phone and call Kwame to talk about his consulting fees, which have been worrying me since yesterday. A woman answers the phone and identifies herself as Alice.

"Hi, this is Walker," I say, guessing she may already know who I am.

"Yes, hi Walker. Dad couldn't stop talking about you and your family last night."

"Oh, I am glad to hear that. You should've come, too."

A silence interrupts the conversation. But then she continues, "I am sorry we couldn't go, but mom was not feeling good last night. Next time, though."

"Sure, I look forward to meeting you both. Anyway, is your dad available?"

"He is in his office, and he asked not to be interrupted for two hours. I think he's very busy."

"Then I'll call back in the afternoon. Tell him that..." A new voice, much louder, from an older woman, starts talking on the phone.

"Hi Walker, this is Amy, Kwame's wife."

"Hi Amy, nice to meet you."

"Kwame will be with you in a moment. From the things he says about you, I know he would like to talk to you."

"Oh, thank you. By the way, how are you feeling? Kwame told me about your operation. How are you recovering?"

"Fine, thank you. I've been out of my bed for some time now and I am feeling better every day."

"I am glad to hear that. Health comes first, you know."

"Kwame tells me," she continues, "that you are an avid student and want to learn everything in one day. Well, I need to tell you this, he is very dedicated and an excellent teacher. One day, when we were dating he started to explain to me all this stuff about math and geometry, and you won't believe it, but I understood every single concept. It was so fun..."

And she keeps talking and talking. I just wait for a chance to interrupt her, but she doesn't stop. She starts coughing very hard with a weird noise coming from very deep in her lungs. It sounds horrible.

"Excuse me, Walker." And she disappears from the line for a moment. When she comes back, the conversation continues as if nothing had happened.

"And when Alice was born," she tells me, "he was so excited that... Oh! Here is Kwame. Well, we can talk some other time. It was very nice to talk to you, Walker. Bye."

"Bye Amy. Nice talking to you, too."

She passes the phone to Kwame, who with his grave voice says, "Hi Walker. Are you still there?"

"Hi, Kwame. Sorry for interrupting your work."

"Oh, don't worry about that. I was making some drawings for my book. I haven't told you, but I am writing a textbook on optimization. It's more challenging when you do your own pictures, but I have more control over the final product."

"Gee Kwame, you really work hard for your age. I hope to get a signed copy of it when it's finished."

"Sure. You will."

"I'm calling because I want to sit down with you and discuss your consulting fees as soon as possible. I don't know how it never crossed my mind to talk about that before. I'm very sorry."

"Don't worry, Walker. I told you, I do this more for fun than for money. We'd better sit together to give you a lecture on optimization, not to write a receipt. Money can always wait, but learning is always urgent. Let's get together the Monday after the Easter holiday. Is that O.K. with you?"

"Easter? ... Oh, yes, Easter. Yes, that sounds like a good idea. There is a lot of information we need to process, and if I take a vacation just before you come, I'll be more attentive. How about meeting in my shop at 9:00 AM? The address is on my business card. Is that okay?"

"Sure, I'll be there Monday, then. Have good holidays, Walker. See you then."

I say goodbye and rush to the kitchen to talk to Emily. After so much work lately, I forgot all about the Easter holidays, but I am sure she made some plans already. I walk to the kitchen where she is making breakfast for the kids, and preparing the morning coffee.

I approach her, stand by her side and ask, "Emily, what are the plans for the Easter vacation?"

"Finally, you ask!" She says with an angry voice and that crushing gesture of her brows that make them curl like two snakes. Now I understand her mood from last night, before going to sleep. She hates when I forget about our vacations, her only chance to spend time together with me.

"Well, don't be so harsh," I reply, "I didn't ask before because I've been very busy at work and had no time to talk about it."

"Work, work, work. That's the only thing you think about. Don't you see that years are passing by, and we are getting old without having fun?"

Hard words again, but I'd rather evade confrontation so early in the morning. "Are you going to tell me or not? Do we have any plans?" She looks at me very defiantly. I return the look.

Christina, who is in her bedroom, hears the loud tones of our conversation and comes down to the kitchen to find out what is going on. She is not happy with the situation and to calm things down she says, "Dad, Mom, please no more yelling. Why don't you guys stop arguing and enjoy the breakfast. And yes dad, we are all going to the Upper Peninsula for a week-long vacation."

She is right. There is no need for yelling. Gabriel comes down from his bedroom too, singing the latest hit from the radio, as if the world were perfect around him. Happy as always, he sits at the table. I sit quietly and begin drinking my coffee, slowly, thoughtfully, minding my own business, but also with echoes of Emily's words —getting old without having fun, old, fun, old, fun.

Emily also sits down to eat cereal with yogurt, ignoring the entire situation. Christina approaches us and gives sweet kisses to each of us. What a daughter we have! Emily and I have been having trouble for a while, actually, for a long while, more than a year I guess. We need to talk about our feelings, but neither of us has the courage to bring up the subject.

The breakfast is almost over. Emily picks up her plate, and says, "We are leaving Friday afternoon, after school. I reserved a cabin for us by a small lake. It should be nice up there. I hope you like it." She looks down, with a defeated gesture; tired of so much fighting for so many months, over so little things.

"Sure we will. I definitely need some days off," I say with confidence, looking at her eyes with a sincere smile that elicits one from her.

I finish my breakfast, pick up the plate, put it on the sink, and walk away with no more comments, no more talk. Gabriel goes upstairs to his room. I take the newspaper and go downstairs to read about a fire that broke out last night in a furniture store downtown. The owner of the store is a friend who I see each morning when I go to work. It must be devastating for him to loose all his life's efforts in one night.

As soon as I finish reading the newspaper, I take some guitar sides and begin heating and bending them as usual. It takes me an hour or so to get the exact curvature I need in each side. I stop for a moment and think about our future, and the things I would like to do and the goals I want to reach in life. I drop my tools and go upstairs to talk to Emily. I feel it is time to talk, but when I pass by Gabriel's room I see him playing video games.

"Hey Gabriel. Are you winning?" His fingers jump from one button to the next; push, steer, shake; the red button, the yellow one, push again; there are three seconds left before the end of the race; jump, jump, push, two more turns and the race is over.

"Gabriel! I asked you if you won!" I say louder. He is hypnotized, and can't hear me.

"Hey Gabriel!" I scream.

"Oh, hi dad. I didn't know you were here."

His eyes are puffy, his fingers red, and he's still in his pajamas.

"Gabriel, I'll have to put some restrictions on video game time for you. I can't accept it any more. You spend hours and hours playing alone. Your eyes get red. You don't socialize with the kids on the block. Why don't you go and watch some educational programs on the TV?" Then I realized the oxymoron of what I just said. Gabriel turns off the game, turns on the TV, and starts explaining.

"Dad, I want to tell you why TV sucks. From channel 1 to 7 there are the local channels with not-for-kid programs; channel 8 is for video music and Hollywood stuff that you don't let me see. Channels 9 to 11 are for little kids, you know, for four-year old babies. Channels 12 to 21 are the movie channels that you asked me to watch only with you or mom. The only thing left are news channels that only talk about war and politics, and the educational channels that are boring... very boring."

Then he turns the TV off and says: "You'll have to admit, Dad, that a video game is my only choice."

I see his well-defended point. I feel sorry for him. My childhood was much simpler than his. The TV wasn't great in those days either so, my only choice was to go out and talk to the boys in the neighborhood and in school. Those were happy days, indeed. Ah, I see Emily's point now. She complained about being old and having no fun, compared to being young and having as much fun as when we were children.

Anyways, what bothers me the most about Gabriel is that he feels bored and his only pastime is video games. I don't want him to be bored; boredom is the preamble to problems. I try to keep him and his sister engaged in any activity to avoid boredom.

"Gabriel, let's sit on your bed and have a little talk." He puts on his face of frustration, but follows my request.

"Okay, let me see. You are just twelve years old. You have a mom and a dad who place high emphasis on learning and working hard. But you, little spoiled boy, you don't care about all that, do you?"

He is unmoved. He's been always difficult to convince.

"Dad, I know what you are trying to say. You have told me that before, and I know what I should do. But I am just having some fun like any kid these days."

"Well, I will tell you once more, in different words perhaps: nobody knows what is ahead of us, and because of that, we need to prepare ourselves by doing our best at the current point in time."

"I've heard that before," he says with confidence.

"Probably. It is not new. But how about if I tell you that everybody is constantly getting prepared for something ahead. For example: you learned to read and write to be prepared for high school; where you get prepared to go to college; where you get prepared for getting a job; where you get prepared for getting married; where you get prepared for having a home and children; where you get prepared for saving money for their college and you retirement; where, finally, you get prepared for, some day, dying in peace. You see? I can always portray any activity in life as a preparation for something. I hope you now understand what I mean, because now I am going to tell you how you get well prepared.

He stays attentive, which is very rare for him. So, I better use this opportunity to teach him something about life.

"Let me tell you three things, three talents, that you must have. Once you have them, you will be ready for any change in life, for any event you don't expect, for any new decision you'll have to make. They are: *passion, knowledge and discipline.*"

"Why do they have to be three?" He asks. "What if I only have one or two, but not all three?"

"Well, you may be able to compensate for the lack of one, with the abundance of the other two."

"What do you mean by compensate?"

"Well, if you have too little of one of them, you can get away with it and be prepared and successful by having a lot of the other two."

"Are you telling me I have no discipline?" he complains.

"No, but you may not have it in the future. If you continue playing video games instead of learning, then your passion and knowledge may not be able to compensate."

He looks confused, so, as always, I invent a story to make it fun and interesting.

"Okay, I have this story for you," I say. "Suppose there are three friends: Albert —the apathetic, Ignace —the ignorant, and Lori —the lazy.

"Albert lacks the passion to take any initiative and risk, but because of his college degree in biology and his discipline and good habits in following instructions he is progressing in life beyond expectations, always prepared for the unknown.

"Ignace, on the contrary, did not have the chance to go to college, but also manages to be among the top in his work and has the answer for any problem because of the passion and discipline he puts into any assignment he takes."

"Then there is Lori. She comes late and leaves early from work. She sleeps on her desk at noon and never works beyond the required time. But because of her knowledge in computers and her passion and eagerness to do her job, she is also doing very well in her life. Nothing takes her by surprise. Now let me ask you who do you think will do better in life? Who is better prepared?"

Gabriel was listening carefully, and I know he is puzzled by the question. Before he says any word, I say, "Don't worry about answering. It is a tricky question. All of them are able to do fine. As long and they compensate for their weaknesses with their other two talents, they will do better and better."

Gabriel smiles as a sign of understanding. "Who wrote that story?"

"I'll tell you later. Now suppose, there are three other friends, with just the talent that Albert, Ignace and Lori don't have. Let's call them like this: Peter —the passionate, Katherine —the knowledgeable, and David —the disciplined.

"Peter always takes his life and job with passion, but makes too many mistakes because of a lack of knowledge and tends to be lazy and indulgent quite often. Katherine, after many years in school, has an engineering degree, but she is so apathetic and lazy that she has been unable to keep any job beyond three months. Finally there is David. He is very good at following instructions, wakes up early, works more hours than his coworkers, but is not very much interested in his work, and doesn't have any skill or knowledge.

"Now comes another tricky question you don't have to answer either. Who will be doing worst in life, Peter, Katherine or David?" Gabriel laughs and understands the point I want to make.

"Finally, Gabriel, this is the last part of the story. There is this person named Alfred Irwin Lawrence. And if you have been following the story, you should be able to tell me what kind of person he is. This is not a tricky question; you have to answer. Tell me, how is he?"

He laughs and shouts: "He is apathetic, ignorant and lazy, and won't find a job ever in his life!

"Good Gabriel, good! The moral of the story is easy. Can you tell me the moral?"

"Well, you have to have at least two out of the three talents to be prepared in life, and be ready for changes, and be successful."

"Great Gabriel," I tell him while I mess up his hair. "It's enough for now. I hope you get something out of this conversation."

"Dad, how did you learn all this?"

"The hard way son, making mistakes. I had to learn slowly from my own mistakes." I stay quiet for a moment, thinking about my own answer.

"So, what are you going to do to with the video games?" I ask him.

"I'll have to change my habits, dad. I want to be like you."

"What a nice answer." I hug him. "Do you want to be a luthier too?"

"Why not? I like the smell of the wood," he says for my satisfaction.

I walk out of the room and while going down the steps I realize what a good time I just spent with Gabriel.

19

Self-Control

T IS NOW SUNDAY MORNING AND WE are packing our stuff into the mini-van for our trip to the Upper Peninsula, or U.P., as it is called by Michiganders. The U.P. is the prettiest country in Michigan. There are waterfalls, beaches, lakes, rivers, and plenty of wildlife. It is very uninhabited up there; but, at the same time, I still feel like I am close to home. A beautiful five-mile long bridge, the Mackinac Bridge, connects the lower and upper peninsulas. From home to the bridge is 250 miles, and from there, we need to continue for about 60 miles to get to Paradise, a small town where Emily reserved a log cabin.

We take highway I-75 all the way up to the Mackinac Bridge. It takes five hours without stops. By then we are so tired and hungry that we begin looking for restaurants. I stop in a gas station to pump some gas, and ask the attendant whether he knows of a good restaurant around. He gives me directions to what he calls 'a small but good tavern where the best chicken noodle soup in the UP is served.'

I follow his directions and in few minutes we get to the tavern. It doesn't look nice from outside, but this is good enough for now. The girl at the front door guides us to the table where, as soon as we are seated, the waitress appears from nowhere asking if we want to order any drinks. I hate when they do that. Why are they always in a hurry?

"Not yet," I say firmly. "We need time to sit, to relax, to read the menu, and then we are going to order drinks."

Emily and the kids look at me, surprised by my rude answer. The waitress looks at me and says, "I'll be back in a sec."

This waitress is like many others. She follows a script of instructions, phrases, and manners that are the standard in many restaurants.

She comes back. "Have you decided?"

"It has been less than a minute since we were seated. We need more time," I say. Emily is becoming nervous and impatient with my rudeness. When the waitress leaves, Emily looks at me.

"Walker, what are you doing to this girl? She is doing her job. Besides, don't you see how scared she is?"

"Yes, dad," Christina says. "I think we should order now."

"I just want some time to relax before we order, that's all. We are on vacation; remember? I don't need to hurry. She is pushing."

A couple of minutes pass and a man comes out of the kitchen, grabs a pad from the counter and approaches our table.

"My waitress is feeling sick all of a sudden. May I take your order?" he asks.

"Sure," Emily jumps to say before I say anything. "We'll take this family dish that you have on special."

There she goes again. Cost is more important than quality. I can't take it. First the waitress, and now Emily with her cheapness.

"Could you give us some time to discuss it? I don't want the family dish," I say emphatically.

But before I finish my sentence the 250-pound man bursts out. "What's the matter with *you*? My daughter told me you were a pest. Now I see what she meant. We don't waste time with people like you around here. You better tell me what you want now, or leave."

He is really mad, but I have no patience today. What is he thinking? That I can't beat him up because of my problem? I tighten my fist. My adrenaline runs high. My first punch got to be to the face, otherwise I won't beat him. But then I realize I am in front of the kids. I breathe deeply, one, two times, and calm myself a little. I regain my composure and start thinking how to reply to this guy. We all reflect the feelings we received. If I respond with violence he'll do the same. If I respond with respect, he will too. I take another deep breath before I respond: "We'll leave, but I would like to talk to your daughter first."

The man, looks at me with little trust, but turns to the kitchen and shouts, "Emily, come on here. He wants to talk to you." And crosses his 25-inch biceps in front of his chest, as a police waiting for any minor misconduct in order to reprimand. It is a good coincidence that she is named Emily too. She steps outside the kitchen and begins walking to the table, fearfully. Fear of her father, not of me, I sense.

"Hi Emily," I say.

No answer.

"Do you know my wife's name? Emily, like you." I smile, and she smiles. Christina and her mother look more relaxed now that the waitress is smiling. Gabriel is waiting for me to react.

"I just want to tell you that we came here to eat after a five hour trip from Chelsea. I was tired, they were tired," I say pointing to the kids. "I apologize if I was rude to you."

She changes her face and looks more confident and serene. She looks at her father as if asking permission to talk. "Do whatever you want," he says and goes back to the kitchen.

The girl smiles at Emily, at the kids, and at me at last. And without losing the smile, she asks, "May I take your order?"

Gabriel sighs. He has said nothing since we entered the restaurant. I look at my wife, and say: "I think we are going to order the family dish, but could you also include your homemade chicken noodle soup?"

"Yes, sir," she responds with a bigger smile.

It is always true —people are like mirrors, they reflect the treatment they receive.

After we finish our meal, we jump happily into the car with the only thought of getting to our destination as soon as possible. In less than two hours we get to Paradise, and find the log cabin where we are going to spend the week. Christina runs straight to the lake and Gabriel takes his bike to go for a short ride along the pier.

"Guys, be careful!" Emily yells at them. Yes, parents never rest.

Emily and I go inside to inspect the cabin. We already decided what places to visit on this trip. We'll go to White Fish Point to see the migration of birds and the museum of the Edmund Fitzgerald, a famous ship that sank in Lake Superior. We'll also go for a fishing trip in the Seney wildlife refuge. We will tour Tahquamenon Falls, and the locks in Sault Ste. Marie. It's going to be a good vacation. I feel so peaceful when I come up here. I wish I had a summer house near this place.

I feel tired from the driving. I need some rest, soon. I tell Emily I am going to take a nap before dinner, and she reminds me that I promised the kids that I'd give them a ride around the lake with the canoe.

"Yes, I know. I will," I say as I walk to the bedroom. I put a blanket on the mattress and quickly fall fast asleep.

Less than five minutes have passed when Emily runs into the room screaming: "It's Gabriel; it's Gabriel. He is in the lake! Run! Help him, Walker!" Emily is hysterical.

I run out of the cabin, but I realize I am naked! I don't know what happened. I feel I have to keep running. People in other cabins are coming out and watching the scene with despair. Emily continues screaming:

"Here, here, Walker."

I don't understand how she got there before me. She is already at the pier pointing to the bottom of the lake.

"He fell with his bike!" She screams.

I keep running, but my legs are getting tired with each step. There are people all over. I feel embarrassed being naked. Emily keeps screaming:

"Walker, please, faster; he is drowning!"

I can't go faster. I wonder if I will be able to pull him out of the water with my arm.

"Gabriel!" I scream.

"It is ready! You can come now," he answers.

I don't understand. People come to help me run and they begin grabbing and shaking my legs. I don't know why.

"Walker! Walker! Dinner is ready," Emily says very calmly.

"What? Oh God! It is a dream. Oh!" I sigh.

"What a relief! Where is Gabriel?"

"He is in the kitchen, honey. He called you for dinner already. You didn't answer, so I came to wake you up. What happened?"

"I was dreaming that I was naked and Gabriel was drowning in the lake. Oh! What a nightmare! People were watching me. Can you imagine that?"

"You are sweating, Walker. Use this towel and come to the table."

It was the most realistic dream in years, worse than those dreams of my mom.

When I get to the table the kids are laughing about me. "Dad, how does it feel to be naked in front of strangers?" Gabriel asks.

"Not funny, son. Let's eat," I say firmly and a bit upset.

20

Honesty

EXT DAY, I WAKE UP EARLY IN THE morning. It is seven; the sun is shining over the lake and birds are singing all around. Our plan is to visit the Seney Wildlife Refugee first. We can go fishing, if I convince them, and spend some time in the Nature Center afterward. I go to the bedroom to call Gabriel and Christina to wake them up.

"Hey kids ... time to get up." They are deeply sleeping and give me no answer. I pull their blanket, and finally they wake up. "Sorry, kids, but we'd better get going."

I go to the kitchen and prepare some coffee, cut the bread, cheese and ham. I put out the marmalade and set the table. Emily wakes up with the smell of coffee. The kids tumble towards the table. It is a fresh breezy morning. We all sit in rustic wooden chairs ready to start breakfast. I begin the conversation about the trip to Seney. I believe that the best time to convince people to do something is when they are happy, and happy they are when they are eating.

"How about if we go to Seney earlier and try to catch a big fish for lunch?" I ask.

Emily looks at me with a disapproving gesture. She hates it when I let the kids make the decision. Gabriel and Christina both nod at my question. Emily stays quiet, looking at her plate, ignoring our conversation.

"Emily, we'll have time for other activities as well. Fishing will be no more than an hour. I promise."

"I'll stay in the car reading a book, while you go fishing. Is that fine with you kids?" She asks.

They both agree, but I am now uncomfortable. I didn't mean to change Emily's plans, but she took it personally, as always, as if I didn't care about her opinion. If she knew how much I need to see her happy too.

We finish our breakfast, clean the kitchen as quick as we can, and jump into the car to visit Seney. It is a nice trip just to get there. Scenery in the U.P. is beautiful all year long, even in the winter. Gabriel brought his new fishing pole and I will lend mine to Christina because she left hers at home.

Once in Seney, we look for a good spot to park the car and throw our lines. After fifteen minutes inside the park I realize there are so many small lakes that we could spend days fishing. I see a good spot at the right side of the road and stop the car. Gabriel is rushing to the trunk to take his stuff out of the car and runs to the lake to prepare his line. Christina comes after and joins me to go together to catch Gabriel.

"Are you sure you want to stay in the car?" I ask Emily, trying to make her participate in the fishing adventure.

"Yes, I want to finish this book," she responds as she grabs the book from her bag, and opens it at the page she had marked. I say nothing in return, and continue walking with Christina.

Gabriel is already sitting and patiently waiting for a tug on his line. He is always quick and focused on his job. Christina is with me watching how I set the hook and the rest of the equipment. This is going to be a nice time, all three of us sitting together. The sun is shining hot now, and the reflections on the lake hurt our eyes. I propose to make a competition before any fish is caught. "To make it more fun, why don't we give a prize to the one who catches the first fish? Let's say I will let the winner drive the car inside the park for five minutes."

Emily is listening from the car and yells: "I don't like that idea." She is scared of giving the car to the kids. Gabriel and Christina look at each other and, after smiling, they agree to my offer. They both start bragging about who is better at fishing and talking about how fast they are going to drive the car. Now they both are concentrated on their fishing, and since I have nothing to do, I begin a story to entertain them.

"Okay kids, let me tell you this real story while you fish: When I was young, long before I met your mom, I was trying to create a company that would harvest trout for restaurants in our home town. It was a very good idea, I thought, because I knew what we had to do and because I had already talked to some potential clients in town. I went to the local bank to ask for a small loan to start the business; but, because I was too young and had no credit history, the bank didn't want to lend me anything. Then I began to look for a person with money to be my partner. It was difficult to find, but after few weeks your uncle Phil told me about this man who was a 'professional investor.' His name was Carl. He was a nice person, a bit reserved, but convincing when he talked. We decided to create a partnership called 'Shell Fish for Chelsea.' Gabriel begins laughing, and Christina follows.

"Don't laugh! It was my first dream, my first business. It didn't matter that trout were not shellfish. It was a fun name, that's all. Later, Carl hired three men to do the tough labor while I would do the management. The business started making money quite fast after our first batch of trout, and was running steadily with profit from the very beginning."

"I got one! I got one!" Gabriel shouts. "A fish, a fish." The nylon line is running from left to right and back, very fast.

"I think it is a big one," I say. "Loosen the line to tire it, and then reel it in slowly."

He unlocks the reel and the fish starts going around. After a couple of seconds Gabriel begins to reel in the fish as I said. He is very excited. Christina is watching jealously. When the fish is just two feet from Gabriel's hand it makes a fast twist, gets loose and goes back to the water. What bad luck! Gabriel is about to cry. He drops the pole and says nothing. Christina pats him on the back and comforts him. That's nice of her.

I try to make him forget about it as soon as possible by continuing the story. "Don't worry Gabriel, you'll catch another one. Well, as I was saying, 'Shell Fish for Chelsea' was doing very well. Actually, it went so well that I hired three more men after six months. One of these men was Carl's brother who had been unemployed for a year and was a certified accountant that could help me to handle all the tax forms I had to fill out and submit. In the seventh month I noticed we did not make the profit we made the month before, but Carl told me that it was normal for a small business to have a drop in profit after the first semester. So, I believed him because of his reputation as a 'professional investor,' but I wasn't happy. In the eighth month…

"Oh yay, a fish, a fish!" Christina screams. This time it's her turn.

"Okay Christy, do as I told Gabriel, tire the fish first and then reel it in." But even before she unlocks the reel, the fish is also gone. She looks at me with such disappointing eyes. Then she looks at Gabriel, who approaches her and says:

"Don't worry sis, it was the same fish. It was already trained." Christina laughs and quickly forgets about it. I am glad the bad luck has not made things worse.

"Well, as I was saying," I continue. "In the eighth month my company reported losses for a second time, and I began to investigate the problem more closely. I talked to other people in the same kind of business, and they told me nothing about drops in profits after the first semester. Then I went to check the books of the company and found the problem."

"What was it?" Gabriel asks.

"Unfortunately, I found that Carl and his brother had been transferring money to their bank accounts and were driving the company into bankruptcy."

"And then what did you do? Christina asks.

"I broke up the partnership and the company disappeared altogether."

"So, what is the moral of the story this time, dad?" Gabriel asks again.

"That when you are going to build a company, honesty is one of the most important characteristics you have to look for in your partners. Honesty leads to trust, and trust leads to productivity. Trust is not only important in companies, but in everything. Do you see your mom there inside the car? She is relaxed and peaceful, enjoying a good book. She can do that because she trusts me; because she knows I will take care of you both. When you trust someone, or something, you feel confident and you can concentrate your energies on other aspects of your life. If you trust someone, you let the trusted person take care of your responsibilities while you explore new ideas and projects. Trust is essential in life. Without trust we crumble to pieces. We become unproductive. We fail."

"And what's the relation between the moral and us being here fishing?" Christina asks me with a confused face. I am about to begin the answer when I see both lines moving back and forth. What a coincidence!

"I am going to reel it in now. I won't wait," Gabriel says.

"So am I," Christina replies.

Both are fighting for a fish, pulling the lines, reeling in as fast as they can. Finally, Gabriel and Christina take their fish out of the water almost at the same time. They look at each other to find out who was first, and when they see both fish out of the water, they laugh and I proclaim a tie in the contest. I'll let each of them drive the car for five minutes. That way, everyone will be happy except, perhaps, Emily who didn't like the idea to begin with. I pull a knife out of my pocket, and grab a bag for the fishes, but then, without even asking me, they take their fish off the hook, release them back to the lake, wishing them good luck. When I ask why they did that, Christina responds: "Before entering the park, Gabriel and I agreed on not eating any fish we'd caught in the park. We can eat one already caught, from the supermarket."

Days have passed very quickly and we are in our last day in this wonderful countryside. We will start on our trip back to Chelsea at about 10:00 AM, early, with the intention of stopping for lunch in a restaurant that is like no other restaurant in the area. It is located a few minutes south of the Mackinac Bridge in a small town called Cross Village. The name of the restaurant escapes my mind, but nobody can miss it once in town. I still remember the first time we ate there. A friend of mine convinced me that I should visit the restaurant, and it was good advice. It has an atmosphere like no other restaurant in Michigan. It is a mix of American Indian and European decoration, with lots of hand carved furniture. The food is mainly Polish and American, though. There is a large room with lots of tables, and a souvenir shop for tourists. And if the weather is good, people can eat outside in a large patio with a view of the lake.

The people that go to this restaurant are not typical Americans either. I remember this weird fellow sitting next to us when we first visited the restaurant. He had a long white pony tail. He was Caucasian, tall, with blue eyes, and a long white beard too; he was probably in his 70's, but very energetic. He used suspenders for his pants, I remember. His wife, a woman in her 60's, had a small hammer inside her purse. I saw it when she opened the purse to look for her glasses. I couldn't resist and asked her what the hammer was for. She told me she did not mean to carry it into the restaurant, but it was there by accident, because they were building a house by themselves just north of Cross Village, and the hammer was left inside the purse by their dog. She was very talkative, compared to the old guy.

I also remember I had asked my kids to tell me what they thought this couple did for a profession. Gabriel said that the old man was a medical doctor, and the woman was a painter. Christina said he was a physics professor and the woman was a writer. Emily said they were rich people that never worked and had a hippie life. We could not ask them, and never knew their real occupation, nevertheless, they were indeed very special people. Along with them there was another man with a European accent. He was in his forties, fine nose, dark eyes, wearing glasses. He was drinking beer from a large glass. The old man and he were talking about mathematics; that is why Christina said the old guy was a physicist. They all seemed to be very good friends, as they laughed quiet often, especially the European guy. I was tempted to chat with them, but before I could say anything they were leaving the room. We waved goodbye and never saw them again. We had a good lunch that time, and since then, we always stop by this place when we go to the U.P.

Suddenly I remember something that happened that first time in Cross Village. It's like a flash of memory: when we were leaving the restaurant I saw a piece of paper, a napkin, on the table where the white-pony tailed fellow and his friend were eating. I remember that I approached the table to read what was written on the napkin. It was pure math symbols to me, and a couple of words here and there. I remember I could read words like *min max*, and *optimality*. I did not care at that time because these words had little meaning for me, then. But now, after talking to Kwame, those words carry weight.

Today is a hot day. The kids are hungry and anxious to have their feet under the table. We get to Cross Village very quickly; but, unfortunately, the restaurant is closed. They don't open until May. What a pity! The kids are angry, now. When we are about to take the road that heads back to the highway, Gabriel sees the white-pony tailed old man and his wife. What a coincidence! They were walking down the street with their black dog. He is still using his suspenders, but is not wearing any shirt this time. I suppose it is because of the heat today. I wave to them, and they wave back to us.

"I think he remembers us," I say.

"Yes, I think so too," Christina replies.

"It was nice to see them again, I wonder if they finished the house that they were building here," I say.

"It has been two years since we first saw them; they should have finished already," Emily replies as we head towards the highway to look for another restaurant.

We get to I-75 and head south. We stop in a fast food restaurant. I hate them, but we are so hungry that we can't wait anymore. At around five in the afternoon we are back in Chelsea. It was a nice vacation with fun and good family time, as we planned. Tomorrow is Monday, when Kwame is coming to visit and give me some lectures on design optimization. This is going to be interesting. I'll play being an engineer, and he'll play being an artisan, a luthier.

21

Natural Designs

T IS MONDAY MORNING. I WAKE UP, TAKE a shower, dress, and prepare toast with butter, ham and cheese for breakfast. I look out through the window and see a shining sun and a blue sky. I prepare coffee, eat as quick as I can and keep going. Emily and the kids are still in bed, resting from the long trip we had yesterday. I cannot stop thinking about today's meeting with Kwame, and the benefits Manuel and I will get from his advice.

I open the front door of the house, but a phone call stops me from going out. Who could be calling so early in the morning? It must be a wrong number.

"Hello?"

A voice from the other side responds, "Walker? Is this the McBride's residence?"

I recognize it. It's the sweet voice of Laura. Oh, how sweet she sounds. "Laura, how are you?" I say with the softest voice I can. "I am so glad to hear your voice. But, how do you know my phone number at home?"

"I have my sources, dear. I was feeling lonely at home, and suddenly you came to my mind. How have you been? How are the replicas?"

I am feeling uncomfortable talking to her, especially because of the way she is talking to me, so soothing and inviting. "Laura," I say, "why don't I call you when I get to my office. Everybody is sleeping here, and our conversation could wake them up."

She doesn't answer for a long instant, and I suspect that she is hurt by my response. "Okay, but don't forget to call me!"

"I won't."

"Bye," she replies with a sad, angry tone, the same tone one hears from a child left at the door of the school the first day of class in first grade.

I hang up the phone, and walk to the door again when, suddenly, I see Emily walking down the stairs. Her eyes still semi-open but staring at me to catch my gestures. "Who was calling so early?" She asks.

"It was a client from Europe. Did I tell you I got a client when I went to Europe for the workshop in Spain?"

She nods at me, but I can see in her face that she is not totally convinced of the truth of my answer. I have to fill the silence with more explanations. "I am building two guitars for this customer for a very good price. It's the best deal I've ever made."

She nods again, but asks, "Is this customer a *he* or a *she?*"

"Does it matter?" I reply, shrinking my shoulders.

Finally, probably because of the tiredness or the sleepiness, she nods one more time, turns around, walks up the stairs, and goes back to bed.

I finally get to the shop. Kwame's car is already in the parking lot. I enter the shop and see him talking to Manuel. "Hi, Kwame!"

He turns around to greet me and says, "Walker! How are you? How was your vacation?"

"It was very good. I needed it. We went to the U.P. and had a nice week fishing, boating, biking, reading and many more activities for the kids."

"Nice to hear that. We stayed home; you know, Amy's problem."

"Mmm ... " I stay quiet on this subject. I feel so sad to hear that. I try to change the subject by inviting him to the office. "Manuel, how are you?" I ask as we walk.

"I am fine. I didn't go anywhere, though. I have two exams this week."

He is talking about his computer science studies. It's tough to study and work at the same time, but I know he will make it. Once in the office I bring up the issue about Kwame's fees, but he refuses to charge any consulting fees since he is just teaching us optimization, and not doing engineering for us.

"But at least charge us the teaching fees!" I insist.

"Well, I could do that, if you want," he replies. "But remember that my book is taking time from me, and you can't count on me a hundred percent of the time."

"Deal!" I reply to close the subject. Manuel smiles.

"Okay Kwame, now that we are clear about your role in our business, let's start the lesson."

"I have to tell you that this is not a one-hour thing, Walker. Optimization is a lifetime career for many. You will grasp the generalities of it, but, as they say, the devil is in the details. Please don't expect to become an expert in a few hours."

"I know, I know, but I trust your teaching skills and hope to be your best student. You'll be surprised how quickly I learn."

He asks for white paper and pencil. "Well, before I start the lesson I want to tell you what Leonhard Euler, one of the greatest mathematicians in history, said a long time ago in the eighteen century. He said, and I'll paraphrase, 'since the universe is made so perfect, everything in it can be explained by methods of minimization and maximization.' I tell you this to open your mind, and make you realize that optimization is not just math, but a way of viewing all phenomena in the universe. There is always something being minimized or maximized that results in what you see, do and feel around you. Even in the way we approach life, our happiness, our worries and hopes are connected to some sort of maximization or minimization of a measure. This measure may not be easily quantifiable, like in the case of feelings, but we still, many times unconsciously, are solving optimization problems minute by minute."

"That is very philosophical, Kwame, very deep. Thank you for that quotation. I'll keep it in mind." His last comment raises some interesting thoughts in me. I start seeing some connections that I didn't see before. What he said makes a great deal of sense. *'Our worries, our happiness'* resonates in me for a while.

He rests his left elbow on the table, and his chin on his left hand. He closes his eyes and seems to be thinking, meditating. He then opens his eyes. "Before continuing, I want Manuel to listen to my definition of a natural design."

Manuel, very much interested in what Kwame is going to say, grabs a chair, sits down with paper and pencil, and stares at Kwame with that gaze that says 'teach me all you want.'

Kwame smiles to him, and begins, "When the BBB concept was first used centuries ago, there was no need to worry about the damage we, humans, had made to Nature. We were so few on earth that the use of natural resources was minuscule, and we didn't have to measure the cost of such resources being depleted. Nowadays, we are in a totally different situation. We have now reached a point where in order to guarantee a sustainable civilization we have to consider the total cost of natural resources used in every product we make. However, most of the time, most companies all around the world don't consider this aspect of their business plan."

"I see what you mean," Manuel says.

Kwame continues, "Disposable eating utensils is one example. They seem to be the cheapest —most profitable— alternative for fast food chains, but the total cost to our civilization, and to our future generations, is immense, if you factor in the cost of non-biodegradable garbage. I am talking about the tons and tons of plastic forks, knives, spoons and glasses that are dumped every year and require decades to be re-absorbed by the earth."

"But including such cost is very difficult to do," I say.

He seems disillusioned by my reply, but continues. "What happens, is that each individual company is trying to maximize its profits without considering the future cost to Nature and to civilization as a whole. The plastic silverware manufacturers want to sell their products to increase their *own current profit*. In turn, fast food chains want to use more disposable silverware to reduce their cost, and increase their *own current profit*. Finally, the garbage-collecting companies want more plastic silverware to be used to keep running their businesses and increase their *own current profit*. They do not consider the total future cost to society, but only the individual and current cost to them alone. On the other hand, Nature had been running the show for billions of years until we showed up with our egotistical and greedy attitudes. Nature evolved and reached a point of equilibrium that is now threatened by big corporations and individual comfort and interests."

"So, how do you propose to change that?" Manuel asks.

"My proposal is simple in concept, but takes time and effort to implement. Each new product we design must be conceived accounting for the total cost to Nature. I mean the cost of material, manufacturing, disposing and recycling it. How do we do that? Simple. Imitate Nature, its methods and its evolutionary approaches when posing and solving the design problem. Imitation of Nature allows us to be part of the whole, entire and complex environment, which in turns makes us aware of the cost, monetary or energetic, of each design intention we pursue. That is the basic idea. If we merge our products with Nature, then whatever we do and make will be part of it, and the impact will be minimized." He pauses and waits for our response.

I am still thinking about the complexity of his proposal. "Now I understand what you meant about BBB and Nature when we talked in Denmark," I say.

"Yes, Walker. Nature has provided the most beautiful designs ever found, the most beneficial, and the most inexpensive designs

—actually free— ever built. Therefore, it is a good practice to imitate Nature as much as possible and find its ways of evolution to improve our lives without jeopardizing our future generations. In summary, we need to make our designs BBB and Naturalistic."

"Oh, Kwame, you could not say it better. It is so clear now. I think I can use this lecture not only in my guitars, but also in my life."

I propose a break, and invite him and Manuel for a cup of coffee across the street. As we walk, my mind keeps remembering what he said before —*our happiness, our worries, our happiness, our worries ...*

22

Design II[*]

E ARE BACK IN THE OFFICE, energized by the coffee, the fresh air, and the walk. Manuel goes to his desk and begins working on the guitars we are delivering next week.

Kwame grabs a pad of paper. "Okay, let's review the mathematics I have taught you so far. We talked about a couple of concepts that I want to recall. First we need to be able to measure things in order to compare and formulate conclusions. The ability to measure is the most basic tool in engineering. When doing design optimization we pick one of these measures from the guitar and call it *the design objective.* The design objective will be maximized or minimized. For instance, if we are talking about the guitar cost as design objective, you want to minimize it, but if we are measuring the guitar quality, then you want to maximize it. Clear?"

"Yes, that is clear," I say while a flash of memory comes to me again. I remember the paper napkin in Cross Village's restaurant.

---

[*]This chapter may be skipped if you have no interest in the design optimization subject.

The Guitar Maker

The piece of paper left on the table where the pony-tailed guy was sitting. I remember the words 'min max' written on it. Mmm, this is becoming interesting. I keep quiet and listen.

"We also talked about *design variables*," Kwame continues. "These are the parameters that you can change to increase or decrease the design objective. Do you remember when I was in your house's basement last time? We talked about the design variables in guitar design. I remember that the sound plate thickness was a very important variable.

"Yes, you are right. You have a good memory."

"We also talked about *sensitivities*. They are quantities that measure changes in the design objective, or any other measure, when we change the design variables. Remember that?"

"Oh, yes. I remember that, too."

He pauses for a moment, smiles, and says, "What I have not talked about is constraints, right?"

I shake my head, "no."

"Well, it turns out that quite often you have many measures to consider, not just one. If I take the guitar design as an example, you may want to increase performance, reduce cost, increase beauty, reduce manufacturing time, and so on. All these measures have a mathematical name; they are called *functions*. Do you remember from your math classes in high school what functions are? At any rate, an optimization problem, the simplest one, is usually posed as the minimization of one of these functions while imposing some limits on the other functions. Those functions that are limited are called *constraints*."

"Kwame," I interrupt, "suppose you want to maximize your design objective. How do you solve the problem?"

"It is simple. In mathematics this is done by changing the sign of the design objective. Suppose you call f the design objective, then minimization of f is the same as the maximization of the negative of f, that is, $-f$. Do you see? It's that simple."

"Okay, I understand. What do you do with the other functions you need to impose limits on?"

"All other functions are then treated as *constraint functions*. They define or limit the designs that are allowed to be considered as an answer to your problem. For example, in a car design you may say that the weight of the car cannot exceed two tons; or that the gas efficiency must be greater than twenty miles per gallon. All these extra requirements are called constraints, and along with the design objective plus the design variables, form the optimization problem. In mathematics, all possible designs put together, if there are any, are called *the design space*. It is simply a collection of all possible combinations of design variables that satisfy every constraint in the problem. For instance, a 130 lb guitar is out of the design space, right?"

I laugh. "What if there is not a single design that satisfies all constraints?"

"Oh! You are thinking fast! In such a case, we say that the optimization problem is *infeasible*. Which means that there exists no solution for the given constraints."

"Okay, I need an example. Let's say I have three measures in a guitar: sound intensity, weight and cost. How do I pose the problem?"

"Well, first of all, I see you did not pick beauty as a measure," he says.

"Because, I can make it beautiful anytime I want with good wood, good polishing, and a well made sound-hole rosette. I know that at the end, the beauty will be there."

"Good argument, but not always valid for other types of products. Before we continue I want to say this. You know that mathematicians need short names for the entities they use. They do that in order to write short equations. Let's use three letters for the three measures you mentioned: S for sound intensity, W for weight and C for cost. Now you pick the most important one. What is it that you care more about, among these three measures?"

"I would say that out of those three the sound intensity is for me the most important measure in a guitar."

"Great, now give me an upper limit for the cost and another for the weight."

"Well, it is hard to say. How can I come up with such numbers if I don't know the final product?"

"Well, you can guess now, and then use other numbers later. This is common practice in the initial stages of a design. We try with the information we have, and then refine as we improve the design."

"Then I would say that the cost cannot be more than $3000, and it should not weigh more than three pounds. These numbers are just a guess based on my experience."

"That's fine. That is what experts are paid for, to provide opinion and knowledge based on their experience. Now we need to decide what are the design variables. For simplicity, I will let you pick only two variables. They need to be variables such that the measures you already picked are sensitive to them," he explains.

"That is easy, the two design variables could be the thickness of the sound board and the height of the internal braces to stiffen the board. I also know by experience that these two parameters will affect the sound intensity, the weight, and to some degree the cost of the guitar."

"Good Walker, we are getting almost ready to pose the optimization problem. There is one more thing I need to do. Let's call these two design variables t and h. Each design variable usually has a lower and an upper limit, called *simple bounds*. Give me the upper and lower bounds for t and h."

"Okay, let's say that the thickness of the plate is between 2 and 3 millimeters, and the height of the braces between 5 and 15 millimeters."

Kwame takes the piece of paper and begins to write. When he finishes, in less than 15 seconds, he shows it to me.

"This is the optimization problem posed as you described it, and written in plain English."

I take the paper and read it. It makes a lot of sense to me. It is easy to understand too. It says:

Find The values of T and h ThaT maximize S, such ThaT W is less Than 2, C is less Than

3000; T is between 2 and 3 mm; and h is between 5 and 15 mm.

"Kwame, I know by experience that this problem has a solution, but if I am a novice in the field, how do I know if this problem can be solved?"

"Well, a lot of mathematics needs to be used to prove that. I don't think you need to know about it. For the moment, we accept that all problems we will pose to improve the designs of your guitars have at least one solution."

I feel excited. I think I understand everything. "Okay Kwame, why don't we solve this problem now?"

"Wait, wait a minute. We haven't finished. We need a very important piece of information here. We can't solve the problem until we have that."

"What is it? I though we would crank numbers in your calculator and solve the problem. Can't we?"

He smiles with that smile I've seen on him before. He is smiling at my ignorance. "Walker, we need to find a mathematical expression for each function in the optimization problem. If not, we are walking in the darkness. These expressions will allow us to compute sensitivities, and eventually, will give us the numerical value of any measure we consider important in the problem. For instance, how does the sound intensity depend on the height of the internal braces? How does the cost depend on the thickness of the sound plate? We need these expressions before cranking numbers."

"Oh, you are right. I forgot about the sensitivities. But then, how do we find these expressions?"

"I am glad you ask. This is probably the most important part of the optimization problem. You need to model the physics of the phenomena. In your case, you have two options: either you build several prototypes with different combinations of variables and take measurements, or, what I recommended to you in Denmark, you build a numerical model inside your computer to perform numerical experiments. You do so for each guitar you want to design."

"A computer model!" I say. "I can't afford that."

"In the long run it is more expensive to build prototypes for each guitar," he replies. "A computer model costs more at the beginning, but you'll recover the cost soon. In the computer you can change variables many, many times. You can simulate different woods, try different brace heights, and so on. I do recommend that you find a company that can build a computer model for you. I can help you in assessing the quality of the model if you want."

"A computer model..." I say again. I never thought I had to deal with such things.

"Once we have all functions modeled," he says, "we can find out how sensitive your functions are to changes in the design variables. Having sensitivity information will tell us what kind of variation we need to make. For example, we will know where to decrease or increase the thickness of the sound plate, but most importantly, we will be able to solve the optimization problem we just posed."

"A computer model ..." I say to myself again.

23

Love

AM ABOUT TO ASK MORE QUESTIONS to Kwame when Manuel enters the office. "Walker, I want to review with you what I did."

This is a good opportunity to bring Kwame to the shop where we transform wood into guitars. I suggest that we take a break and go with Manuel to the other room. While we walk, Manuel takes the opportunity to bring up the question that has been pending since last time we talked.

"Walker, did you ask Kwame about your aspirations of building high quality but inexpensive guitars?"

Kwame smiles because we already talked about this, and says, "Look, Manuel, I promise that Walker will be able to answer that question in a couple of lessons. He already knows the answer, but I want him to grasp other concepts before giving an explanation to you."

Manuel smiles back and realizes that Kwame and I are in agreement. We take a short tour through the shop while Manuel explains many details of the construction process. He has learned so much since I hired him. I am proud of him.

It is already noon when we return to my desk. Kwame tells me he has to leave, and we agree to meet again in a couple of days. We go together to the parking lot and before he opens his car door he pauses and looks at me.

"Walker, the lesson you received today is not only for your guitars. In fact, the design optimization of a product is an easy optimization problem we engineers know how to solve. The real optimization problems are in life. Since I learned optimization, I realized how much I can use it in my life, how it can guide me to make decisions, to sort out my priorities, and to achieve what I consider to be one of the most important goals of life. Any guess what that might be?"

"Happiness?" I say timidly.

"Correct. We spend our lives maximizing happiness and minimizing suffering, but some people don't know the steps to follow, or the direction to take to achieve maximum happiness. The difficulty comes then when we want to solve the optimization problem of our own lives. People suffer because they don't know how to pose the problem with so many constraints they face in life. They only look at the objective —to be happy— but don't know the design variables, or the constraints, much less the concept of sensitivity applied to their lives. Let's see, could you tell me one constraint in life?"

I look at his eyes, and with no hesitation I say, "Money."

"Yes, a very concrete and quantifiable constraint, but there are many more. Many of them come from the fact that we live interacting with other people in our society, therefore, material resources need to be shared among us, creating a limit on the amount we can use. This limitation in material resources is the source of so many disputes, oppositions and wars around the world. The goal is to solve the optimization problem for the entire society, for the entire human race and not for each individual. Only then we will live more peacefully. However, we need to act individually in order to attain the goal. This is also difficult since it requires a hierarchical structure to measure happiness at different levels."

"Another constraint, Walker, is time, lifetime I mean. We have only seventy-some years to achieve the objective of happiness. Now think about this idea: happiness is like a substance that has passed from generation to generation. Therefore, we have to make the effort to ensure that we don't destroy it for our greedy, personalized, egotistical benefit. Don't you think that it is more ethical to be happy by guaranteeing to those who come after us to be happier than us? We can provide the means to our children, and the children of the world, to maintain the continuity of the substance called happiness."

I think I understand what he tries to tell me, but I don't see a practical application of his theory of happiness. "This *substance* of happiness, Kwame, where did it come from?"

"Good question, but it is not as important as where can we find *more* of it, so we are sure we don't deplete it"

He pauses, looks at me as if waiting for an intelligent answer, but since I stay quiet, he continues. "Since material resources are limited, that is, there is only one Earth for all of us, then happiness, which we want to be eternal, cannot depend on external entities like material resources. In other words, we can't use external means to maintain happiness in the world. We need something more secure, unlimited, that is able to keep going as long as the human race, right?"

I nod.

"Then, let me repeat the question: where can we find more happiness?"

"From inside," I finally realize.

"And what comes from inside you that can make you happy? Money? Obviously not. What is it?"

Another pause breaks the flow of his conversation, but I don't answer this time.

"It is love, Walker. Can you be sad while being loved or while loving someone? Love is, for me at least, the seed of happiness that we all need to cultivate. It is that simple for me. We then maximize our love, express it towards our family, our friends, our coworkers, our entire surrounding world in order to achieve the maximum happiness we can within the limited time on Earth, and the limited resources we have."

I see his point now. He smiles to me, waiting for an answer.

"Great, Kwame, this is great," I say while I suggest to him that he can go to his car now.

But he stands firmly and says. "I haven't finish with this design problem. I have not talked about the design variables yet. I told you about the objective and some constraints, but what about the variables you can change to solve the problem of happiness maximization?"

"I don't know, it is difficult for me to see it," I say.

"Ask yourself this question: what can I change to increase my love in a limited amount of time, with a limited amount of material resources?"

"My attitude?" I ask.

"Yes, you got one, but there is more than that."

I think and think, but nothing comes to my mind.

Then he says, "Values and principles, Walker. Let me summarize for you. People need to improve their attitude, values and principles in order to achieve happiness through love, within a limited amount of time and resources. This explains why it is so difficult to solve the optimization problem of life. Changing your attitude towards people, improving your values and principles are not easy things to do."

"I know. Few are willing to do it, and fewer are able to," I say. "But Kwame, you argued that engineering is based on measurements, then how do you measure values and principles?"

"Great question, Walker!" He says. "I didn't say we engineers need to rule the world. In fact, I think it's better if we don't interfere in such matters. We are a tool to be used by society to reach happiness. From a mathematical point of view we can't measure values and principles like we measure the speed of a car, or the size of a shoe —with very precise numbers. This is another reason life becomes so difficult; we haven't found the way to measure what we need to change in order to reach happiness, which by the way, isn't measurable either. Can you buy ten kilograms of happiness?" He smiles.

I say nothing, because there is no point to refute. He then takes a deep breath, pats me on the back, and gets inside his car. We say goodbye, and I return to the shop as soon as I can.

It's getting late and I need to return the call to my Danish *client.*

24

Trust

I GRAB THE PHONE AND PUNCH THE NUMBERS. I am feeling anxious to hear her voice again. One ring, another ring, and she answers: "Is it you?"

I stay quiet for a moment, pondering the things I want to say.

"Hello?" She insists.

"Yes, it's me, Walker. How are you?"

"I am fine, but you sound nervous. Is there any problem?"

"Not at all. It's that, well, you know, you caught me by surprise this morning when you called me at home, and I wanted to ... well, it doesn't matter. Just remember not to call home next time."

"Okay, I won't."

"Good. I have to tell you that I haven't started with the construction of the replicas, but..."

"Don't worry, Walker. I wasn't calling to talk about that."

A pause that lasted like centuries makes me think more than what I should. I know she wants me to ask why she called.

"Walker, are you still there?"

"Yes, I am. Sorry, I was thinking."

"Well, I was also thinking. I was thinking about you, and I had this impulse to call you. How are you doing?"

"I am fine, fine." My pulse is going faster now. I can feel it. "Laura, I am very busy now. I called you back because I thought you wanted to know about the replicas. I'll call you later in the week once we have some news for you." I hear a sigh in the other side of the line.

"Please call me. Bye." And she hangs up.

I was too rude to her, I think, but I need to set my priorities. Kwame was right. It is so difficult to changed values and principles.

When I get home, Emily is again in the garden, planting some flowers before it gets too hot in the summer. When I see her it reminds me of the many times we have missed the opportunity to talk. I feel we have lost so much by not sharing our thoughts and feelings for such a long time. If she knew how much I need her.

"Dad!" I hear from the window upstairs. It is Gabriel.

"Dad, come up here. I want to show you something."

Emily turns towards me, says hello, and keeps working in the garden. I want to talk to her, but she looks busy and indifferent. I keep walking to the porch, and as I take the steps and open the front door I feel the weight of her sight over my shoulders. I know she also wants to talk, but I keep walking. Gabriel is waiting.

I get upstairs where Gabriel is working on his homework. "Hi, son. What are you doing?"

"Dad, I am preparing this report for the Social Studies class. It is about entrepreneurship in America. I think you can help me because you are an entrepreneur. You have your own business. The teacher gave us some questions we need to answer by tomorrow, and I am sure you know the answers better than I do."

"Gabriel, I think you should do it alone. Once you finish, then I can make corrections or answer any question for you."

"That's what I did already! What I want is to check my answers with you. Here is the first question."

He grabs his notebook and stands up.

"What is the most important characteristic of an entrepreneur? My answer was that they have to be intelligent, otherwise, they won't be able to run the business," he says.

"That is a good answer, son. But if I were you, that would not be my first choice."

"What is your first choice, then?"

"It is hard to choose only one characteristic because people are very complex in their behavior. I would say that the first thing an entrepreneur has to have is leadership. However, there are many types of leaders and not all of them are successful. They need more than leadership to reach the top. I would add they must be good decision makers; they must be very disciplined and hard workers; and because the business is just starting, they must put the production of results as their first priority, otherwise people won't take them seriously."

"Okay dad, but what is, in your opinion, the most important characteristic?"

"Write down *leadership*," I reply. He writes it down and proceeds with the next question.

"The second question is: how do you know whether the business will be a success? I wrote that the business would succeed if they make a profit. What do you think?"

"Well, that is not the answer to the question, I think. Your teacher is asking whether you know if it will be a success even before you start the business. I am going to tell you what our friend Kwame would have said. If the product or service you are planning to sell is beneficial, beautiful, at the lowest price, and friendly to Nature, you can be confident that the business will be a success. These are called BBBN products."

"BBBN? What's that?"

"It means a product with four qualities: betterment, beauty, bargain, and naturalistic."

He scratches his head, takes a pencil, and asks, "But what if another company has a better product?"

"Oh yes, I forgot to tell you this: all four qualities, must be optimized; that is, if your company makes the best BBBN product in the market, then customers will come to you. No other company will be able to compete with you."

"But dad, you always say that anything can be improved."

"Yes, this means that you need to keep improving the BBBN product until there is no more room for improvement, or until you introduce new technology to improve it or to manufacture it."

"Gee, dad, it means that a new company has to come up with a really new and different product to compete with the big companies."

It is incredible how a young boy can reason through this mess of economics when it took me years to understand. When one learns by experience, knowledge comes slowly and often painfully. I am glad Gabriel is getting it at this young age.

"Yes Gabriel, new companies must bring something new to the market, otherwise they will be eaten by the big fishes. Look at me for instance; I went to Spain to learn more about guitarmaking. I needed to inject knowledge into the company to maintain its competitiveness. If I just keep repeating what I know, sooner or later, my business will go bankrupt. These are the rules of the game. Big corporations have research departments to keep up with the new methods and technologies, but I can't have a research department. I need to educate myself as much as I can, use my creativity to produce new guitars with excellent quality and price that appeal to demanding guitarists. But going back to your homework question: there are many ways to make a successful business, but I am giving you one that is the most important. Offering BBBN products or services is a way to succeed, maybe the most certain one."

He writes down the four letters and their meaning. He then asks me the next question. "The third and last question is easy: how do you choose your partners? I wrote that you should start with your friends first."

"Good, very good answer, Gabriel. This is how most businesses used to start. Nowadays things are a bit different, but you are right. When you start a business with your friends or family there is a lot of trust between partners and that single fact facilitates and speeds up the business pace. Keep that in mind for any business you start and for the rest of your life, son. My mom, your grandma, used to say 'tell me who your friends are, and I will tell you who you are.' This is true inside and outside of business. Choose your friends carefully, those with attributes that complement yours and who strive toward being the best, with good values and principles. That is something that will be beneficial to your career and life forever.

He opens his eyes, like waiting for more information to digest. He's like a sponge absorbing anything that comes its way.

"When a company becomes larger and larger," I continue, "the original owners begin to lose contact with the people they started with. Big firms have to hire people who will hire people. They are called Human Resources people. If I had a big company some of the most important employees would be those in Human Resources. The reason is that they are in charge of bringing new, talented and trustworthy people to the company. If this fails, if employees are not trustworthy, the company is doomed. Trust builds a healthy employee-employer relation that eventually gets translated into better and more successful companies. Fortunately, I have a small company, and I don't need to worry much about all this. I hire a person after I know him very well. If I have any doubts about trusting him, I simply forget about it, and keep looking for the right person."

I feel the presence of someone else in the room. I turn around and I see Emily standing at the door, listening to our conversation. She is serious. I have no idea what she is thinking, but a serious face is always a bad sign.

"Hello boys," she says. "I got one more question for you both. When do you know that the trust between two partners has disappeared?"

I feel a cold knife through my heart.

Gabriel does not get it. "I think that when one partner hides something from the other, the trust disappears. But I don't have to answer that question for my homework. I'm done. I'm gonna play some soccer outside. Bye." He leaves the room.

Emily and I are now alone in the room. She is looking at me, waiting for an answer. I have been trying to evade this confrontation for a long time, but now it seems inevitable. Maybe it is better to face our problems once for all. She takes a chair and sits, while I change my posture to feel more comfortable.

"How long have you been listening to the conversation?" I ask. "Not for long," she says while resting her elbows on her knees, leaning towards me. She is waiting for me to start the conversation. The truth is that we simply don't feel like talking to each other anymore, and we have opted for not sharing anything. A few seconds pass, but it seems like hours for me. I better say something to start the discussion.

"I think Gabriel is right," I say. "When one of the partners hides something, even a simple thought, trust starts to fade away until, eventually, it is all gone."

"Does that apply to us?" She incisively asks.

"Maybe, maybe not. I have nothing to hide. How about you?"

"Yes, I do. I hide my sadness, my loneliness, my disillusion. I hide my crying when I am home alone. I hide my needs for you. I hide ten years of waiting for something to happen. I hide..."

"Emily, honey, we have been over this many times. I have to work hard, ten, twelve, fourteen hours a day to keep up with the expenses of the family. I give all my energy to you and the kids. What else do you want?"

"I want you. I want my husband back."

A tear rolls down her cheek. She looks down.

"I know, I know. I have been thinking about us lately. Since I met Kwame things make more sense in my life. I am able to organize my thoughts easier. I think I know what the problem between us is."

I put my hands together, interlacing my fingers. "It is simply that our objectives in life are different. You go in one direction, and I am going in another. When I fell in love with you I thought we had the same goals in life, the same final stage. But lately I don't see that. I never criticized the way you approached life, and I felt we were going to the same place, the same destination. But I am not sure about that anymore."

"And what does Kwame have to do with this?"

"Well, he says that life is about solving an optimization problem. Each person picks the objective that most fits him or her. Then you spend your life solving it."

"What happens when you get married? How do you put both objectives together?"

Tough question, as all questions coming from her. I'll give my best answer. "When marriage comes the objectives of both partners must be pointing to the same place. According to Kwame there are four categories of objectives. One that accounts for the benefits you want from life. Another objective considers the aesthetics, the beauty, and the artistic side of life. The third one has to do with how much money, energy, and time you want to spend to achieve your goals. Finally, the last objective is to try to do it all in a naturalistic way, without imposing an unrecoverable burden on nature beyond the minimum required."

She sits back, straightening her torso against the chair. "All that sounds nice, but now tell me how can we use it to improve our relationship?"

It is hard to come up with a good answer when one is part of the problem. When one is an outsider sometimes the diagnosis and the solution are easier to find. "Well, I guess that we need to sit down and talk about our future and see if we can put our individual objectives together. I propose this: you and I take a couple of days to write down our objectives, classify them in the four categories I just told you, and see our differences and similarities. How about that?"

She shakes her head; her sadness is obvious. "This is nonsense. I am talking about feelings, love, future, and you ask me to write down objectives in four categories. What is that, Walker?"

"Then you propose something!" I reply with a stentorian voice.

"Don't get angry. I'll do what you say. It is that I don't think it will solve our problems."

"I know that, but it is the beginning. First we need to know what the problems are."

She stands up, puts her hand on my shoulder, looks in my eyes, and leaves the room with no more words.

I stay in the room thinking, pondering. Life seems difficult, but it is just a matter of prioritizing and resolving small problems one at a time, I think.

25

Design III *

$\mathcal{T}$HE MORNING IS WARM; SUMMER WILL SOON arrive. Kwame is coming to the shop today, so I'd better hurry up and get ready for him. I take a shower, groom my beard, and get dressed. I go downstairs, eat a quick breakfast and rush to the shop to arrive before Kwame.

When I get to the shop I see Kwame's car in the parking lot, a well maintained old car. It must be more than fifteen years old. Manuel is already in the shop and as soon as I enter the door, he points to my office to tell me that Kwame is waiting for me. I've gotten used to Manuel's gestures. He points to things with his mouth because, he says, it's quicker and easier. So, now I do it too, which is even more useful for me.

"Kwame, it is eight in the morning. Did you fall out of your bed?"

He smiles. "Excuse me for coming so early, but I need to quit around eleven this morning. Is that okay with you?"

*This chapter may be skipped if you have no interest in the design optimization subject.

"No problem, Kwame. Let's start right away. I have some questions."

"Great."

"First, I want to know how to compute the solution of any optimization problem. You told me how to pose it, but how do I solve it?"

He smiles again, suggesting this is an easy question; but he is a good teacher and answers gently.

"Walker, first you must understand that not all problems have solutions."

"What? You taught me so much last time, and now you are telling me that the problem may not have a solution?"

"Yes Walker, it is simple. I mentioned this to you last time, but I guess you didn't write it down. Let me give you an example. Suppose you want to maximize the sound intensity of your guitar imposing an upper limit of five ounces on the weight. Obviously, you won't be able to even build the guitar, much less to maximize its sound. This means that there is no design that satisfies the constraint functions plus the bounds in the design variables. In mathematical terms it is said that the design space is empty. If you remember, I told you that mathematicians call this an *infeasible problem*."

"How do you know that?"

"Sometimes by logic or by studying the formulation of the problem you may be able to figure out the feasibility of the problem, but sometimes it is not that simple. Especially when there are many design variables and constraints, it is very difficult to prove that there is at least one solution to the problem. Most of the time, the method you pick to solve the problem will determine this, and you will reformulate the problem again, if necessary."

"That is good news. That means I just pass the problem through the computer, and if an answer is found, I am done; if not, I reformulate. Is that right?"

He shakes his head from side to side. "You are wrong again. If the computer finds a solution, it may not be the optimum."

"What? You're kidding, aren't you?"

"Well, what happens is that there may be more than one optimum."

Now I am getting frustrated. First, there is the possibility of no solution at all. Now, if there is one solution, it may not be the optimum. What kind of mathematics is this? He senses my frustration, and continues explaining.

"I need to teach you a new concept that will help you to understand what I am talking about. Have you seen those camels with two humps?"

"Yes, I have. They are the bactrian camels."

"Oh, you surprise me, Walker. How do you know?"

"Well, when I was in seventh grade, I had to prepare a report about camels. I still remember my drawings. I was good at drawing before, you know.

"Well, good enough," he wisely continues. "Now imagine that the back of one of these camels is the function you want to maximize, and that there are no constraints. As you can guess, there are two possibilities, two solutions: the maximum of the front hump, and the maximum of the rear hump. Most likely, the heights of these humps are not equal. That means that if a computer is trying to find the highest hump, it may choose the wrong one."

"Why can't the computer just identify the tallest hump?"

"Because computers don't have eyes like humans. However, some methods are powerful enough to get you the right answer. They are called *global search methods*. If you have patience, these methods will provide the real —global— optimum for you."

"Now imagine the other type of camel, the one with one hump only."

"The dromedarian camel," I quickly reply.

"Excellent. For this type of function, there is only one maximum. If you find it, you have found the optimum solution."

"Okay, how do you put camels and mathematics together now? Do you have names for these functions?"

"Of course. A function with only one hump is called a *concave function*, roughly speaking. They are very special since they always have only one maximum, which is called the *global maximum*. Since mathematicians prefer to deal with minimization problems, however, they'd rather work with the negative of concave functions, which are called *convex functions*. For example, imagine the Chinese cooking plate –the wok. This is a convex function with only one minimum called the *global minimum*, at the bottom of the wok."

"And what do you call the two-hump function?" I ask.

"Those functions are neither concave nor convex, and have no special properties for us. The problem gets more complex when we add constraints. For example, the same two-hump function can be considered as a concave function if we constrain ourselves to look at only one hump, discarding the other one. This is good because now, with the problem being concave there is only one maximum which is the solution. However, this is not always the case. Many times the addition of constraints to a minimization problem may transform it from a convex problem to a non-convex problem, and that is bad news. It all depends on the type of functions used to describe the design objective and the constraints."

"Are you telling me, that a problem with non-convex functions cannot be solved?"

"No, it is simply that it is more difficult to find the global minimum, but not impossible. It means we have to use more powerful methods that may take longer to find the optimum."

I am getting confused with all this, so I change the subject to take a rest. "Kwame, I want to ask you a question that has nothing to do with optimization."

"Go ahead, but I bet you it will have to do with optimization."

I don't know how to say it. It may be too private to ask. I think it over twice before asking, and finally it comes out like this: "I see you are a successful man. You earn good money consulting, you have traveled a lot, and you seem to be in good shape economically, but how is it that you drive such an old car?"

He listens carefully, but changes his facial gesture and becomes very serious. He interlaces his hands, looks at me firmly, and suddenly, starts laughing, which confuses me.

"Oh, Walker. You were so serious with the question that I couldn't resist teasing you. Let me answer the question, which as I predicted, has to do with optimization. I learned from my grandfather that we humans are among the most wasteful beings on the planet. We waste so many resources for unnecessary reasons. But let me answer your question: *a major challenge in life is to live it to the most, while using the least.* I hope you realize this is an optimization problem, a difficult one. It is very easy to live a life with abundance and unlimited resources; the difficulty lies in being happy with the least amount of material needs. And that applies to money as well as to power and fame."

He stands up, goes to the window, sees his car and says, "So my friend, I drive a seventeen year old car because it works perfectly, because I don't need more than that, and because I don't need to show to anybody my social status."

"I guess I got a full lesson today," I say.

He smiles. "I am waiting for the next question."

"What?"

"Well, if I have a minimum consideration for Nature, as I have stated so many times to you, why do I choose to keep using old technology that pollutes so much compared to the technology in new cars?"

"Yes, that is a good question. Why?" I reiterate his own question.

"And here comes the second part, my friend: *it is not how you look from outside, but what you are inside.*"

I lower my gaze, feeling a bit uncomfortable with his comment. He seems to notice it, and quickly continues:

"Don't feel offended, it's not about you or your problem. It is that my 'old car' is not so old inside. I have many friends in the automotive industry, and every new technology that is out there in the market is already in my car. If you open the hood you'll see the latest engine running smoothly and as clean as any car in the street."

I'm glad he was not referring to me, so I change the subject to forget about it. "Why did you mention power?" I ask.

"Walker, some people don't care about money, either because it is not attractive to them, or because they already have plenty. But they seek power. They love to be at the top, giving directions, handling other people's lives. Sometimes they don't even care about which side they are fighting for, as long as they are in the power position. I hate those people. They are cynical; they switch sides when it is convenient for them."

He begins to change his face again. He seems angrier as he speaks. I guess he is remembering someone. I approach him and pat him on the back. It is the first time I see him this way, a bit out of control. He takes a chair and quietly sits down with a vague gaze.

"Kwame, do you want to quit for today? It is fine with me. We can continue next week."

"I am fine Walker... I am fine. Sometimes I remember a person whom I love with all my heart but his thirst for power and wealth makes me sick and sad. But don't worry, let's continue with the lesson."

"Okay. I have a second question. Remember when you told me about something called Pareto? What is that?"

"Very interesting question. I thought you had forgotten about it. This has to do with having more than one design objective. In order to answer this question I need to give you an example. Let me formulate an optimization problem where there are two functions. Suppose you want to build a guitar as stiff as possible, and as light as possible. We know by experience that these two objectives go in opposite directions. By that I roughly mean, when the stiffness increases, weight also increases, which is opposite to what we want.

"You can imagine that if we fix the amount of wood to build the guitar," he continues, "we could optimize the design until we find the stiffest of all possible designs for such an amount of wood. Then, we could optimize for another, different, amount of wood, and so find a different optimum design for a second amount of wood. If we repeat this for several amounts of material, we obtain a set of designs that each could be associated to a pair of numbers. Each pair is made of the stiffness and the weight for each optimum design we just found. Finally, we simply plot these pairs in a graph having stiffness, S, on the horizontal axis and wood amount, W, on the vertical axis. This set of points is called the Pareto set. Each S, W point in this graph is an optimum design, but different. At this point the decision is in the hands of the designer, that is you, who is asked to choose which, among all Pareto points, will be the one to build."

"This seems like a long process, isn't it?"

"Yes, indeed. There are other methods to find the Pareto curve but it is not important now. Now let me answer the question that Manuel asked you. Since quality and cost are also conflicting objectives —that is, objectives that go in opposite directions as Manuel pointed out— we could use the same steps to obtain the Pareto set for quality, Q, and cost, C."

"But Kwame, I remember that you told me that we could solve the problem by maximizing the ratio quality-to-cost. Why should we use the Pareto curve?"

"Because the Pareto curve gives you the opportunity to choose among a set of optimum designs."

"So you recommend the Pareto curve method?"

"Well, you have to realize that Pareto works easily for two design objectives, but as soon as you add more objectives, things get more complex, lengthier to compute. Then, other methods are required to compute the Pareto set, which by the way, cannot be visualized so easily. The set belongs to a surface of many dimensions."

I look at his eyes and say, "I don't get what you say Kwame."

"I know. This is more difficult to understand. You don't have to worry about this right now. Things will be easier to understand as you learn and practice these methods."

I nod, and watch the clock on the wall. It's getting late for him.

"I have to leave soon," he says, "but before I leave I want to know something about your warranties. If a client comes back with a defective guitar, do you account for the time, money and material spent to repair it?"

"Why do you ask? I usually fix the guitar, and don't care about how much time or money I put into it. I always want my clients to be satisfied. That's what matters, I think."

"You are right, but it also matters that you don't go out of business, otherwise you will not be able to sell more guitars. What I am getting to is that the cost-quality issue is more complex than it looks. Let me explain."

"If you build poor quality guitars," he says, "it may look cheap up front, but later when the customer comes back with a complaint, you have to add the cost of repair —the cost of the warranty. Hence, in reality the product costs more, and even worse, you develop a bad reputation as a luthier. So, in terms of the three Bs, you are failing in two aspects. On the other hand, if you build super high quality guitars, a quality that nobody can match, it will be so expensive to build that nobody will be willing to pay what you ask for them. Therefore, there is a *sweet spot* in between the two extremes. At this sweet spot, which is found with optimization techniques, the quality will be high, the cost will be adequate, and there will be a minimum of customer complaints. Only then you will be making BBBN guitars."

"You are right Kwame. Fortunately, your argument may work for mass production manufacturing, but in my case, the number of guitars I make is so small that warranty is not a concern. However, it is good to know about it."

He takes a look at his watch. It is time for him to go. He sits still and quiet for a while, with eyes closed. I wonder what he is thinking. He takes a deep breath and opens his eyes, this time with a worrisome gaze.

"Any problem, Kwame?"

He says nothing. He stays quiet for a moment, and then starts talking about his wife.

26

Death

I LEAN FORWARD TO LISTEN TO WHAT KWAME is going to say. I've never seen him so sad before.

"Walker," he begins, "I did not want to talk about this, but I think it will be good for me to tell you what is happening."

I don't like his tone. He is not talking with the confidence he normally does.

"Amy is dying."

He said it very quickly and with a sad tone. He is holding back his tears. I don't know what to say. He caught me unprepared. Death is almost a bad word and a worse reality. I don't like it. Before I can say anything, he continues.

"The doctor says the prognosis is less than a month."

I keep thinking of what to say, but nothing comes to me. I then go back to my dad's theory of interfaces to figure out an explanation to passing away. I try to tell him something at the same time I am thinking about it.

"Kwame, I know it is hard to loose your lifetime partner. It is painful and very sad. The only thing I can say to you is that you might try imagine being in her shoes. Imagine her situation. Ask yourself what would you think, do and say if you were dying instead. Share her point of view."

He looks at me surprised by my comments, and then stares at the wall, thinking, I guess, about what I just said. His eyes come back to look at me, and says, "Thank you Walker, those were very comforting words."

I can sense his anxiety, his sadness and desperation. Life is so mysterious sometimes. It is understandable that people take shelter in religious beliefs. I suppose it is good to believe in God in these situations. When there is no logical answer, there is no other resource than to accept things as they come, with faith. We have never talked about religion before, but now it could be the best moment. It may help console him.

"Kwame, do you ... eh, do you believe in God? Don't answer if you don't want to."

He gives me that strange smile, where only one corner of the mouth moves, and that can be interpreted as happiness or nuisance, depending on the situation. "I want to believe now," he says. "I want to know where she is going. I want someone to tell me if she is going to be fine there. I want to be there with her after I die. I want to continue the timeless romance we have had for thirty seven years, and keep it so forever."

He pauses and looks at me with the saddest face I've ever seen in a man. I want to say something, but I see he needs to vent his feelings.

"Walker, tell me, how can I help her?" He opens his hands and rests them on his laps.

"Kwame, I only know what my dad told me once: to die is a transition from one state to another. It is an interface of two worlds. Every time there is a transition, there is a problem, a pain to go through. What you need to do is to accept that there will be a transition for her and for you. Then time will smooth the pain out and will heal the scar in your heart."

Kwame listens with attention and seems calmer. He stands up, turns and walks to the window. A Cardinal lands on the outside sill. Kwame smiles at the bird, and it looks at him too. This is a very rare thing to happen.

"I think I should go," he says.

I accompany him to his old car in the parking lot. His posture is tall and straight, and conveys the confidence he always has. "Take care Kwame."

"I will."

After he enters the car and closes the door, the Cardinal flies from the sill and lands on the hood for a moment, jumps a couple of times, and flies away. Kwame smiles as if he understood something from the bird.

As soon as Kwame leaves, Manuel yells from inside the shop, "Walker! Your daughter is calling. I think it is an emergency."

27

Betrayal

RUSH TO MY OFFICE, RUNNING AS FAST AS I can. Manuel's face is of panic and uncertainty. He passes the phone to me, and I, frightened of what I am going to hear, grab it from his hand. "Christina? What happened?"

She is crying. She cries as when one feels deep pain. "Tell me, what happened? Why are you crying?"

"My friend Adlin, she says we can't be friends anymore."

I feel so relieved. For a moment I thought the worst. "Oh, God! You scared me! I thought you had an accident, or something."

She is sobbing, and I can feel how painful it is by the sound of her breath between sobs. "Who are you talking about? Adlin, your friend since first grade?"

"Yes, the only Adlin you know."

I can't believe Adlin would harm Christina in any way. "But what happened?"

"Her parents told her that she should find better friends. She doesn't want to break our friendship, but she told me she had no choice."

This is so irrational. How could she? "Christina, let's talk about this tonight, could we? But please don't cry over that. You are too old for this. A kiss, honey."

"A kiss," she replies between sobs.

I hang up the phone, and go back to my desk. I keep working in the shop for a couple of more hours, but Christina's problem stays in my mind. Some parents say weird things to their children. What were they thinking?

Manuel passes by the door and I ask him to come inside my office.

"Manuel, I have a question for you. What would you say are the reasons people have conflicts?"

"What?"

He was not expecting a question like this. I then tell him about the incident with Christina's friend.

"… Then I saw you passing by the door and thought you may help me to understand why people engage in conflicts sometimes."

"Well," he says, "a quick answer is *money*. The desire to be rich creates conflicts."

"Yes, that sounds reasonable. Our greed always interferes with another person's greed. Material goods are limited, so not everybody can have them all. Thank you Manuel, I'll think about it." He smiles, and goes back to his guitars.

Greed is a common reason for conflict, but some times there is more than that. Kwame was talking about power as a source of problems too.

Manuel, who was already bending some guitar sides, stops and comes back to say, "Walker, nationality is another reason people don't get along."

"Nationality?" I say, and then stay quiet, thinking about it. "It may be, but it goes deeper than that. I think it is about moral values, ethnicity and beliefs. Nationality is just an euphemism we use to talk about different cultural values."

"But how do you explain that countries with similar values also enter in conflict?" He replies forcefully.

"You are right, Manuel. This subject is not as simple as making guitars, is it."

"I could give you plenty of examples of how nationality is a reason for human conflicts," he continues. "When you come from another country, you see it from a different perspective, one that you can't realize if you are a native from this place."

"Oh! I think you are talking about patriotism. Yes, I agree with you, then. Patriotism is a separatist philosophy. Those who call themselves patriotic are simply dividers of the world. They don't love their country, but their land, life style and possessions. They are not who look for unity or for harmony with no boundaries, but instead, they prefer well marked divisions that separate them from the rest.

He seems convinced with my argument. In any case, at least I have identified three reasons to be in conflict —*greed, power and values*. This is a good starting point for my conversation with Christina, tonight.

I am about to make a call to the place where I buy the wood from, when I see, clearly in my mind, these relations. A greedy behavior happens between people engaged in a materialistic pursuit, like in a business; power conflicts happen between people set in a hierarchical relationship; and value conflicts happen between people of different backgrounds. Yes, it really makes sense. Christina's problem with Adlin should fall in one of these three categories.

I finish my day with the last touch of French polish on a beauty we made for a customer in Los Angeles. This guitar was made with Alpine spruce and the sound-hole rosette took me days to complete because of the special design the client wanted. Now I am free to begin making the two guitars for Frederik. I am planning to use the wood that arrived yesterday afternoon from Brazil.

As I am going home, taking my time at the stop signs and enjoying the nice bright day, I keep thinking about the triad of greed, power and values. I think it can explain all possible problems in human relations. But how are they solved? Can I use my dad's interface theory? I should keep thinking until I find an answer to this.

When I get home I see all the lights off, and the street lights are also off. I step in the house and yell: "Anybody home?"

Christina, from upstairs yells back, "Yes, dad, I am upstairs."

Emily is in the kitchen, lighting some candles. "Walker, we'll need the camping lamps to have dinner. We are lucky that I finished cooking before the power went off."

"I'll do that in a minute. I need to talk to Christina," I say. She nods at me and says, "I know, I know. It's awful."

I walk upstairs while thinking about the three things: greed, power and values.

"Hi, honey," I say as I sit next to her on the bed. The room is very dark, and there is one candle on the middle of the floor that creates an even sadder atmosphere in the room.

"Hi, dad," she says without even looking at me. Her eyes are puffy from crying so much. The trash basket is full of wet tissues, and her bed is covered with even more of them.

"How are you feeling?" I say.

"Well, I am fine now, but I was really sad when Adlin told me that. Dad, I could not believe what she said."

She is sitting with legs crossed, elbows on her knees, and hands holding her chin. Her diary is on the other end of the bed, open and with a red pen next to it.

"What was it? Why did she say?" I inquire.

"She was like, you know, don't ask me."

"No, I don't know. Like what?" I insist.

"She told me that her dad said that since we were not of their class, she should not be with me any more." She covers her face with her hands, and starts crying louder.

"You need to calm down first, Christina. What class is she talking about?" I put my arm over her shoulders, trying to make her feel loved and nurtured.

"You know that her parents are rich," she replies. They own a furniture factory in Adrian and, and a real estate business in California, I think. And they go to the clubs we are not members of, and go for vacations to Europe or Australia each year. So... I think she is right," and she keeps crying.

"This is awful, honey." Well, as I suspected, her problem fits into one of the three categories. The reason behind this problem is the difference in social values. They think they belong to another *class* that does not have the same values as ours. "Honey, let me tell you something. Your are not the first person in the world to suffer discrimination. What happens is that because they don't know us enough, they are in a defensive position. They need to know you, and me, and all of us, better. There is an obstacle, an interface between her parents and you that is creating this discomfort for them. Besides, you also need to know them better. You need to talk to them and understand their point of view. If you are in their shoes, and they are in yours, everybody becomes more open, forgiving with each other. Don't you think?"

She looks at me and says, "Why do you think this is going to work? We are not new friends with them. Remember, we've been going to the same school since first grade, and mom knows her mom too."

She is right. This is an unexpected behavior from them. "Well, I am going to tell you what I was thinking this afternoon. I think that human relations are a combination of these three kinds: material, hierarchical and value relationships. If your relationship with another person is in terms of material possessions, then greed may disrupt the relationship. For example, suppose two friends decide to create a company and so begin a material relationship. In this case, the two partners may enter into discord if one of them becomes greedy and tries to take more possessions than previously agreed upon."

She listens with attention as she plays with her hair, looking calmer, and crying less.

"If your relationship with another person is hierarchical," I continue, "then we are talking about relative positions within a group of people. For example, a soldier and a sergeant; an employee and his boss. They are in a hierarchical relationship. In this case, two persons may get into discord if the rules of relations are broken by any of them. If the soldier disobeys, or if the sergeant abuses his power, then the relationship becomes conflictive."

Gabriel walks by the door and watches us sitting together and talking. "Hi dad, I did not know you were here." He doesn't stop and keeps walking to his room, while holding a candle in his hand.

"Finally," I continue, "if your relationship with another person is in terms of values, then we are talking about the most difficult type of relationship between two persons. This is the relationship at the level of human beings, a presumably leveled relationship where neither material nor hierarchical issues should be present. We should treat each other with respect and honor other people's values within the norms of our society."

She suddenly stops playing with her hair and ask, "What values are those?"

"There are many: friendship, honesty, loyalty, love, care, responsibility, and many others. They all contribute to a relationship based on values. Religious, cultural and ethnic backgrounds can be included in the list too. When your values are the same as those of your partner, then your relationship is easy to maintain. But if not, then you need to make an effort to make it work."

She nods, but stays quiet and thinking. "Dad, to me, and this is my personal opinion, all problems in any type of relationship are some kind of *betrayal*. This is what I feel about Adlin. She betrayed me. I thought she was my friend, my real friend, but she wasn't." Tears roll down her cheeks as she takes the last tissue from the box next to her.

I am surprised by what she said. She went one step further than I, and is telling me that all human relations are broken for only one reason: betrayal. But is she right? If a person betrays another one, then conflicts emerge immediately, and the trust, the hard-to-build trust, is lost. She may be right. It seems that no matter how I name problems in any relationship, all of them are a betrayal of some sort. I hug her and wipe away her new tears with my hand. "You are such a clever girl, Christina. I am very proud of you. I think you are right, Adlin lost a piece of your trust today, and that loss is causing so much pain in your heart."

"Yes, I don't trust her anymore." And her eyes are watery once more. She rests her head on my chest, and I put my arm around her.

"There must be some reason for all this," I say. "If they know our family for so long, and suddenly they bring up this issue, it's because something wrong is going on in their lives that we don't know about."

"Well, I know something you don't know, dad. It happened two weeks ago, but she asked me not to tell anybody. Her parents are divorcing."

"That could explain the entire situation, Christina. Divorce is not an easy thing to handle, and I am sure they all are going through lots of problems right now."

The electric power comes back, and the lights are on again. Gabriel enters the room and says, "Dad, now we can go out and play something. I am really bored. Can you play soccer with me in the backyard?"

I don't feel like playing now. Besides, Christina is still sad and needs my company. I look at her and ask her how she is feeling. She seems better now. "You can go with Gabriel if you want," she says.

When I hear Gabriel or Christina saying that they are bored, I never let them down. Being bored is the preamble of bad things to happen. I always make the effort to be with them when they say that.

"Okay Gabriel, let me change my shoes first. Wait for me in the backyard."

Christina kisses me, hugs me, and thanks me for our conversation. "Thank you, dad. Thank you for listening to me."

As I put on my tennis shoes, I keep thinking of Christina's words. Looks like all problems between any two people could be described as a betrayal. But how can we solve a betrayal problem?

I change my shirt and put on a baseball hat. I keep thinking. If I do what my dad would have said: put myself in the place of the betrayer to understand him better. Mmm ... I think I know what the problem is. It's lack of love. How can I betray someone

# The Guitar Maker

that I love unconditionally? I can't, simply, I can't. Yes, I think this explains many situations, many problems in life.

"Dad! What's taking so long?" Gabriel yells from the backyard.

I have to hurry up before Gabriel gets tired of waiting. I go downstairs and when I pass by the kitchen, Emily looks at me with a sad glance. I look at her too. No words, no gestures. I know we haven't talked in days.

When I step out of the house I see Gabriel playing with the ball. "Hey Gabriel! Kick it to me."

He juggles the ball three, four times in the air, and then passes it to me. "There it goes, dad."

I run to get the ball, but after few steps, I can't believe how tired I feel. I ran no more than ten feet and I am already exhausted, breathing like an asthmatic. I must be in very bad shape, I guess. I kick the ball back to Gabriel; he makes a dive to stop it and sends it back to me again. I start running to get it, but my legs tumble with the tall grass and I fall flat like a board.

Gabriel runs to me. "Dad, what happened?"

"I am fine, I just tripped on myself, but I think I can't play anymore. You are too good for me, Gabriel," I say to disguise my pain. What a shame. I can't even play five minutes with my son. I remember my dad used to play with us until he was in his late fifties. I've got to do something about this. Having fun is an important part of parenthood, and I am failing at that.

"Dad, you promised to play with me! You can't quit now," he complains.

"I know Gabriel, I know, but I am tired already, maybe hurt." I know how he feels, betrayed. Yes, the same feeling I was talking to Christina a few minutes ago.

"Then let me call mom. Mom! Dad is hurt!"

Oh, no. I didn't want Emily to see me here, laying on the grass. Emily runs to me, but realizes it is nothing serious, and helps me to stand up. I put my arm around her waist, and she sighs as she feels it. I look at her eyes, and they are like screaming for the tenderness of a hug.

"Let's play together," I say. "I'll be the keeper, and you both kick the ball to me. How about that?"

Gabriel's eyes shine like stars because she rarely plays with us, and this will be an opportunity to have her enjoying a playful time along with us.

"Sure, mom. That's a good idea. Come on, mom, say yes."

"Okay, okay," she says, "but I prefer to be the keeper. Let's play!"

Christina yells from upstairs, "wait for me guys!"

As we play, the sky clears and the breeze becomes cooler. Trees in the neighborhood dance with a wind that runs through the backyards. I feel happy. We all feel happier. Yes, I feel loved at this precise moment, and I am sure all of us feel the same. Love is the key feeling. Love changes everything; it gives you energy to continue, and desire to build something better.

28

Memories

EXT MORNING, AS USUAL, I GET to the shop at around eight. But this time, when I am about to turn my car off, a beautiful Cardinal lands on the hood, looks at me, and then flies away. Suddenly I remember the first time I drove a car. I was sixteen. My mom had just passed away in a horrible car accident. It was devastating for my dad and for all of us in the family. My older brother and my younger sister were depressed for over a year. I was so much so, that I dropped out of high school for the rest of the school year. Mom was like a lighthouse for us. She always gave us her best advice and never thought twice of sacrificing her happiness for our benefit. She also was the engine of the family. We couldn't figure out how to keep the house in order without her. She was always on top of each detail —the clothes, the laundry, the plants, the food, the homework, birthdays— everything. She really was a person who knew how to run a family.

My dad, who probably suffered the most for the loss, was with me that first time I drove. It was my first lesson with his old car. I remember his first words. "Son, this is a great responsibility, as you well know." He always worried too much, but we both knew why he was telling me that. I could read between the lines. The words "car accident" were never spoken at home since mom's crash. So, when he said 'as you well know,' I knew he was referring to mom's tragic death. My dad was never the same after she died, and began progressively losing contact with all of us at home. I wonder if that precipitated his death too.

I looked at him, firmly into his eyes, showing a courage I didn't have then. "Don't worry, dad, I'll be careful."

His eyes were tearful, but he held them in, crying inside. I knew he could not bear to have a child killed in a car accident. "Okay," he said, "before I tell you anything else, you must remember this for the rest of your life: we are impaired when we drive in reverse gear. We lose more than three quarters of our control over the car when we are in reverse. Don't ever speed when backing up. Understood?"

"Yes, dad," I said in an obedient tone.

Again, he said, "Going forward is easy and predictable, but going backwards is more dangerous. Now, set the gear in reverse and get out of this parking lot." It was the only and most important lesson my dad gave me as a driver. I don't know why I am remembering this now, but sometimes memories come and go without explanation, like the Cardinal moments ago.

I get out of the car and head towards the shop. There, the lights are already on. Manuel is working in the back of the room sanding some guitar plates.

"Good morning," he yells from afar, with a broken voice, quiet rare in him.

I walk towards him to find out if there is any problem. "Hi, Manuel. How are you?"

His shoulders are shrunk, and his face is sad. He presses his lips and lowers his gaze. I approach him and pat him on his back. "What is it, son?"

He hugs me and starts crying. He is such a young kid. "I was just thinking about my grandma," he says. "She meant so much to me." He is really sad. Death is the only sure thing we have in life, but we still don't know how to face it.

I am trying to think what to say... "You did the right thing, Manuel," I counsel. "You visited her and she saw you before she died. You couldn't prevent it."

"I loved her so much," he replies. "She taught me to read when I was five. She taught me to play the guitar when I was ten. She taught me to write poems when I had my first girlfriend. She was so special to me." He takes a chair, sits and keeps crying. "I called her every week since I came to Michigan. We were so close, but now she is gone, gone forever."

"Manuel, let me tell you this. As long as you have her memories, as long as you remember her, she will be alive and with you. She will never be dead if you remember her ideas and follow her advice. Nobody dies, Manuel. It's us, who stay alive and make them die as soon as we forget them. Do you think Thomas Jefferson is dead? He is not! As long as the legacy of your grandma is preserved, her ideas, her philosophy, her words, and all that she stood for, then she will be as alive as you and I."

He looks at me with a glance of hope and happiness. "Walker, thank you for your words. I think you are right. I can't forget her. She is still with me, in my heart, forever. I may not be able to see her, but she is definitely with me."

I pat him once more and walk to my office, satisfied with the outcome of our conversation. He goes back to his work, bending sides. Once in my office the phone rings. I extend my arm to grab it, but I get a bad feeling. I hesitate for a second. It rings again, and I finally lift the phone to answer.

"Hello, this is The Professional Guitarist Shop. How may I help you?"

"Walker, it is Kwame."

I don't like the way he sounds. I notice a sadness in his tone. "Hi Kwame, nice to hear from you; how are you?"

"Walker, I am in the clinic with Amy and my daughter Alice. Amy is in coma," he says nervously.

"What? But, but, you said..."

"Yes, I know," he interrupts. "This is totally unexpected. The doctor has no explanation either."

"How can I help, Kwame?"

"Thank you for your offer, Walker, but we, my daughter Alice and I, are doing fine, so far. I just called to let you know that I may take some days off to attend this."

"Oh, Kwame, you didn't have to. The family comes first. Where is the hospital? I'd like to visit you, if you don't mind."

He gives me the address and I leave the shop as soon as I can. When I turn my car on, I have another flashback, one that I will never forget. The day my mom had her accident, I received the call from dad asking me to go to the hospital to take care of my sister. It was a difficult thing for me. I was so sad that I could barely talk to my sister. I remember the conversation with her. She was ten years old. I was nineteen.

"What happened to mom, Walker?" She asked me while we were in the waiting room. My dad was inside the emergency room with my older brother. I even remember how cold the room was that night. People were running from one side of the building to the other side. The walls were light green and the doors red. The smell of alcohol was ubiquitous. I hate it ever since.

"She had an accident, but she'll be fine. Don't worry," I said to her. I stood up and looked through the small door window. My dad was next to mom. Phil, my brother, was crying, standing in the other side. A nurse was embracing my brother while the doctor was trying to get a response from my mom. I went back to my seat.

"What did you see?" my sister asked.

"Nothing. She is fine." I said to calm her. It felt like a ball was in my throat, and it was hard to swallow. I stood to take another look through the little window, and saw my mother opening her eyes. I was sure she was looking at me. I raised my left hand to wave to her, and she smiled to me. My dad and my brother were not paying attention to me. She then closed her eyes and never woke up again. It was like a goodbye. I felt blessed by her smile. I was blessed by her for the last time. I went back to the chair, next to my sister. I looked at her, probably with the saddest face I've ever had and said, "She is no more." I closed my eyes, tears rolled down my cheek, and my sister hugged me as hard as she could, for minutes, until dad and Phil came back with the news.

Now that I remember it, I feel relieved, and somehow happy for that split second in time, when I saw her alive and I said goodbye. Sometimes memories hurt you, but some other times they heal you, too.

I get to the hospital where Amy was admitted. She is still in a coma. I see Kwame sitting in the waiting room. "Hello, Kwame."

He seems calmed, but clearly worried. He looks at me, but seems to be in another place, thinking about other things. "Thank you for coming, Walker. May I ask you to stay with Alice while I talk to the doctors? It won't take long."

Alice, a young woman in her early thirties, sitting on his side, is emotionally destroyed. Her hair is tangled as if she did not have time to fix it. The room is cold like the one thirty years ago when my mom died. The smell is also the same. Kwame points towards Alice and makes a gesture indicating that he will be back.

I approach Alice, who I have never seen before, and sit next to her. "Hi, Alice. I am Walker. Your dad's friend."

She covers her face with her hands, and starts crying. I wait until she is more receptive, and after a few minutes, she wipes her tears and says, "Thank you for coming, you didn't have to."

"That's what friends are for, to laugh together in good times, and to comfort in the bad ones," I say. "Alice, this is always difficult to accept. You have to be optimist, but you also have to be prepared for the worst."

"No!" she screams. "I don't want to be prepared for the worst. She is not going to die yet." Her tears keep coming out, and falling on her red dress.

I say nothing for a moment, waiting for her to calm down. "Alice, let me tell you this event from my past, so you can appreciate my point of view: when I was nineteen I lost my mom in a car accident. Can you imagine how that event affected me?"

Her face changes immediately, and her tears stop. It's as if she realizes that things could have been worse. She lowers her gaze and sighs. Then, lifting her chin, with a gesture of forgiveness for having screamed at me, she says, "I am sorry." She looks at my eyes and listens with attention.

"Pain is not always bad, Alice. Sometimes we need to go through some anguish to gain a better understanding of the beautiful things in life. Besides, your mom is not suffering at all. She is not aware of what is happening. I am more worried about you and your dad. It all depends on how you take it from now on. She will always be fine no matter the outcome."

She looks relaxed now, with a little smile coming from one corner of her lips. "Thank you, Walker. I wasn't polite with you. I am sorry."

"No, you don't have to apologize. Your behavior is natural and very normal for the situation."

"I felt better when you said that she will be always fine, no matter the outcome. I think it is true. And it is also true that I will have to take care of my dad more closely."

She looks more reasonable now. When people begin talking about the future, they are already accepting the worst case outcome and becoming more aware of the reality. If they keep talking about the past, about the *good old times*, it means they are not yet prepared to face bad results. That is a formula against death. We overcome the difficult encounter with death by facing the future with joy and optimism. We need to nurture courage to accept the changes and challenges that come unexpectedly with death.

Kwame is back, with an even sadder face than when I enter the hospital. "It's over. I don't think she will wake up."

I say nothing and let him vent his feelings. He begins bringing memories of better days. Those memories that bring smiles to one's face. I let him talk as long as he wants, and when he finishes talking I simply say, "Thank you for letting me know all your private and beautiful memories, Kwame."

He smiles as tears roll down his cheeks. I spend two more hours with them in the hospital before going back home.

The Guitar Maker

⌐ ⌐ ⌐

W hen I get home I don't feel the mental and physical strength to get out of the car. It has been a tough day for me. First, my own memories about mom's death, then Manuel's anguish about his grandmother, and finally Kwame's bad news. It was a hard, emotional day. I enter the front door and Emily, from the kitchen, says, "What a face you have on today!"

"Yes, it was a difficult day. I'm going upstairs to get some rest," I say as I slowly walk upstairs, face down, pounding each step, and swinging side to side to ease the effort.

"I have good news instead," she says.

I stop walking to listen what she is going to say. "What is it?"

"Two Cardinals were feeding in the garden for two hours this afternoon. You should have seen them; they were playing around, eating, jumping, and singing. They were beautiful."

"Nice. I am glad you had a good day," I say, as I keep walking.

"Also, Manuel called from the shop asking for you. A woman called from Denmark. Her name was Laura. Do you know her?"

I stop again. "No," I say promptly to avoid further questioning, but then I change my mind and say, "yes, I do know her. She is the sister of the guitarist who wants me to make the two guitars I told you about."

"I don't remember you told me anything about her."

"Oh! I thought I had told you about it. Well ... it's just another customer. What else did Manuel say?

"Well, Manuel said she sounded anxious to talk to you," Emily responds with that ironic tone; the one women use to suggest that we, men, are hiding or lying about something. She is right.

"I'll call her tomorrow," I respond with faked indifference, and keep walking to my room.

29

Mirrors of Feelings

ACH GUITAR I MAKE IS LIKE A FRIEND THAT I meet and hug for several days, and that finally leaves for another home, sometimes far away, sometimes not so far away. It's like having an extended family around the country. Today, I am going to begin the replicas of Frederik's guitar, probably the most important guitar for my future career as a professional guitar luthier. I'd better begin this project before Laura calls me again. I have all the wood I need, including what I ordered from Germany to match the wood used for the original guitar.

The shop is hot even though the large fans are both running at maximum speed. The weather has been dry for several weeks and the sun has been merciless the past two days. Manuel, sitting in the back of the shop, is busy with a new project as well. He is sweating as much as I am, so I get this good idea of having something refreshing. I reach in my pocket, pull out some bills, and call Manuel.

The Guitar Maker

"Manuel, I need a favor. Take this money, go to the store on Main street and buy some ice cream for us?"

He wipes his fore head and smiles at me. "Yes, good idea! We are going to melt pretty soon in here."

He leaves the shop, and I, going back to my business, grab the old broken guitar to see how it was built. I need to disassemble it with care because I want to assemble it back for Laura.

Laura... as soon as I think about her my mind starts wandering around, feeling lonely, and wishing she were here. I'd like to know what you are doing at this moment. I stare at the wall clock, and when I wake up from this sort of trance, I realize that time is running out fast, and that I should be working on the replicas instead of dreaming alone and awake.

I grab Frederik's guitar, and start looking at the details, the curvatures, the polish, and many other things. This guitar is a beauty, signed by a French luthier in 1981. It will be difficult to know how it sounded when it was new. I can only reproduce the measures, and hope that the sound is the same or similar to the original. I begin by separating the neck from the rest with the special, large and curved pliers to take off the pin that holds the neck joined to the guitar. I make several attempts. The pins are very tight. Oh, nice! The neck finally came out and I pull it apart.

Manuel comes back with the ice creams. "I brought chocolate for you. I know you like chocolate," he says.

"Thank you. Good choice. What did you buy for yourself?"

"Lemon," he says as he licks the ice cream. "How is the broken guitar?" He asks.

"It's a beauty. When I finish disassembling it, I'll show you the details. I just pulled apart the neck from the body. Now I have to separate the sides in order to measure the braces inside."

He scratches his head and says, "how do you separate that?"

"With heat and chemicals. It's not difficult at all. You only need patience, because if you do it fast, you break the parts, and then we won't be able to reassemble it."

He is more surprised now. "Reassemble it? Why? You never said you had to do that!"

I lick my ice cream and respond, "You know, this guitar belongs to the sister of the guitarist who used to play it. Even though she is not expecting the guitar to be returned at all, I want to surprise her with that. I am planning not only to reassemble it, but to repair it."

"Is that the woman that called from Denmark a couple of weeks ago?" He asks.

"Yes, she is. Her name is Laura," I say while licking my ice cream once more.

"Oh, I see," he says with sarcasm. "Now I understand."

"No, it is not what you are thinking. This is strictly business," I say emphatically.

"If you say so," he agrees with doubts.

"Besides," I say, "I think that I can do a better job if I repair this one before I build the replicas. So I can hear how it sounds. Don't you think?"

"But look at it. It is almost impossible to repair it," he forcefully replies.

"You'll see. By the end of the day I will have the guitar disassembled, probably with all measurements made, and in two more days I will have it repaired," I convincingly say.

He turns away and as he walks to his place, he says, "I believe you." But I am not very convinced he does believe me.

I finish my ice cream and grab the torch and chemicals to start separating the plates and sides. After about two hours of work my vision becomes blurry. I close my eyes as hard as I can, then open them, but the blurriness is still there. I knock my head in the right side, but nothing changes. I tumble towards the rest room and put cold water on my neck and face. I feel better, and I can see clearer. I guess it was the heat or perhaps the chemicals.

Manuel knocks on the rest room door and as I go to grab the knob I lose my sight for a second or two, hit the wall with my head, and make a loud noise. I've never had this happen to me before.

"Walker, are you okay?" Manuel screams.

"Yes, I think. I'll be out in a minute," I reply with a broken voice. I open the door, and he is outside smiling.

"Hey, I thought you had fallen."

"Almost! I lost my sight for a second. It was weird," I say.

He seems very surprised by my comment, and says, "Yes, that is weird. You better check that out with a doctor. You don't know what it may be," he says very concerned.

"I will," I reply politely, "but you know what, I don't like to go to the doctor. They usually don't know what is going on with you."

"But still, I think you should go," he insists.

I nod to him, walk to my table and continue working. I am sure this blurriness is because of the combination of heat and chemicals in the room.

It is already eight at night, and I'm feeling hungry. Emily called about an hour ago to find out when I was planning to be at home for dinner, and I told her that I had to finish some measurements, and that I had to call Kwame before heading to home. As many times before, she didn't like my long hours at the shop, and said, "do whatever you want."

I am done with all measurements on the original guitar, but Kwame may want me to do some other ones. I grab the phone and dial his number.

"Williams family," Kwame says in the other side of the line.

"Hi, Kwame. It's Walker."

"Walker, I was wondering when were you going to call me. I got a call from Ole Rasmussen a couple of weeks ago. He was called by Laura, you know, the sister of Frederik. She was asking for your phone number."

"Oh, that is how she got the number. Well, yes, I am planning to call her back, but I want to have something done before I talk to her. In fact, I want to talk to you about her guitar. I'd like you to come to see it disassembled. Also, I want to know if you had any recommendation about how to make the measurements and the replicas."

"I thought you were the luthier, not me," he says jokingly.

I notice a humorous tone that I did not feel last time we talked, so I feel comfortable asking for his wife. "By the way, how is Amy?"

He is quiet for about five seconds and answers: "She has been in a stable condition since last time we met. There is nothing we can do now. Nurses are taking care of her."

I feel, by the tone of his voice, that he has a better attitude toward the situation. But still, I don't want to make this conversation just about Amy, because he may feel uncomfortable. "I am glad you sound in a better mood today. When can we meet? Is tomorrow a good day?"

"Yes, tomorrow is fine, I think. I can be there tomorrow afternoon. But let me ask you: did you take all measurements?"

"Yes, I think," I say, "I measured all dimensions and thicknesses, but I don't know how to use the electronic equipment you asked me to rent."

"Okay, I can take care of that tomorrow. We need to measure other characteristics of each part, like frequencies, material properties, and so on. We'll do that tomorrow. Don't worry."

"Great! I'll see you tomorrow, then. Bye, Kwame." He replies with a happy "bye, bye," and I hang up.

Manuel left the shop two hours ago for his class in the community college. I turn off all lights, close the shop, walk to the parking lot, open the car door, and when I am about to insert the key in the ignition switch my vision gets blurry again. Suddenly, I feel tired and disoriented. I close my eyes, take a long breath in and exhale slowly. I open my eyes and I can see clearly again. I turn on the car and get home as soon as I can, before it happens again.

When I get home, I walk slowly to the kitchen where I see Emily reading the newspaper. "Hi Emily."

She notices that something is wrong. "What happened?"

I say nothing and keep walking slowly. I feel like my feet are each carrying a boulder.

"Walker, you are pale. What is it?" She asks anxiously.

"It's that... well, I think it is nothing important. My vision is blurry sometimes... but I am fine now."

She grabs me by the arm and sits me on the couch. She prepares tea while I rest, and brings it to me.

"Take this. You'll feel better. Tell me more. When did this start?

"I told you it is nothing. I am fine," I insist.

"Honey, you don't look good to me," she says kindly, too kindly actually. She hasn't been so kind in years. We look at each other without saying anything. This is the kind of glance we used years ago, when things were better between us. I like the fact that she seems really worried about me, and I feel so connected to her at this moment.

She approaches me, put her hand on my forehead and says, "I want you to be healthy until we die together. You are the most important person in my life."

That is so nice to hear, that I feel happy all of a sudden. I grab her hand, press it against my chest and look at her eyes saying, "I feel close to you, right now."

She smiles and lowers her gaze, mixing happiness and shyness in a single gesture. Then, slowly lifting her face, with sparkling eyes, says to me, "I do too." Her lips are trembling, and about to say something. "I can't even think of living without you, Walker."

I say nothing, not because I don't want to, but because of my emotions are taking me by surprise. It's been many years since we've been this intimate.

It is already 10:00 PM. We are both tired. Happiness makes you sleepy sometimes, too. She rests her head on my chest, as if she were listening to my heart, and we fall asleep on the couch without realizing it.

Next day, when I open my eyes, I see Emily still in the same position as last night, with eyes closed, serene. I feel so invigorated when we both are in tune. She wakes up, kisses me on the cheek, and goes to the kitchen to prepare something to eat. Gabriel and Christina are still in their beds. I go to take a shower and when I come back, the table is all set with a delicious breakfast with toast, coffee, eggs, marmalade, orange juice, ham, and yogurt. This is my favorite breakfast, and she knows it.

When we finish eating she goes to the sink to start cleaning the dishes. I approach her from behind and embrace her, slowly and with fondness. She turns her head and reaches up for a kiss, a long one this time. I say good bye and leave for work.

While I am working in the shop, I remember the nice little talk Emily and I had last night. I am trying to understand how everything started. How all of a sudden were we so nice to each other and so happy? The only thing different was my illness. Was it only that? If not, what else? I felt so good when she treated me gently that I couldn't be but the same to her. I keep working on the guitar and thinking about my own feelings. I think we reflect the way we are treated. How could I be bad to a person that treats me with love? Yes, we reflect back the actions of others towards us. We are mirrors of human feeling. This is like the law of action and reaction in Physics. The better I am treated, the better I will treat back. And it works with mistreatment too: if someone is nasty towards me, I'll have a hard time being nice to that person.

Manuel is watching me quietly, standing at the door of my office. "What are you thinking, Walker?"

I turn around and say, "I was thinking that we humans are like mirrors of feelings. If you treat me well, I will treat you well too. I can't harm you unless, of course, I am insane."

"Mmm, but why are you thinking about that?" He asks.

"Well," I say and pause for a second, trying to come up with a good answer, "I think we can use it in leadership problems. The secret for leading people to do what you want them to do is to treat them well. If you treat them the best you can, they will give you back the best of them as well. That explains why Mahatma Gandhi was such a great leader. He always treated his followers with love; he worked for them; he served them. And he didn't use violence but love against his enemies. This sounds so obvious now. How can somebody be a leader if he or she is hated? You have to be loved and respected before you are a leader."

Manuel looks down to the floor as he thinks for a moment and says, "My grandma used to say that we all should love our friends to keep them with us, and love our enemies to convert them to you. She never hated anybody, and always lived happy."

It seems that love is the solution to many problems. Unconditional love *is* the key. I take the opportunity to question Manuel about what happened to me last night. "Manuel, what happens in a family when there is an emergency? Suppose someone is very sick, about to die."

He quickly says, "I know the answer to that one too. We have had many emergencies in my family, and after years of problems I discovered that the first thing the family needs is a leader. A person who will lead to a resolution. If there is no leader, the family goes nowhere and things become worse. The second thing that should happen is that the family respects the leader and follows without argument. Speed is very important during emergencies. If the family doesn't follow the leader, the solution is delayed and the emergency may become a bigger problem."

I stand up from my chair and walk towards him a couple of steps. His answer is very sensible, but I still have one problem with it, "What if the leader is incapacitated?"

"That happened in my house when our dad got sick," he replies. "He was the leader, the breadwinner, and we did not know what to do. But almost immediately, my oldest sister took charge and we didn't notice the lack of direction. If the leader falls, then someone should take the banner and provide the guidance; more so in a family, where there is trust among brothers and sisters. When there is an emergency in the family a leader is the most needed person. When things are going well, the leader is on vacation, but when the emergency strikes, the leader gets to work. His decisions are vital for the family."

I definitely enjoy talking to Manuel. He has great family values. "So, you say that emergencies put the leader to work and also brings families together."

"Yes," he says, "that has been the case in my family. But why are you so concerned about leadership, and being sick? We were talking about reflecting feelings, and being like mirrors. I liked that idea."

I turn my back to him and walk back to my desk. This allows me some time to give him a disguised reason for my question. "It is just something I was thinking about. It's about Kwame's family, you know, his wife is in a coma these days."

He nods and makes no more comments. In examining our conversation, now I realize how things may be related. The need for a leader is evident in emergencies, but there is no leader unless he or she is trusted by the followers. On the other hand, trust is built through love, and love is produced by mirroring of good feelings. So, to me, it means that a small gesture of affection and love towards a person can start the chain reaction that ends in a better relationship, a good leader, and a good follower, a trusted and loving relationship.

I finish the compilation of all measurements. I write them all on a piece of paper, along with the corresponding drawings that will help us to do the other measurements. I bring out the equipment I rented and set them up for Kwame. He should be arriving soon, and I am looking forward to my first engineering experience.

30

Reverse Art

KWAME ARRIVES AT THE SHOP JUST IN TIME to go for lunch. His face shows some tiredness, but his disposition is energetic still.

"Good timing, Kwame! Why don't we go for lunch before we start working? There's a fancy restaurant on Main street where they serve an excellent tenderloin steak."

He scratches his head and says, "Uh ... okay, sounds good. I've never eaten here in Chelsea."

So, we walk together on a beautiful sunny day. The restaurant, which is always rated as the best in Chelsea, is just two minutes from my shop, and we'll be there before the crowd arrives. "The only problem with this restaurant," I tell Kwame, "is that it's a bit noisy. But the chef is so good, that it is worth it."

Once we get there the hostess takes us to a table next to the front window, facing Main street. As we walk around the tables people are staring at us. Kwame notices it, but ignores them. With a population predominantly white in Chelsea, African Americans

190

are rarely seen in this restaurant. The waitress comes, serves two glasses of water, and leaves the menu on the table —a large one-page menu with a complete description of each plate.

"Kwame, I recommend any steak in the menu. They are delicious. This chef is really amazing in the presentation, and the taste can't be beat."

He begins reading the menu and then says, "I am going to have the pasta with pesto sauce and seafood. I love seafood."

I order the tenderloin steak that comes with buttermilk sauté onions. It's really good. While we wait for the waitress to come, I ask Kwame, "Did you notice how people looked at you?"

"Yes, I did, but I don't practice self-discrimination, so I don't care."

That was the end of the subject. He seems firm and clear about it. The waitress comes and takes our order. We begin a conversation about Amy and all that has happened since I visited the hospital. It is sad to see someone fading away, especially when that person is your closest friend. Kwame seems much more calm now, and to me, he has a wiser perspective of the situation.

"You know something, Walker. Life gives you many chances to be happy. More chances than you think. It is up to us to identify them, to nurture them, and to make them enjoyable. Amy was a blessing in my life, and until now, before her illness, I thought she was simply a good companion. But now, now I realize she was more than that. She was my strength, my engine, and always the source of my laughs. And among all these, what I will miss the most is laughing with her. I think we come to live in this world to enjoy our time here, but we learn the worrisome things too fast, and the enjoyable things too slow. Sometimes it takes us our entire life to discover the good things."

I nod to him in response to his comment. It is a simple comment, but true down to its roots.

The waitress is back with the two dishes. Kwame takes his napkin, puts it on his laps and says, "Walker, before we start eating, why don't we try to guess how these dishes were prepared?"

I have no idea what his intentions are, but he always has good reasons when he asks me something. "Well, let me guess. I think the chef marinated the steak in the sauce and put it in the skillet for about ten minutes or so. That is all that I can guess; I'm not a cook."

He smiles and says, "Is that all? How about the onions? How did they prepare the onions, or the pepper? Any idea?"

"I think they just cooked them along with the steak. Don't you think?"

He smiles again and says, "Do you know why I ask?"

I grab my silverware and as I cut the first piece of the steak I say, "Actually I was about to ask. Why don't we eat first? I am hungry."

He laughs and says, "Yes, go ahead and eat, but the reason I am asking you to guess how they cooked it is because we are going to do the same thing in your shop this afternoon. We are going to figure out how the guitar was built by just looking at the final product. We don't know the sequence of the steps, nor the properties of the original material used. The same happens with your steak. I love onions, and I know they first dip the onions in a buttermilk batter, cook them separately from the steak, and then serve them together with the steak. This afternoon though, you are going to be the expert, not me. You will have to reverse the steps of guitarmaking, and find out the initial conditions and the process to arrive at the guitar you want to replicate. This is called *reverse engineering*, but in culinary and guitarmaking arts, I guess we should call it reverse art."

"Interesting," I say. "Isn't that what computer makers do to competitor's models?"

"Yes. You are right. This is a common practice in the manufacturing industry."

"But we have an extra problem," I reply, "Frederik's guitar is broken. We don't have a finished product in good conditions to start with. How can we do it then?"

"You will have to guess more than usual. That is what engineering is all about: solving problems with limited information and resources."

We start eating our meals that, as expected, are delicious. "You were right Walker," Kwame says, "this food really tastes good." When we finish, we head to the shop to start our important project.

31

*Design IV**

E ENTER THE SHOP AND START right away. The equipment is all set to start taking measurements. Kwame takes a ruler and says, "Walker, this is what we need to know. First, a full set of measurements to determine all possible dimensions, thicknesses, curvatures, etc."

I grab the papers I had prepared and show them to him. "Here, these are all the geometric dimensions."

He looks impressed, and I feel proud of being ready. "Great! We are going to finish very fast, then. Next step is to measure the properties of the materials used in the old guitar."

I call Manuel to make sure he sees what we are doing, so he can learn something from Kwame. "Manuel, come and watch," I yell. "You'll learn something here."

Kwame takes the sound board plate and rests it between two wooden blocks. He then grabs a dial that has a thin metal rod sticking out, and position it in such a way that he can measure the

_____
*This chapter may be skipped if you have no interest in the design optimization subject.

deflection at the center of the plate. He finally sets a quarter pound weight on top of the plate and measures the deflection.

"Why do you want to know the deflection, Kwame?" Manuel asks.

"We are doing engineering, Manuel. If I know the setup of the test, the thickness of the plate, the weights, and the deflection, then I can compute the elastic properties of the sound board plate. This is very basic information we need to reproduce the guitar."

Kwame repeats the experiment several times and explains to me that in engineering, two measurements are never the same, and the more we measure the better understanding we have of the phenomenon. It makes sense to me.

He performs the experiment on each individual part of the disassembled guitar: the bottom plate, the sides, the braces, even on the bridge. He records each measurement and makes sure that we record the variability of the measurements. After two hours without stopping, he stands up, stretches his back, but keeps going.

"Kwame, don't you get tired?" Manuel asks.

"When you are having fun, time does not exist, my friend." Kwame replies. He is right. He is in the zone, in the timeless zone. He then grabs a high precision balance and weighs each part as well.

"And why do you need to weigh them?" I ask.

"Because the weight divided by the volume of the part, will give us the density of the wood, another vital piece of information to predict the dynamic performance of the guitar," he replies.

Manuel, like a sponge of knowledge, is taking notes of everything he observes and whatever Kwame says. "How are you going to replicate the sound quality if the guitar is not assembled?" He asks.

"Very intelligent question, Manuel," Kwame replies. "You guys will have to reassemble it for me, if you can, and I'll come back tomorrow morning to make a couple of acoustic measurements."

"Yes," I reply, "we'll have it ready for you tomorrow. Manuel and I will begin assembling the guitar as soon as you leave. Don't you think so Manuel?"

"We can assemble the sound box by tomorrow," Manuel answers, "but the neck is broken. I don't think we can repair it that fast."

Kwame interrupts our conversation and says, "I don't need the neck now. If you can assemble the sound box I can take the measurements I need."

After about half an hour, Kwame leaves the shop with all the measurements. We, Manuel and I, stay in the shop to begin the assembly of the old guitar to have it ready for tomorrow. I glue the old braces back to the plates, while Manuel make some kerfing blocks that need to be replaced. We set both sides and the sound plate all clamped on the working table, and wait for about two hours until the glue is hard. We loosen the clamps to release the pieces and bring the back plate to be glued. Once the back plate is set, we begin the roping around the guitar to make sure the sound box plate is perfectly tight. All of that takes about four hours from the beginning to the end, and now we can let them rest overnight. Manuel is exhausted; so am I. We leave the shop around ten at night, sweaty, tired, but quite animated by the advances we made today.

Next day in the morning, Manuel and I get to the shop as early as possible, to be ready for Kwame. He arrives at the shop, no more than twenty minutes after us, carrying a suitcase from which he pulls out a microphone, an amplifier, and a small speaker. "Today we are taking acoustic measurements," he says.

By looking at his face I can see he did not sleep very well last night. "When did you go to bed last night, Kwame?" I ask.

"Actually, I did not go to sleep. I took all your geometric measurements and built a computer model for the guitar," he replied.

"Did you do that alone?" Manuel asks, very surprised.

"No, I didn't. I called a couple of young friends that can do this on very short notice and they did it for me. They said they had an old guitar model from another customer and they were able to simply change some dimensions and create Frederik's guitar in the computer."

"Oh my! You are amazing Kwame," I say.

He opens another suitcase and pulls a small laptop computer. He plugs it to the power, and begins showing us the guitar model. "This is incredible," I say. "You are so effective, Kwame. We are in the front edge of technology, now. Look, Manuel," I say while I point to the computer screen.

Kwame can rotate the image and show different views of the guitar, from any angle he wants. He can toggle on and off each part to show the inside of the guitar. He then clicks a couple of dials in the software and begins what he calls a simulation. He can make the computer reproduce some sounds that imitate the guitar's six cords. I can't believe what my eyes are seeing.

Manuel is mesmerized as well. "Kwame, can your computer improve the design?" He asks.

"Of course, that is the whole purpose of this model. We will try to optimize the design," Kwame replies.

"No, no." I say. "I don't want to change the design. This is strictly a replica, not an improved guitar." I say quickly before we proceed.

Kwame turns towards me and say, "Walker, the replicas will be replicas. Don't worry. I am talking about other guitars you'll make from now on. You now have the power of optimization techniques plus the artistic knowledge of a luthier to create the best guitars for your customers. However, let me explain something you have not realized yet. You have two possible routes: to replicate the geometry and materials, hoping that the sound will be satisfactory for Frederik, or to replicate the sound, no matter the geometry of the guitar. You see, when I finish to measure the sound characteristics of the box, we'll have the option to build the perfect replica from a sound point of view, not just by copying the geometry."

Manuel gets excited and says, "Yes, I like this. What do we need to do now?"

I notice a synergy between Manuel and Kwame that I haven't seen before.

"Manuel," Kwame says, "we can replicate the sound character-istics of the replica, in the computer, even though it is broken in real life. What do you think?"

"This is great," Manuel replies.

"Okay, okay, don't get so excited. We need to make the acoustic measurements first," I say.

Kwame is ready to start with the experiments. "The acoustic measurements will be used to check that our computer model is precise. Let me show you. A signal generator is connected to the speaker," he explains, "and the microphone cable goes to the spectrum analyzer. The speaker and the microphone go inside the guitar box and the experiment consists in recording signals at different frequencies."

"Like in radio frequencies?" Manuel asks.

"Yes, but much lower frequencies," Kwame replies. "Each note in the guitar has its own frequency. For instance, the note A has a frequency of 440 Hertz. In addition, each plate and even the air inside the box has its own frequency too. They all interact with each other. We need to understand how they are interacting in order to replicate the sound of the original guitar."

I can't understand how he can know so much about guitars. "Kwame, you said you did not know anything about guitars. How come you are talking like an expert now?"

"Well, I don't know guitars," he replies. "I am just using my knowledge from the automotive industry. In a car, you have the same thing. The roof and the floor of the car are like the two plates of the guitar, and the doors are like the sides. There is also air inside the car cabin and, even worse, there are people inside too. So when we design cars, we need to consider the resonances of air, floor, roof, people, seats, instrument panel, windows, in order to design the car body for a quiet ride. As you can see, the car design is much more complex than a guitar because conditions change constantly. The number of passengers changes, the windows are not all closed, and the origin of the noise is more unpredictable."

I simply stay mute. I can't refute him. He starts making mea-surements and recording what he calls 'fundamental frequencies' for each part in the guitar. He clamps the guitar in different ways, and performs the experiment each time. This is taking a long time. Manuel pays close attention to each move.

After three hours of measurements Kwame stops and says. "Okay guys, I think we finished. I got the Helmholtz frequency with good accuracy."

"What is that?" Manuel asks.

"The Helmholtz frequency is the fundamental frequency of the air inside the guitar box. It is a key number for the validation of the computer model. I think we have all the elements to do the reverse engineering, but now it is your responsibility to do the reverse art."

"You bet we can," Manuel responds enthusiastically.

"Kwame, I have an idea," I say. "Since I promised two replicas to Frederik. Why don't we do one of them by just copying the geometry and the other one by copying the acoustic behavior you just measured?"

"That is an excellent idea. I forgot you were going to make two replicas. This is great. We will learn much more than I thought. We need to work fast."

I feel energized now. We are all excited about this project. "Tomorrow we begin the *geometric* replica and next week, we can start the *acoustic* replica."

We all agree.

32

Leaders

FTER AN EXCELLENT DAY IN THE SHOP, where Manuel and I learned a lot about engineering, I drive home looking forward to a good shower, a good meal and some rest. I park my car in the driveway, but as soon as I cross the entrance of the house I hear, "Dad, dad." It is Gabriel running down the stairs.

"Hi, Gabriel, how are you? What's the hurry?"

"I am glad you came, dad. I have homework I need to finish, and you can help me. Do you remember my homework on entrepreneurship?

I yawn and say, "Yes ... I remember."

"Well, when I got it back, my teacher said it was a well done job. She liked it a lot, but now she wants the students to answer one more question."

I am feeling really tired, and have no strength to sit down with him and do homework. "Gabriel, when is this homework due?"

"Tomorrow, but it is only one question, dad. I know you can help me." He quickly replies, anticipating my negative response. I take a big breath, put away the car keys, and walk with him upstairs. He grabs me by my hand, and almost pulls me up. His room is full of stuff thrown all around. I can't work with so much chaos. "Gabriel, I'll take a shower first. You fix your room in the meantime. I'll be with you in fifteen minutes, agreed?" He knows I can't work in the middle of this disaster and agrees to straighten it up.

I leave his room and go directly to the bathroom. I really feel tired, too tired as a matter of fact. I am about to take my shirt off when my eyes, begin seeing blurry again. I feel dizzy and lose my balance. I sit on the toilet to take a rest and wait to see if it passes. I close my eyes for about a minute and when I open them, my vision is fine, back to normal. I stand up with care, and I feel stable and firm. This is something I should take care of; there is no reason for this to happen today. I did not work with chemicals, plus it was cool during the day.

Ten minutes later I was bathed, in pajamas, and ready for Gabriel's homework. I go to his room and see it's all cleaned up. He is sitting on the floor, next to the bed. The ceiling is dark blue with stars hanging from it, and posters of famous soccer players are hanging on the light green walls. I enter the room and sit on the carpet to get closer to him. I've noticed that when I talk to him at the same eye level, he is more receptive, more talkative.

"This is the question, dad," he says. "If leadership is an important characteristic of a successful entrepreneur, what should be the most important characteristics of a good leader?"

"Very good question," I say. "Let me see. I want you to give me your first answer. Let's think about a leader you know."

He thinks for a little while and says, "How about you, dad? You are my leader."

"Then, what are the things you believe I have that make me your leader?" I ask him.

He stares at me while he thinks, and then says, "I know. You are a leader because you have good ideas that make me happy. How about that?"

"Good ideas... yes, that is one quality for a good leader. What else could there be?" I ask again.

He goes back to his thinking pose, staring at me. "Yes, another one is that you can predict what is going to happen. You know, you always tell me be careful with this and that, and in the end, it always happens as you predict. You have like a magic ball that tells what is going to happen."

I see how innocent he is, and with a smile on my face I say, "Well, Gabriel, I don't have a magic ball. This is called *experience*. When you become an adult, you'll see how you will sense what your children will face ahead of time. It is not magic. But you are close to another characteristic of a good leader: vision. A good leader cannot predict with certainty what is going to happen, like when I predict that your pants will get dirty when you go to play in the playground, but a leader can see what may be the best route to follow and what is the goal to seek. That is called vision. A company without a vision, is like a ship with no compass."

"That sounds good, dad, what is it that you do to make me follow you?" He asks.

And when I was about to answer his question, Christina, who was at the door listening to the conversation, interrupts and says, "because we trust dad."

A silence fills the room for a second, and I turn around to face her. "Hi honey, I did not know you were listening. Come on and sit with us."

She kneels down and after a kiss on my cheek, I ask, "What did you say, Christina?"

"Well," she continues, "after I had this problem with my friend —you know— I thought a lot about relationships and about why I used to follow her. I realized that I trusted her so much that I never thought she could hurt me."

Gabriel is listening with attention, but looks a bit worried. "Christina, she was selfish, that's all," Gabriel replies.

"Selfish! That's it," I promptly say. "A leader cannot be selfish, otherwise, he or she cannot build trust among followers. Yes, definitely, unselfishness is another characteristic of a good leader. This is a great conversation kids. Let's continue. What else is important to be a good leader?"

Gabriel's eyes brighten suddenly and he says, "Of course, dad, we know that all you do is for us, not for you. You are unselfish like a good leader."

I am glad to hear that. He sees things that I never thought at his age. "And the reason I am unselfish is because..."

"Because you love us," Emily interrupts. She is standing in the door of the room, listening to our conversation too. "May I participate?" She asks.

There is no more room on the floor, but she finds a place to sit on the bed, next to me. She poses her hand on my shoulder. I rest back to feel her legs.

"So, again, everything boils down to love. If I love you, I will be unselfish. If I am unselfish, you will trust me. If you trust me, you will follow me. If you follow me, it means I am the leader."

"But that does not guarantee a good leader," Christina replies.

Gabriel points to the list he has been writing and says, "Well, we also said that a leader has good ideas, or is creative, has vision, and has a good goal."

I proposed to name famous leaders to see if they had this love for their followers. "How about Gandhi? Was he a good leader?"

Emily stands and says, "I have to check the food downstairs, guys." And as she walks out of the room, she says to Gabriel, "show me the homework before you turn it in, okay?"

"Yes, mom, I will," Gabriel replies. "Dad, Gandhi was the guy that liberated India from England, wasn't he?"

"Yes," Christina replies, "Don't you remember that dad forced us to watch a movie about him?"

"He was an excellent leader. Don't you think?" I ask.

"Yes, he loved his people, he had good ideas, and a vision," Christina says, "but I remember something from the movie that I saw in him. He was very courageous, even with the small body he had."

"You are right honey, he was a valiant guy, no doubt about it," I reinforce her. "A leader often goes against the mainstream in society, like Gandhi, and has to be courageous to lead. But there is one more thing we need to add to our list. Do you remember Gandhi's method? He used nonviolent disobedience. He won the war without violence."

Gabriel quickly writes my question on his paper and replies, "I know what you want us to say, dad. He was a role model of nonviolence."

I smile and pat him in his back. "Yes, Gabriel, that is the last characteristic of good leaders. They need to be role models of their own ideology. If they don't, people won't believe in them, and the trust will fade away soon."

Gabriel stops writing and says, "Okay dad, this is the list for my homework, so far I have: creative, visionary, unselfish, trustful, loving, courageous, and role model. What else?"

"I think that's enough, Gabriel," I say while yawning.

"Yes," Christina also replies, "you can't add much to it. Besides, it is too late already. I am going to bed."

Gabriel hugs me and says, "Thanks, I think we did a good job again."

"Okay, I'll have something to eat now. Good night guys," I say, and leave the room, heading to the stairs.

The timing is perfect. Emily calls me from the kitchen. "Walker, food is ready!"

As I go downstairs I have a feeling like an electric current in the left side of my brain. "Ouch!" I scream.

"What?" Emily asks as she runs to the stairs. She grabs my arm, and walks with me to the chair.

"I don't know," I say. "It was like an electric shock, here in my left side. I'd better have a glass of water and go to sleep. I think I am too tired."

Emily shakes her head, look down, and says, "I think you should go to the doctor tomorrow. You are not supposed to have such things."

"What things? It's nothing. Besides, I don't want to delay the construction of the new guitar anymore. I'll go to the doctor next month, after I finish the guitar I am making for my client in Denmark."

She doesn't like what I said. "Walker, health comes before work. You know better."

"I know, I know, but this guitar is my first international sale. I've got to do it fast and well. I can't miss the opportunity to open our business to the Europeans."

She is still not convinced. She walks to the kitchen, grabs a glass, and pours water in it. "Take it, and don't bother me again with your illnesses," she says with anger.

I take the glass. "Emily, it's a one-week thing. I promise I'll be in the doctor's office after that."

She doesn't reply and ignores my comments. After she cleans the table, having said not a single word, she goes upstairs to our room. I stay alone, sitting on the chair, trying to figure out what I should do. A visit to the doctor is just one hour, and I could just walk in to his office downtown. He knows me well. But on the other hand, it's important that I am in the shop at the beginning of the construction. Mmm, what should I do?

Then I hear Emily's voice from upstairs, "Why so much interest in this guitar? Is it because of your *girl friend* from Denmark?"

There she goes again. How can she suspect anything? I have not called Laura. I have not talked about her. Nothing. How can she? "No," I reply loudly, "it has nothing to do with my *client* in Denmark. It is just *business.*"

She slams the door so hard that even the glass of water trembles on the table. It seems to me that we always find an excuse to be upset with each other.

33

Romantic Friendships

I WAKE UP EARLIER THAN USUAL TO GET TO the shop before anybody else in order to gain some time. Emily and the kids are still sleeping. I get to the kitchen, clean and shiny as always, to prepare coffee and toast some bread.

I finish eating, set the dirty dishes on the sink, but when I am about to leave, Emily comes down the stairs and stops on the last step. Her red Irish hair is messed up and her eyes are puffy beyond normal. "Why so early?" She asks between yawns, with a tone of suspiciousness.

"I have work to do. I'll be back late today. Call me at the shop if you need me."

I walk passing by her and I feel that burning gaze on me. I slow down with the intention of saying something, something that she may like to hear before I leave. But I don't know what to say. I look at her. She gives me a half smile with sad eyes and then lowers her gaze. I touch her cheek with my hand and she squeezes it in between her cheek and her shoulder, holds it for a moment, and releases it.

"Thank you," she says. She turns back and goes upstairs to our room. "Bye," she softly says without looking back to me.

I go out the front door, get into my car, and sit there for half an hour, examining my feelings, my behavior. I turn on the car and get to the shop as quick as I can.

I love to be in the shop. It is the smell, the woods, the glues, the stains, all combined. It is delicious to me. My grandfather used to be a carpenter, and I used to go to his shop on Saturdays to check the new furniture he had made during the week. I guess this is why I like wood so much.

I collect all papers with measurements and templates for the first replica. I pick the new wood pieces and copy the templates to the two boards. After half an hour, Manuel enters the shop. He is singing and showing an unusual happiness today.

"Manuel," I call, "could you come here for a second?"

He drops his backpack on the floor, and when he is in my office I tell him what happened yesterday in my home with Emily. I also tell him about my 'brain shock,' and how I felt when that happened.

He listens with attention, and then says, "I understand your indecision. You want to finish the guitars, but you know that your health is more important. Why don't you do both: go to the doctor and make the guitar. You know, my mom used to say, 'It is not that you have A or B, but also neither or both.' Meaning that sometimes we think we are forced to take one choice, when sometimes we can simply take nothing, or take both."

"Interesting," I say. "Then I'll take your advice and do both. But I will need you to take care of my duties while I am gone at the doctor's. I'll be back in a couple of hours if there are no surprises."

"Not a problem, Walker," he answers promptly. "I'll take care of everything.

I leave the shop and start walking to the clinic, slowly and meditatively. As I walk I begin thinking about the consequences of this being a serious illness. I can't imagine Emily taking care by herself. She would be defenseless, unemployed, with two children and no work experience in more than a decade. She got a law degree, but that was many years ago. She only practiced for a year before we got married. Then she got pregnant and had to quit her job. After that she never worked outside the home again. Now she is probably outdated in the practice of law, and it will be difficult for her to find a job. What should I do then?

I stop in the ice cream shop to think more about this. I enter the shop and sit in the first chair I find. I ask myself, what if the doctor sends me to the hospital right away? That would be a disaster for us. I'd better not go. I have to be more prepared before going to the doctor. I step out of the ice cream shop and head back to the guitar shop.

When I enter the door, Manuel quickly asks me, "What happened? You are back too fast! You didn't go, did you?"

I don't want to look like a chicken. I better make up something quick. "The doctor could not attend to me. He has a long line of patients and gave me an appointment for next month. I thought I could just walk in and see the doctor, but he did not let me."

"Oh! That's a pity. I guess you have no other choice but to wait a month, then."

I am glad he believed my alibi. There is no need to talk about the doctor anymore. "I guess," I reply.

He looks at my eyes and says, "I was about to get working on the guitar when you entered. I really wanted to work on this one. Do you mind if we work together in the replicas? You know, I am interested in learning from Kwame too."

I see the eagerness to learn in his eyes. He knows how much emphasis I put in learning and knowledge. "Of course, Manuel. I was thinking on asking you, anyway. I want to finish both guitars as soon as possible."

"Great! I knew you were going to say so. I'll put in extra time for the other guitars we have pending. Don't worry about them."

I enjoy working with responsible people, and Manuel definitely is one of them. He is going to get far in life. "Okay, let's do this. I finish repairing the original guitar, while you start with the replica's neck. Take these papers where I have written the original dimensions. Just duplicate the geometry for this replica. The second replica will not follow these dimensions. You know that the second guitar is the acoustic replica, and Kwame said that most likely dimensions will be different."

He grabs all the wood pieces for the neck, the tools he needs, and with a big smile on his face walks to his table.

Dust is everywhere, but the work is going smoothly and fast. Manuel is almost done with the main piece of the neck, and I am almost done repairing the old neck. Actually, I had to make a new one because the old one was too damaged. I can't imagine how this was broken. I am ready to connect the neck to the sound box so I can begin the finger-board. I found wood that is the same type, color and design of the original. The finger-board is the single piece of the guitar that is most likely to be recognized by Frederik. Professional guitarists know their finger-board better than their palms, so I'd better make the new finger-board as an exact copy of the old one.

It is getting hot in the shop, and I set the fan it to the highest speed. Manuel has taken his shirt off already. "Hey Manuel, why don't you turn on your fan?"

"Good idea," he replies.

I finish gluing the finger-board and check that it is absolutely flat. The worse defect in a professional guitar is the lack of flatness in the finger-board. Now I have to begin installing the frets. They are the little metallic rods that separate each semi-tone. This has to be very precisely copied from the original. A minor difference and the notes will not reproduce the original.

After a couple of hours, the frets are all installed. I measured them and they are all at the same height and distance as the original, one by one. The head-piece is finished too, so I can start sanding with the #120 paper. Manuel is also about to finish the neck of the replica. He is fast. I am going to miss him when he leaves the shop. Unfortunately that is the way things work most of the time. People want to have their own business, and I can't stop him.

We have been working for six hours without stopping, and I am feeling tired. Manuel is probably as tired as I am. "Hey Manuel, how is it going?"

He stands and stretches. "Good. I think I can start the plates and sides tomorrow."

I am done with the sanding and begin the painting and polishing of the neck. It is going to be hard to duplicate the color of an old guitar, but I'll try. I am sure Laura is going to like it. I know her.

Manuel walks to my table. "Why are you smiling?"

"Oh, well, because I think our client is going to like this guitar," I reply.

Manuel looks at me with a different smile, like trying to catch me saying something. "Which guitar do you like better, this one, or the one in Denmark?"

I look at his eyes, but mine betray me. He steps backs and says, "You don't have to answer. I shouldn't have asked." He leaves the room while I stay alone, trying to answer the question to myself for the rest of the day. Manuel leaves the shop, and I stay for a while more, until I finish to repair the guitar, passed 1:00 AM.

Next day in the morning, back in the shop, I feel inspired and accomplished. The guitar is fully repaired and ready to be tested by Manuel. I enter my office and hear the phone ringing. It cannot be a client; it's seven in the morning. I turn on the lights and grab the phone.

"Hello, it is Walker talking."

A soothing voice on the line says, "Hi, handsome man. How are you?"

"Who is this?" I demand.

The sweet voice replies, "don't you recognize me? I am disappointed."

Oh! There she is. I can't believe I am talking to her again. "Hi Laura. What a nice surprise so early in the morning. And you sound so clear. Where are you?"

She doesn't answer. The silence is killing me. A fraction of a second seems like hours. "I am closer than you think," she finally says. "I am in the hotel at the Metropolitan airport. My airline sent me here last night, and I am going back to Europe this afternoon. But I want to see you before I leave."

"Of course," I quickly say.

My mind starts thinking fast, looking for an alibi for Emily and Manuel. I've got to leave now, before Manuel arrives.

"Laura, I also have a surprise for you. We can meet in your hotel. What is your room number?"

"I'll wait for you in the lobby," she says.

"Well, that's fine too. I'll see you in forty minutes at most."

I leave a note to Manuel dated yesterday saying, "Manuel, I'll be late tomorrow. Don't call home for me." This should take care of everything, I hope.

I take the repaired guitar, go to the parking lot and rush to the airport. The traffic seems to be going very slow today. As I get closer to the airport my mind begins to think about what I am doing, but I ignore it. There is even more traffic near the hotel too. It's been more than an hour since she called and I am just entering the parking lot. I park my car and walk as fast as I can, straight to the hotel lobby.

The hotel is crowded with tourists. People, as always, staring at me. There she is, standing next to a large vase full of red roses. She is as beautiful as the first time I saw her. I approach her from behind just to contemplate her without her knowing it. She is winding strands of her golden hair with her fingers. She is wearing a blue suit from the airline, I guess. It fits her contour like the bag of a guitar. I put the instrument behind a column and go around to face her.

"Good morning," I say.

She looks at me and with her shiny smile says, "Better morning for me."

She seems even more confident than when we were in Denmark. She approaches me and hugs me so exquisitely. Then with a very romantic voice, next to my ear she whispers, "I missed you."

I can feel the goose bumps on my neck, on the same side she just whispered to me. "So did I," I reply. "Why don't we go to your room?"

"We can't. My friend is still in bed," she says while sitting on a white leather sofa.

"Your friend? And who is he?" I ask surprised and disappointed.

She laughs and replies promptly, "It is a she, not a he."

I feel stupid, but before she says anything else, I reply, "Wait here. I have something for you."

I grab the guitar behind the column, still in its bag, and say, "Close your eyes first. This is something I am sure you'll like."

"Now, open your eyes." She does, and after realizing what I have brought, her eyes are big like a pair of moons. "Oh! The replica! Walker, I though you said it was going to take months! Oh! What a nice surprise!"

"Well, it is not the replica. It the original guitar."

She looks at me with a confused face. "What? You don't want to make the replicas anymore?"

"Oh, no. It is not that! Let me show you." I unzip the guitar bag and pull the fully repaired old guitar, clean and shiny.

She is so surprised that she can't talk. She can't believe it. Her eyes become watery, full of joy. "You... you repaired it? I can't believe it! And ... and how does it sound?"

"I finished it last night. My apprentice, Manuel, who tests all my guitars, has not seen it yet, so I don't know how it sounds. You know... I can't play it. Besides, you won't be able to take it with you because Manuel doesn't know you are here." She drops her shoulders.

"But don't worry," I continue, "I am still planning to make the replicas, so I still need this one to finish my job. I brought it with me because I knew you would like to see it repaired."

She stays quiet for a while until a smile appears in between her two round cheeks and says, "Well, I hope you finish them soon. Frederik is very frustrated with the guitar he has now. He complains every single day."

"I'll do my best, Laura. I am working with Kwame and Manuel to do it fast and with precision. You won't believe what we are doing."

She smiles again and touches my right hand with her thin, long and terse fingers. "I really wanted to see you, Walker."

I contemplate her eyes deeply and read how sincere her comments are. I am not sure if I feel the same this time, but it feels good to be next to her. It's like being seventeen again. My palm is sweating, my heart is pumping, my mouth is dry, and my voice stuttering at times, but she always smiles. I want to say something sincere too, but my thoughts of Emily's image keeps coming to me. I evade her glance and she notices it immediately.

"What is it?" She asks.

"Nothing. Well, I just wanted to say that ... well, long time ago I read something."

"What is it?"

"It was something like this: *friendship is too important and valuable to risk over a romantic affair, plus sex is too pleasant and exquisite to destroy with guilt.*"

She looks away from me, a sign of repulsion I recognize, and looks at her watch. I know she didn't like my comment. "Well, I have to go. The airplane is leaving for Denmark in one hour."

I feel she is not telling the truth. "Okay. I guess we have to say good bye again. I will call you when I have the replicas ready for your brother."

She seems more uncomfortable now. She looks at her watch again and firmly say, "Please, do so. Good bye."

We hug a second time, but now I feel the coldness of her chest. I hold her for a split second and say, "Sorry."

She ignores my comment and replies, "Bye." And walks to the elevator where she disappears among the rest of the people.

I feel lonely and confused. I don't understand my own feelings. It is so intense to be with her, but a torment at the same time. It is like watching a sunset with sunglasses. The beauty is there, in front of you, but you can't see it and feel it fully. I feel imperfect, restricted.

I pick up the guitar and put it inside the bag. I walk taciturn, with dropped shoulders, carrying the guitar I brought with so much enthusiasm. I pass by the screen with the list of departing flights. There are no flights to Denmark for the next four hours. I knew it; she lied to me. I keep walking, slowly, looking at the marble of the hotel floor, looking at the asphalt on the street, looking at the cement floor in the parking lot. I get to my car and drive back to my guitar shop.

$$34$$

Crippled for Life

HEN I GET BACK TO THE SHOP IT IS almost noon. I park the car in the same place where I had it this morning. Slowly, with not much intention in each step, and carrying the guitar, I enter the shop, silently, to avoid Manuel seeing me with the repaired guitar.

He has finished the neck of the first replica and is already working on the sound-hole rosette. "Walker, I am glad you are here. Let me show you what I've done so far." He seems very happy this morning, or it may be my own mood that makes me think so. He walks to the other table and shows me all the cuts he's made. He is amazing. He has the sides, the braces, the bridge, and the sound boards all ready and set to be glued.

"How can you do it so fast?" I ask, faking naiveté to give him a reason to show off his skills.

He looks at me, trying to figure out what to say. He then shows me his two palms, shrinks his shoulders, opens his eyes wide, and says nothing.

But I knew what he meant. So I change the subject immediately. "Well, this is the thing. Since you are so fast, why don't you finish all the parts, and I'll assemble them later this afternoon? Is it okay with you?"

He gives me a nervous smile, with trembling lips. I guess he thinks he may have offended me with his mimic reply. "Yes, Walker, it sounds good to me."

"I'll go home for lunch, and will be back around five. See you then," I say.

He waves a good bye to me, and goes back to the working table to finish what is left. Manuel has been my best apprentice in many years, and I trust him like a son. He would never say anything to offend me. Besides, I am too old to let my problem interfere with a friendship that I am convinced will be forever.

When I get home I take a look at the backyard to see if Gabriel is playing ball. Nobody is there, but then I realize he must be at school, still. It is just my habit of being sure that he and Christina are home when I come in the afternoons. I enter the house expecting to see Emily working in the kitchen as usual, but she is not there. I go upstairs, enter our room and hear the shower. It must be Emily taking a shower. I open the door of the bathroom trying not to call her attention. Once inside I see her blurry image through the shower glass door, a bit fatter than some years ago, but still inspiring. I feel tempted, but I decide to step out of there in the same way I entered. With my hand still on the door knob, I try to examine what I am feeling. It's a desire I can't hold back, but that I don't want to be expressed. I definitely don't understand my own feelings all these years. A few hours ago I was with another woman that I like very much, but couldn't commit to. Now I am with the one I think I love, but somehow I can't commit to her either.

The shower stops. She is probably putting soap all around her body. I remember when we used to do that to each other, during long hours of showering together. I am still holding the knob trying to decide what to do. I open the door again, but this time I make enough noise, so she can hear me coming in. She doesn't say anything. I call her name to grab her attention.

"Emily!"

'Oh! Walker! You scared me."

I open the glass door and look at her from head to toe, and back from toe to head. She understands what I want.

"Don't look at me like that," she says. "Get out of the bathroom."

Her words are like a thousand daggers through my heart. I close the door, and walk away taciturn again, but this time in my own territory, in my own home. I walk out of the bathroom, looking at the gray carpet of my bedroom. I go downstairs, and now feel no desire to stay or eat here. Why should I? I leave home and head to Main street, to the fancy restaurant where Kwame and I ate last time. As I get closer to downtown, my appetite is less and less. I decide to skip lunch, and go straight to the shop instead.

It's been only twenty minutes since I left the shop, and when I enter, Manuel takes a look at his watch and says, "You came back earlier than expected. It there anything wrong? You look awful, too."

"Nothing wrong," I say kindly to avoid more comments. "How is your guitar going?"

"I will be done in two hours, at most, and then you can take all the parts and start gluing them together."

"Good! I want to finish all these damned replicas as soon as possible."

He looks at me with surprise. "Damned replicas? I thought you liked them. You've always been happy about making these replicas. Now they are *damned* replicas? What is happening to you?"

He is right, but he doesn't know what I just went through. "I am sorry, Manuel. You are right. I had a problem at home. Forget what I said. It is that sometimes women put you down so easily."

He smiles and says, "Do you know what my grandma used to say?"

There he goes again with one of his grandma's saying. "What?"

"She used to say *amor quieto es amor muerto,* which means that love stays alive if you keep changing it."

"Changing it? What do you mean? That I should change my wife?"

Now he laughs even more. He gets closer to me and say, "No, Walker. It means that you have to change how to express your love for her. Tell her how much you love her in different ways; share new things with her; make new plans and visit new places together; pay attention to the details; give her surprises; take her for a vacation; give her a red flower when she does not expect it; and so on."

I guess his grandma was a clever person with lots of experience, but I am not in the mood to be receptive. "It sounds like good advice, Manuel. Thank you. I'll think about it." I walk away, but then I turn back to face him and say, "I'll do the guitar assembly as soon as you give me all the pieces."

He goes back to his table and I go to my office. I close the door, turn the light off, close the window shades, disconnect the phone, and sit still on the chair. I close my eyes, recline back, and start thinking. Since the day Gabriel was born my life changed from day to night. I hate to remember that day, but every time she rejects me, I can't have other thoughts but those. That day was so painful, physically and emotionally. I was driving to the hospital where Emily was in labor to deliver Gabriel. It all happened so fast that I can't remember how exactly it was. The only thing in my memory is that I had my left arm hanging out the car when a huge red truck lost control, couldn't evade the collision, and side-swiped my car on the left side, where my arm was. It sliced off my hand so fast, that I didn't realize what had happened until I saw the blood all over my shirt. My left hand was lying in the pavement, probably crushed by the other cars in the road. I put my left arm, whatever was left of it, in between my legs to stop the bleeding. I pushed the gas pedal to the bottom and got to the hospital when I was about to faint inside the car. The last thing I remember is the valet parking guy trying to open the car door and calling for help.

They couldn't find my hand because they didn't know where I had lost it, and their only concern was to stop the bleeding to keep me alive. The next day, when I woke up, the feelings were mixed. The joy of a newborn son, and the sadness of losing my hand forever. I didn't know if I was crying for my hand, or for my son. The worst part was when I realized I could not play the guitar for the rest of my life. My career as guitarist was over. And since that day everything has been a struggle for me. My career and my marriage changed dramatically, so fast and so abruptly, that I haven't had time to think about how to adjust to it. It is a nightmare that haunts me, and I know haunts Emily as well.

Months passed trying to figure out what to do with one less hand. At first, I thought of abandoning all I knew about guitars, but I couldn't be without them. I had played guitar since I was ten years old. I was the lead guitarist of a folk music group that had signed a record deal weeks before the accident. Everything was lost, trashed. I had to provide for a growing family, an unemployed wife, and an arm without a hand. The following year I went to Boston to learn guitarmaking from a luthier that also had a crippled arm. It was inspirational, and enough to convince me that I could also do it. The best way to encourage anybody to pursue a dream is by talking to someone who has made it. From that day I knew I could make guitars as good as anybody if I had the right tools and enough time.

The other side of my life, the familiar side, was fast and steadily deteriorating. Since the accident, Emily has been very inconsistent in her feelings towards me. Some times she would be nurturing and inspiring, but some other times, very often, she would not even let me be close to her, with a repulsion that I feel as intensely painful. That has been my struggle for many years. So then, when someone like Laura lays eyes on me, with a fresh start, without even looking at my arm when we are together, my feelings are deeply moved, and my heart flourishes with each encounter, each sight, each possible touch.

Someone knocks on the door. It must be Manuel. "Yes?" I respond.

"Walker, the parts are ready for assembly," he says.

"I'll be out in a second. I am finishing something here."

I open the shades, connect the phone, turn the lights on, and open the door. "You were fast again, Manuel."

"It took me what I said, no more, no less, just two hours. All parts are on the table. By the way, where is the repaired guitar? I was looking for it to try it out, but I couldn't find it."

"Oh, I am sorry, Manuel. I took it last night to show it to Emily. There it is, next to the wall. Please try it and let me know how it feels."

He grabs the bag, open it, and tune the guitar for about five minutes before playing the first scale. It sounds beautiful. The scales are precise and clean. He goes up and down, repeating a C-major scale. All notes sound perfect to me. Frederik will enjoy this guitar again.

"This is a one-in-a-million guitar," Manuel says. "I can't find a defect in it."

"I am glad to hear that. It was hard work to replace the neck," I say proudly. "Keep playing it, while I begin assembling the first replica."

He goes from scales to cords, then from cords to songs. He tests each fret several times. I am glad Manuel knows how to play guitar. I taught him the scales some time ago, the best I could, and now he tests all our guitars before they are sent to our customers.

While I listen to him, I take the sides, boards, neck, and all other parts to build the first replica. I grab my glue and begin with the braces of the sound board. I have all marked to make sure it has the same pattern as in the original guitar. After three hours of work, and three hours of listening to good folk music from Central America, I get to the point where the assembly is all wrapped with the elastic strips to tighten and hold the shape. After this, the only thing left is the polishing, and in a couple of days Manuel will be able to try this guitar too. I hope I don't have to reject this replica. I hate rejections.

35

The Letter

$\mathcal{I}$ AM IN MY BASEMENT SANDING THE NECK OF a guitar I started many months ago, but that I haven't had the time to finish. It is mid morning, the sun is shining after a dark and rainy dawn. The kids are in school. I hear the steps of Emily coming down the stairs. She rarely comes down here, so I wonder what she has to say.

"Hi," she says as she arranges her hair, exposing her left ear. She is wearing an almost transparent nightie that I gave her many years ago, but that she has never used. Now I know what she wants.

"Hi," I reply. I continue sanding as if I didn't notice anything. I don't feel like touching her after what she did to me in the bathroom last week.

"I want to talk to you," she softly says.

"I'm busy right now," I respond firmly.

"I know, but this is important," she insists.

The Guitar Maker

I begin thinking of what she is going to say. She'll say that she feels alone, that she loves me, blah blah blah. "I know what you are going to tell me."

"Perhaps, but that doesn't mean I shouldn't say it," she replies with the wit of a lawyer. "Remember the list of goals in life that you asked me to prepare some time ago? Well, I did it yesterday, and I want to give it to you."

She shows me a piece of paper, all crumpled. "Here it is." And she leaves the basement, going back to bed, upstairs.

I take the paper, wait until she is completely out of the basement, and read it. It is a short letter.

> Walker,
> It has been very difficult for me to get used to you since Gabriel was born. You went from a cheerful man, with hope, optimism, happiness and passion, to a sad man, with traumas, pessimism, hopelessness and apathy, especially toward me. Honey, I still think you can find the old Walker in you, and I want to help you. This is the list you asked me. My goals in life, my BBBN objectives, as you put it:
>
> To soften our hearts; to perfect our marriage; to raise our children the best we can; to nurture our talents; and to live happier together every day.
>
> I don't know if they are what you wanted, but this is what I want.
> I love you, Emily.

My hand starts shaking. I had never read something so moving and thoughtful from her. My tears wet the letter, and I feel overwhelmingly happy and blessed. How can I not agree with these words? Why did she never tell me this before? I always thought I was recovered from my accident, and that I was living a normal life. Oh, how could I not see it? How?

Now I realize we are both aiming in the same direction, and to me, that is what counts. The differences might be in style, but not in content. This is the secret of living together: to have the same goals that eventually converge, sooner or later. Differences in style cannot derail us from being happy with each other.

I drop my tools, the sanding paper, and clean myself up. I walk upstairs to our room. She is sitting on the bed, resting her back on the back board. She is still with the same nightie, and I see much more through it. I look at her, and she looks at me. I approach the bed. Every gesture is a word, every hug a sentence, and every kiss a paragraph. And without pronouncing a single word, I feel we have told more words to each other than ever. Hugs are followed by kisses, kisses are followed by our private expressions of love. That love that throws you into the timeless zone, with loud muteness that emanates out of each pore of the skin, along with the salty sweat of your lover. There we are, one for each other, until we confessed our needs and our pains.

Once relaxed, with that feeling of fullness that one experiences after satisfying carnal desires, we kiss one more time. A long kiss that takes our breath away, where darkness, smells and flavors are shared. "I don't want to leave," I say.

"You don't have to," she replies.

"I do. Kwame and Manuel should be waiting for me in the guitar shop.

She changes her face and with disappointment says, "Why do you always have to find an excuse to be at the shop?"

"They are not excuses. I am working in one of the most important projects I've ever had, and Kwame is helping me with it. Honey, bear with me for some weeks, and I promise that we will be fine again. I promise."

She looks at me in silence, with eyes of desire. I sit on one side of the bed, pick my underwear from the floor, and when I am about to stand to get dressed, she holds me by the waist and says, "I don't want promises. I want a proof now. I've been without you for too long, and I don't want you to leave that fast."

"But honey, I ..."

When we finally exhaust our energies on each other, after having the best time with Emily that I remember, I leave home with a sense of security and invincibility that I haven't felt in years. On the way to the shop, I start thinking about what happened. All these years I thought she was the problem, and it never occurred to me that *I* could be the problem. It is so hard to do a self-examination without falling into the trap of blaming others. Foolish are those who think they can diagnose their own problems. It is impossible.

I get to the shop, and enter the main green door. "Good morning guys!" I say to Manuel and Kwame, who have been here for a couple of hours already.

"Good morning, Walker. I guess you had a warm bed this morning!" Kwame sarcastically says.

"You are completely right, Kwame. It was really warm," I promptly reply.

"I am happy to hear that, Walker. Manuel and I have been working on the acoustic replica for some time and we were just waiting for you so we could make some decisions."

Manuel nods to Kwame. "Yes, we are ready to start the reverse engineering for this replica."

"Great, let's begin with the lesson then," I say.

"Well, I told you guys how it works," Kwame explains. "In essence, this is an optimization problem, too. The objective is to match the properties of the new guitar with the properties measured from the broken one. We set some constraints on the thicknesses of plates, on some dimensions, and that's it."

I scratch my head and say, "But Kwame, we have many acoustic properties we want to match. There are many objectives."

"You are right; we will treat them as constraints in the problem. For instance, the objective could be to match the Helmholtz frequency, and then we set other constraints to match string frequencies, plate frequencies, sound intensity, and so on. This is going to be a difficult problem, but I feel we can do it.

"What we want to do," Kwame says, "is to find the same acoustic properties and sound quality of the original guitar using a different geometry. Now we need a starting geometry that is different from the original, but that can be 'tuned' until we attain the acoustic properties of the broken guitar. Walker, could you find any of the drawings you use in your guitars?"

I go to my office, and come back with a very special guitar, one that has been in the cabinet for years. "I have this guitar that we can use as the starting geometry."

Manuel's eyes cannot be wider. "Walker, I've never seen this guitar before. Who's the owner?"

"I am," I say. "This is the guitar I used to play when I was part of a folk music group, some years ago. My father gave it to me as a Thanksgiving gift."

I hold it with care, and pass it to Manuel. He takes it and stays astonished for minutes. Kwame is also somehow puzzled too. I take a long breath and tell him what I've never said to anybody before. "Yes, Kwame, I used to have both hand. Actually, they were very good with the guitar. I played the lead guitar in my own band at the peak of my career when I lost my hand in a car accident."

Manuel, noticing that I am kind of sad, plays some cords to cheer me up. It sounds like years before, rugged and metallic. "Walker, this is a beautiful guitar with a sweet sound," Manuel says.

"I know. It's been a while since I played, though. I just wanted to see if we could take some dimensions from my guitar and tune it to get the sound of Frederik's guitar."

Kwame nods to me, "Yes, let's try that. The worst thing that can happen is that we get a replica of your precious guitar, which I am sure you won't mind."

"No, I don't want that to happen. Actually, a classic guitar and a folk music guitar are quite different. It would be impossible to get the right classical sound from my guitar. We should copy some dimensions to start the process, that's all."

Kwame and Manuel look at each other, and then nod to me as sign of agreement. We made some measurements of my guitar, and Kwame put them into the computer. Now we have a model of my guitar and the acoustic characteristic we want to match. As he explains to us, he sets the objective and the constraints in such a way that we can tune some dimensions and thicknesses until the reverse engineering is complete.

We wait several hours for the computer to give us the final answer, but it was worth it. Kwame reads each piece of information the computer provides and then says, "I think we got it. It sounds crazy, but your guitar was very close to Frederik's guitar."

"Close?" Manuel asks. "What do you mean by close?"

Kwame smiles and say, "It's just an expression of us, optimizers. Imagine that the two designs are two points in the sky, then we can say they are close to each other, and we can measure how far they are from each other, too."

I don't understand what he is saying. What sky is he talking about? "Well, it doesn't matter, Kwame. Just tell us what changes have to be made to build the acoustic replica."

"It does matter," he forcefully replies. "The point I want to convey is that because both guitars are so close, we don't have to make many changes. According to the computer, we only need to increase the thickness of the front plate by 1 millimeter, change this radius, and increase the back plate by 0.5 millimeter. That is all."

Manuel and I look each other with disbelief. How could these two guitars, being so different geometrically, produce the same sound by just changing the thickness of the plates? "I can't believe it, Kwame," Manuel says, as I nod to him.

"Guys, don't be so incredulous. Let me show you the graphs," Kwame replies.

He takes the computer and plots some curves on the screen showing how the replica will perform after the changes proposed by the computer. Then he plots the same curves for Frederik's guitar. They are basically the same! I guess he is right. I can't refute him.

"But the ultimate proof," Manuel says, "is going to be when we build the guitar, and play it. That is going to be the real test for us."

"You are right, Manuel," Kwame replies. "You are right. So, I leave you now, and will come back in a couple of weeks. By then you should have the new guitar ready for the ultimate test."

36

Changes and Dreams

HREE WEEKS HAVE PASSED SINCE EMILY and I began talking more, understanding each other, and feeling much more the togetherness we had lost. They have been the best weeks of my life in the last ten years, with no fights, no sadness, no remorse. I don't know how I had lived as I was living. I feel so inspired, so compelled to do more for her, for me and for the kids. I have finished all my guitars that I have procrastinated over so many times down in my basement. I wrote new songs, new lyrics, as I used to do before the accident, one better than the next. I have found the way of existing that I had lost.

Even more, our intimacy has grown so much, so deep, so tender and secure, that I feel invincible. Our romanticism returned and the kids notice it. Our dinners are a delight and Emily is always with a smile on her face. We even went for a 'date' a couple of days ago. It was in the fancy restaurant downtown, with candles, wine, a rose I bought for her, a delicious meal, and of course, sharply dressed for the occasion. "Emily, what happened?" I asked, then.

She, with a smile of red lips that crossed her face from ear to ear, replied with "We never gave up." She paused for a second, and continued, "You have always told us that *love* was the key for everything, and I agree. But there is something that is needed to make a marriage succeed, besides love." I stayed quiet waiting for her argument. I grabbed her hand, and she said: "commitment; In the bad times, when things go sour in a relationship, the commitment to stay together is what keeps the marriage alive. Eventually, as is happening with us now, love will take over again." And that was a lesson I took from that date that I'll never forget.

I am about to leave home, heading to the shop, when Emily, Christina and Gabriel approach me by surprise and start singing Happy Birthday. I had forgotten completely about this. I am one year older today, forty nine, but I feel ten years younger. What a nice way to feel! I hug them all, kiss them all, and leave home with a sense of completeness that I've never felt before.

The second replica is almost finished. I think we can test it today. I get to the shop and grab the phone to call Kwame. I ask him to come in the afternoon to see Manuel testing the guitar, but he insists in coming right away.

Manuel enters the shop. I sense a bit of tension in his manner. "Walker, can we talk for a second?"

I approach him, and notice he has written something to read to me. "What is it, Manuel?"

"Walker, this is going to be a difficult thing for me to say. I wrote it down and I'll read it."

He is trembling. I don't like how he looks at me. I am clueless about what is written there.

"My good friend Walker," he reads, "you have been my teacher and mentor in guitarmaking all these years, and I am grateful for that. However, there is a time in every man's life where some decisions have to be made. I am leaving Michigan and going to Texas, closer to my family. I dream of opening a guitar shop as good as this one and hope to continue our friendship forever. Accept my apologies for this decision, but it is time for me to depart. You are my best friend and my best teacher. I will never be able to pay back all that I learned from you in this shop, and outside it. Truly yours, Manuel."

His eyes tear up, as do mine. We hug each other, and cry some more. Manuel has been like an older son for me, and I will never forget him.

"I knew this would happen some day, Manuel. It is the natural course of life. Don't worry about me. I will find someone who can test my guitars, but I will never find anybody to replace our friendship."

"I'll pay you back all you spent for me in college. I will," he insists. We talked and talked, remembering our good and bad times.

"Behind my office's door, there is a picture hanging." I say to him. "Go and take it. It's for you."

When he comes back, we laugh together. It is the picture of both of us, the first day we met. I wasn't bald, and he had long hair. Now we look older, but it does not matter to either of us.

Kwame enters the shop and approaches us. "What is going on here?"

I show him the picture, and he says, "Oh boy, where did all this hair go?"

We all laugh. I tell him the news about Manuel's departure. He seems sad too, but he knows well that we can't stop these things from happening.

"Changes and dreams are essential in life," Kwame says, "If we don't change, we don't prosper, and we die quicker. If we don't dream, we don't see ourselves changing. Nature never gives you the same events every day, so we humans should try to live with change. It is because of changes that we can improve; otherwise we would be stuck in the same place forever. And improvement is the fundamental step towards perfection, quality, beauty, and all those attributes that we can maximize in our journey through life, until we get, if possible, to the *optimum*."

It always amazes me how Kwame can come up with such an intelligent answer to any situation.

"Well, let's see how the second replica sounds," I say.

I feel a little nervous. Kwame looks confident, and Manuel a bit anxious as he grabs the original guitar first. He plays some cords to get used to the sound and feeling. Then he grabs the replica, and before playing a single note, he says, "It feels strange. It's lighter than the original."

"It doesn't matter." Kwame says, "What matters is the sound. Remember, this is a different guitar that should sound the same as the original."

Manuel nods at him, and plays each string separately. They all sound fine to me. Kwame keeps observing. Manuel goes for his first chord, C-major, a strong one. He then grabs the original guitar back, and plays the same chord. We listen to the echo inside the shop. They sound identical to me, but Manuel is the one who can tell the real difference because is feeling the vibrations of the box, and is closer to the guitar. He then looks at me and Kwame, but says nothing. He closes his eyes and plays several chords on each guitar. His gestures seem to indicate a disappointment. He opens his eyes and says, "They are the same to me!"

We all jump from our chairs. "Yes! I knew it." Kwame says. "We did it right!"

I was scared for a minute, but now I feel good. I am so happy about what we have achieved. We now have three guitars that sound identical, and we learned how to make them consistently well.

"I can't wait to see Frederik's face," Kwame says.

"Yes, Kwame, Frederik will be impressed with all this," I affirm. "I'll call Laura tomorrow. We have to go to Denmark as soon as we can. Manuel, do you want to go with us? This will be our last trip together."

"Of course," he quickly says. "I already have one foot on the airplane."

37

A Poem

ERE WE ARE IN THE DETROIT METRO airport, waiting for our flight to Copenhagen. Manuel, who has never been to Europe, is with me tonight. "Manuel, please, stop tapping your foot. You make me nervous too," I say. He stops. I am carrying the original guitar, and Manuel the two replicas. They are our most precious luggage on this trip.

"Walker, do you know that girl near the window?" He asks me as he points to her.

"Don't point at her. She'll notice we are talking about her," I say as I push down his arm. "No, I don't know her. Do you?"

"Yes, I've seen her in downtown Ann Arbor. I think she is a college student. I find her so attractive and sweet. Look at her. See how she moves. But you know..."

"What?"

"Well, girls like her will never notice me. I am a poor guy, with no professional degree, no properties, nothing; and she is probably a wealthy beautiful girl that can afford going to an expensive university in the US."

"But why are you discriminating against yourself?" I ask angrily.

"You don't know anything about her. Listen, before coming to any conclusion, you need to talk to her. I can help you with that, if you want."

He looks at me surprised, but nods to me. "How can you help me?"

I say nothing to him, walk towards the window, and when I am close to her I say, "Hi, I need to put this guitar next the window. It's better for the guitar to be next to a cooler place. Do you mind if I sit here?"

She is a pretty brown-haired girl, in her twenties, blue eyes, tall, with sensual dimensions, wearing tight blue jeans and a turquoise blouse that exposes her belly. In one hand she carries the most popular gadget nowadays —a cell phone— and in the other hand, a black leather purse worn by use. A brown freckle stands out near her right eye to unbalance the beautiful symmetry of her face.

"No, sir. Please help yourself."

As soon as I sit, I signal Manuel to come. When he is close to us, I say to the girl, "This is Manuel, my guitar maker apprentice. He'll take care of the guitar."

Manuel stretches his arm to greet her, and she does the same. I see how Manuel is already happy. I sit two rows away from them, where I can see the guitars and listen to the conversation as well. I like to see how romance and love evolves between couples. I want to see how they connect, or disconnect.

Surprisingly, she strikes first and says, "I like guitars a lot. My brother has three at home." I can't see how she won't like Manuel, a young handsome man, with black hair, strong build, soft spoken and intelligent.

"I can't live without a guitar near me," he replies to her. Great line from Manuel.

"Where are you guys going?" She asks.

She is showing interest in him now. Manuel checks on me, and says, "We are going to Copenhagen to deliver three guitars to a customer."

She looks more impressed now, "Nice. Do you make guitars and travel around the world to deliver them? That's a cool job."

Manuel hesitates for a second. I nod to him, and without saying any word, and making sure she is not looking at me, I articulate with my mouth "yes, yes."

"Yes ... sometimes we need to travel to deliver our guitars," he finally says with a serene confidence.

"Where have you guys been before?" She quickly replies, trying to check the truth of Manuel's claims.

I then intervene before he is uncovered. "I think we should get ready for the flight, Manuel."

"Yes, Walker. I'll be there," he replies looking at me, while I see how she is looking at him from head to toe, checking him out, taking the opportunity of his distraction.

I leave them alone, walk to the counter, and watch them talking for about ten more minutes. She pulls out a piece of paper, writes her phone number, and gives it to him. He got it! I am happy. Maybe he won't leave Michigan after all.

Once inside the airplane I ask him. "Did she say anything about you being a poor person, or any other discriminatory word? Of course not. You see? Don't discriminate against yourself."

"You are right, Walker. She is a sweet girl. Her name is Natalia, and she studies literature in the University of Michigan. I got her phone number. She gave it to me without me asking for it."

"I told you, silly boy. She likes you," I say while I give him a friendly nudge on the shoulder.

We sit in the always uncomfortable airplane seats, and start the long trip to Copenhagen, the city of historical buildings and ancient streets. Shortly after the plane reaches the cruising altitude, and seconds after the seat belt light goes off, Natalia shows up.

"Hi Manuel," she says, "guess what, the seat next to me is empty. You may come over if you want." And as quick as she came, she leaves heading to the restroom.

"See? I told you." I say as I hit him in his ribs with my elbow.

"Easy, easy," Manuel replies. "I don't want to create false expectations."

"Okay, now it is your turn, Manuel. Be aggressive, don't waste time, ask her out, say something that impresses her, and ..."

"Walker, please. What is the hurry? I have time. I know what to do. 'Fast courtship, stupid man,' my grandma used to say."

"That doesn't rhyme," I reply.

"Because she didn't speak English. The original version is in Spanish: *rápido cortejo, hombre pendejo.*

"But anyway, you should listen to me, I have more experience."

He ignores my comments and leaves me alone. Unfortunately, experience is something you learn after you need it. He has to go through it, and realize by himself how things are. I hope they get along well.

I put a blanket over me, stare at the window, and begin remembering my two kids and Emily. She prepared my luggage this time, like many years ago when I had to travel with the band. She has been so sweet with me since we had our conversation. I now feel that all of our problems are behind us, and I look forward to good times together.

The flight attendant stops by to offer a drink, and when I see her, I can't avoid remembering Laura. It is going to be a difficult encounter with her. She doesn't know anything about my improved relation with Emily, and she is probably still angry with me since we met at the Detroit airport weeks ago. I'll see how it goes. I close my eyes and try to rest as much as I can.

Someone is tapping my shoulder. "Walker, Walker, wake up!" It's Manuel.

"Uh? What?"

"Walker, I am in love," he says delightedly as he nods his head. I can see his excitement. "She is one of the sweetest girls I've ever met. She is caring and has a heart fill with compassion. I am telling you.

She is my type of girl, Walker. She smiles a lot, and even laughs at my terrible jokes!" Manuel laughs, smiles, then adds, "She's smart and has strong values, like those my grandma used to teach me. You'll like her too, Walker. Oh man! What should I do now?"

In the middle of my sleep, the only thing that occurs to me is, "I don't know. Write a poem, I guess."

"A poem?" He says with wide open eyes. "Yes, a poem! I've written many poems before. I can do that."

He grabs a pen and takes a napkin from the sleeping passenger next to us. He begins writing effusively a few lines. "Here is the first one. Read it for me, please."

I grab the napkin and read,

> When you are not with me
> I feel breathless,
> like drowned in a deep ocean
> waiting for your rescue
> with the hook of your smiles,
> of your words, and
> your sweet caresses

"I don't quite understand it," I say.

"It doesn't matter," he replies. "She will. That's all that matters. A poem is like an arrow —Cupid's arrow. It has an end and a point. The end is touching my heart, and the point is touching hers. Only she and I are able to decipher what the poem means. It's like a secret between us.

"Nicely said, Manuel. I like it. You could use it as lyrics for a song. Now tell me, did you ask her out?"

"Not yet. The thing is that ... I can't. She won't be back to Michigan until next month."

"Then let's concentrate in our task for this trip. When she gets back to Michigan, you'll have time for her."

He smiles and nods to me. We buckle our seat belts and prepare for the landing. He calls the flight attendant and asks her to deliver the poem for him. I stay quiet thinking about this simple, but intense romantic event. Men and women very often attract each other instinctively, with little reasoning or logic. Manuel, without realizing it, just talked about the most basic expression of love that connects a woman and a man: laugher. If a couple doesn't laugh, something is wrong. In our occidental culture, during the courtship period, men tend to behave humorous, almost clownish, to impress women in most things we do. On the other hand, women tend to laugh to men's pirouettes as a response to the courting routine. In some couples, this pattern goes on for many years, some times forever. I can relate to that very vividly with my own wife. She used to laughs anytime I said something, or did something funny, until Gabriel was born. Then the laughs disappeared until three weeks ago when she and I reunited. Now I feel like joking and jumping, and she is laughing again. As long as the man is humorous, and the woman laughs at it, love will be present. And when love is present, happiness is around the corner, waiting for you.

We arrive to the Copenhagen airport at around nine in the morning. A taxi takes us downtown and drops us near the City Hall. Manuel is mesmerized with the beauty of Danish women. Who wouldn't be? "Hey Manuel, be careful when you walk. Look at the cars and bikes around you," I warn him.

We get to the hotel, check in, and I make the call to Laura. A man with a serious voice responds.

"Good morning," I say after his Danish greeting. This is Walker McBride. May I talk to Laura, please?" A couple of seconds later she responds.

"Walker! What a surprise! Where are you?"

I notice a nervous tone. "I am here in Copenhagen, with my apprentice Manuel and three guitars in hand. We finally made it, Laura. We have the original guitar repaired, plus the two replicas, as promised."

"That is great, Walker. Frederik will be amazed to hear that. You took a risk to come to Copenhagen without calling me first. I was not supposed to be here today."

"Yes, I know I should have called, Laura, but I had a plan B in case you weren't here. I read that Frederik has a concert in few days here in Copenhagen, so if I didn't see you, I could have given the guitars directly to him.

"When can we see each other?" She asks. "Tomorrow is a free day for me. Frederik is in Paris today, but I can take care of the guitars."

"Oh, what a pity. I want to see Frederik's face when he plays the replicas. But anyway, where can we meet?" I hear her talking in Danish to the man. I wonder who this guy is. She comes back and in a very soft, almost inaudible voice says, "Call me in half an hour." And then loudly, immediately after, says, "Let's meet here in my apartment at three in the afternoon, tomorrow. Bring your friend as well."

I realize she is scheming behind her friend's back. "Okay Laura, tomorrow at your apartment is fine. See you then. Good bye." And I hang up the phone.

Manuel is anxious to know the plan. "So, when is it?" He asks.

"Tomorrow at 3 p.m. The guitarist is not in town, but she can take the guitars."

"Oh, no! That is bad news. I wanted to meet the guitarist," he complains.

"I know, I know. Maybe we can stay a couple of days before going to Spain, so we can meet him."

He doesn't seem happy with my answer. "Well, okay," he responds.

"Why don't you walk around downtown while I take a nap?" I ask him.

He still seems disappointed, but grabs his jacket and leaves the room quietly. I plop myself down on the bed, and wait until it is time to call Laura. I keep thinking about Emily, Gabriel, and Christina, though. I don't know how to tell Laura what I am feeling now. Besides, who is this man who was with her? Maybe she already has a partner and I don't have to worry about it. I pull over a pillow to cover my eyes, and rest my head on another one.

Half and hour has passed. I wonder what her intentions are. If she is hiding something from her partner, it's not a good sign. I grab the phone, and put it back. I walk around the bed, back and forth, twice. I grab the phone again and I make the call.

"Hi, Laura, are you alone now?" I ask.

"Hi. You are a clever man, Walker. How do you know he is not here?"

"It doesn't matter how, but just to satisfy my curiosity, tell me, who is he?"

She hesitates for a moment, and responds, "I'll tell you when we meet in private. Do you have some time tonight? We could meet in Nyhavn. I know a good restaurant there."

I think for a moment and remember that Manuel is with me on this trip. "Well, I could, but what about Manuel? I cannot leave him alone."

"Oh, I forgot about him," she says. "The problem is that I leave for London the day after tomorrow, so I have no other chance to talk to you in private."

I try to come up with a solution, but I can't think of any. "Well, let's meet at 7 anyways. I'll see what I can do with Manuel."

She gives me the name of the restaurant —Fyrskibet. We finish the conversation and hang up. I go back to bed, and fall sleep, tired of scheming; tired of feeling disloyal; tired of faking and hiding feelings; tired of figuring out what to say and do each time I talk to her; tired of living two lives in one. That's is the price to pay for having a relationship like this.

Some hours later, when the sun is already gone, Manuel shows up in the room, "Hi Walker."

"Hi Manuel, how was your walk?"

"It was very nice. I walked along the cobblestone street called Ströget. You can't imagine how many stores they have. Anything you want to buy, you'll find it in that street. I walked all the way to the end of the street, where there is a statue in the middle of a round plaza. Also, I noticed they like bikes around here. I can't believe how many they have."

"It's great you like it. I had the same impression when I first came here," I reply.

"I am so tired!" He says. "I am going to bed right now, until tomorrow, nonstop."

I am lucky that I don't have to come up with an excuse to leave him alone. He'll stay in the room while I go for dinner with Laura. I encourage him to go out anyway. "But it is only 6, Manuel, the night is still young."

"No way I am going outside tonight. I'll see you tomorrow," he says and goes to the bathroom.

I dress up as soon as I can and get ready for the event of the night.

38

Fyrskibet

I GO DOWN STRÖGET STREET TO NYHAVN, a twenty minute walk from my hotel near the City Hall. I get to the Nyhavn area and start looking for the building where the restaurant should be. She said I couldn't miss it, because the canal is very short. I walked all the way to the last building in the canal, but the restaurant is not here. I ask for directions to a man on the street: "Sir, I am looking for a restaurant called Fyrskibet. Do you know where it is?"

"You passed it already," he replies. "Go back and you'll see a white boat with many lights on your left hand. The restaurant is *on* the boat."

"Thank you, thank you very much."

How could I know that the restaurant was on a boat? She didn't tell me. I am late already, five minutes after seven. I walk as fast as I can and get to the boat. This has to be it. I walk over the wooden platform connecting the sidewalk and the boat, and enter it. I see her sitting at one of the tables. She waves to me, and I go directly to her.

As I approach the table, she begins to stand. As always, her beauty leaves me perplexed. I approach her, and she hugs me like never before, and before I know it, she is kissing me as intensely as she can. I feel it is too long of a kiss, and back away my face from hers. She looks at me and says, "What happened?"

Now I know why time is relative. For me, the kiss was an eternity, but for her was probably a split second. "Nothing, it's that we are in public. You know, I don't like kissing in public."

"Oh, you silly Americans. All over Europe people kiss in public, what could be wrong with that?"

"You are right, but you also got me by surprise."

I grab her hand as we sit down. "You didn't tell me this was a restaurant on a boat," I complain.

She takes the napkin, put it in her lap and says, "I thought you might figure it out. Fyrskib means light boat in Danish."

"Well, my Danish is not *that* good," I reply. "So, let's be frank first. Who is the man who answered my call this morning?"

She smiles, stays quiet for a moment and says, "He is Viggo, my ex-husband. He wants a reconciliation." A silence fills the table until she says, "but I don't."

I notice that most tables are with couples, except one with seven people next to us. They are celebrating something. They have already had three toasts since I came.

"Oh, I see. Well, I have to be frank with you too."

She changes her posture and moves away, resting her back to her seat. "What is it?"

I am still distracted by the crowd at the next table. Specially because one of the guys at the table looks familiar to me, but I can't remember where I saw him before. They are laughing and laughing, and then I remember. Yes, this guy with glasses is the same person I saw in the restaurant near Cross Village in Michigan.

"What is it?" She asks again.

"It's about Emily and me," I say. "We are back together again."

I watch her body language carefully. She passed her hand behind her neck, and look to the side, vaguely, to the horizon. I can tell she is not happy with the news, but I have to continue: "It happened about three weeks ago. It was a very emotional moment for both of us. We found each other again after many, many years."

She's still looking away. She releases her hand from mine, and hides both of them under the table. "You should've told me before coming here," she says, still looking away.

"I preferred to tell you in person. We were going to meet anyway, so I thought it was better to do it face to face, in private, like now."

She looks down and tears falls on the red cloth of the table. The cloth soaks them, one by one, and the darker red stain grows slowly, as her pain grows with each beat of her heart. "I think we have nothing to talk about, then. Excuse me. Call me tomorrow about the guitars," she says while standing up, and grabbing her purse.

"But we don't have to end it like this," I say. "Please stay for the dinner. Give me a chance to explain."

She wipes her face and says, "I am sorry, but I can't. Sometimes, life doesn't treat you well. The person you don't desire is after you, and the person you do desire rejects you." And she turns around and leaves the boat before I can say anything else.

Why is it so difficult? Human relations are the most intriguing things in the world. It's all my fault. I sit and ask for a beer as I watch her disappearing in the crowd.

"Hello." It's the familiar man from the table of seven. "I think we know each other from Michigan, don't we."

I am still in shock from the abrupt departure of Laura. I should've followed her and convinced her to talk. But it's too late now.

"Helloooo," the guy insists.

"Oh, hi. How are you?" I say. "You are right, I was going to greet you when I saw you, but I was busy with my companion."

"We saw her leaving the boat," he tells me, "so I thought you could spend some time at our table, instead of drinking alone."

"Sure, why not. Her departure was unexpected," I say. He introduces me to his friends, all of them colleagues from the university, who are celebrating a doctoral graduation of one of their students, who actually is not here at the table. His colleagues are Joakim, a Swedish guy with an intense sagacious gaze; Ole, the typical well-mannered Dane; Pauli, a white-bearded smiley guy; Erik, who comes from Aalborg, a city far west of Copenhagen; Sine, the only woman at the table; and Giovanni, a visiting professor from Costa Rica who was enjoying the night in this uncommon restaurant.

This is a very rare situation. Danes are shy by nature, and rarely come forward to a stranger to invite them to a celebration. The guy I know from Michigan, whose name is Martin, seems a very sociable person, always laughing, and the heart of the conversation at the table. "What are you doing in Copenhagen?" He asks me.

"I came to deliver a guitar to Frederik Jacobsen."

"Frederik Jacobsen?" He exclaims.

"Do you know him?" I ask.

"Of course, everybody knows him. He is not only the best guitar player in Denmark, but one of the richest persons in the country, from a wealthy family owners of the largest beer company in Denmark. But tell me, what is so special about this guitar?"

The other guys keep drinking beer, while Martin and I begin talking about guitarmaking, "I am a luthier. I make custom-made guitars. Frederik commissioned me to make two replicas of an old guitar he had broken. After several weeks of work, plus the help of a design optimization expert from Michigan, I came up with two replicas that are as good as the original guitar."

"Optimization? What a coincidence, because all of us here at the table teach design optimization."

"Really? This is too much of a coincidence. By any chance, do you know Ole Rasmussen?" I ask out of curiosity.

"We all know professor Rasmussen. He was our teacher, a pioneer in the field. How do you know him?"

"Well, my friend from the States knows him, and we met one time here in Copenhagen when Frederik commissioned his guitars." Now I feel like being part of the company, surrounded by people that understand my problems in design. "And this friend of yours in the U.S., the old guy with the pony tail. How is he?"

"John? I talked to him last week. He finished his home in Cross Village, and is doing fine. He's been a friend of all of us here at the table for many years."

We keep talking about many different subjects, from life in Denmark and in the U.S., to the consequences of immigration in Denmark. We are all having a good time as more beer is poured in our glasses. In less than an hour I'm fully integrated, screaming 'SKÅL!' —the Danish word for 'cheers'— every time I have an excuse to do it. It's late already. I gather the strength to stand up, say good bye to my new friends. "SKÅL," I say once more before leaving the boat.

When I get to the hotel room, Manuel is still in bed snoring loudly with lights on. I try unsuccessfully to operate the switch for the light. I can't do it, not because I don't know how, but because my head is going crazy, the bed is moving, the walls are wavy, and I can't even grab the switch. A minute later, tired of trying and still with the lights on, I fall like a log on my bed. I couldn't change my clothes, but it doesn't matter now. I am almost dead.

Next day I wake up in the morning with a big headache, very disoriented, and feeling a hole in my stomach. Manuel is sitting on his bed, watching television, quite serious. "Hey Manuel, what time is it?"

He faces me, and says angrily, "Passed eleven." He keeps watching television.

I wonder why is he in a bad mood. "What's the problem?"

"Go to the bathroom, and you'll see," he replies with his teeth very tight.

I go to the bath, and I see what happened. It is a puddle of vomit from last night. What a disgusting smell and appearance. I take the paper towel and clean as much as I can, and go to the room to talk to Manuel. I don't know how to start. This is too embarrassing. I can't even remember when this happened.

"I am sorry, Manuel, very sorry. It's the first time this has happened to me," I say to him apologetically.

He nods to me, stands up, goes to the door and says, "I'll wait for you in the lobby, downstairs. Remember that the meeting with the client is at three."

He leaves the room, and I begin getting ready for the day. I take a shower, shave, and dress. I am all set. I need to call Laura before we leave. This is going to be an awful conversation. I dial the number. It's ringing, once, twice, and she answers. I talk before she can even answer. "Laura, it's me."

The line is mute for a second, but then she says. "Mr. McBride, I am glad you called. I was waiting for you to set the appointment."

It hurts when someone you feel fondness for, treats you so distantly, so cold. I have no other choice but accept it for now. "Well, are we still meeting at three?" I ask.

"I can't make it so early, but I am available after five. Can you make it?" She asks with a dry, sharp tone.

"Not a problem, I came to Copenhagen just for this, and I can arrange my visit at your convenience. Five is good."

"Okay then, I'll see you at five in the same restaurant where we ate with Kwame and Ole the first time we met." And she hangs up the phone.

I go downstairs, and find Manuel sitting in the lobby. He seems in a better mood now. "Manuel, we'll meet our customer at five. We have time to tour the city. What do you think?"

He is still mad for the mess in the bathroom. Quite seriously, he replies, "It's fine with me. Where could we go?"

"Let's go to the Royal Deer Park. It's a nice place to spend a couple of hours."

We agree and take a taxi to the entrance of the park. According to the tourist information, this park used to be the place where the royalty would come to hunt deer for fun. A herd of deer still roams and grazes in the park. As we walk along the green paths I begin to question Manuel about his girlfriend from the airport.

"Tell me, Manuel, this girl Natalia, what does she want to achieve in life?"

"She told me she would like to live in Alaska, in a big house with lots of rooms for guests that could visit us during summers."

I can't imagine Manuel having such a life. He is probably dazzled by her beauty, and can't see what problems he'd encounter in that life style. "And what do you want to achieve in life, Manuel?"

He looks at me, and realizes that I am being very objective. "Well, I always wanted to be a good guitar maker, even before I met you. But I also wanted to have a big house too."

I smile and say, "In Alaska too?"

He senses my sarcasm and replies, "Okay, I see your point. I have no intentions of living in Alaska, but she is flexible on this."

"Flexibility, mmm. That is very important in a relationship. As long as flexibility comes from both sides, and as long as your final goals in life are similar to hers, the relationship is likely to succeed. On the other hand, if the characters and opinions are rigid, if there is no flexibility in either side, or when goals are diverging, then the relationship is doomed to fail."

We reach a small castle in the middle of the park. This is the place where kings would sleep during the hunting season. There are lots of people around. Families, bikers, runners, all of them enjoying the fresh breeze and the green pasture. I check my watch and see that is time to go back. The time passed quickly.

"Manuel, let's go back to the hotel. We have just enough time to pick up the guitars and get to the restaurant."

We get the guitars from the hotel and head towards Lyngby, the suburb where the meeting was arranged. This is exciting for us. Manuel can't disguise his emotions about delivering these guitars that have been so carefully made.

We enter the restaurant, take a table, sit and wait for Laura.

"What does she look like?" Manuel asks.

"She is tall, thin, blue eyes," I say with a tone of indifference.

"Is she pretty?"

"Well ... yes. She is pretty. You'll see." We both turn our attention to the main door, and see Laura just coming in. "There she is," I say.

Manuel looks at me with that mischievous face, one that says 'aha! I got you.' I ignore him.

"Good afternoon, gentlemen," she says very politely.

I have the feeling this meeting is going to be short. "Good afternoon, Laura. This is Manuel Castellanos, my apprentice."

They greet each other and then she goes directly to the business. "My brother couldn't be here today, but I can take care of the replicas for him."

She opens her purse and pulls a check for the amount agreed. "This is your payment. Thank you very much for your work Mr. McBride. I heard from Ole that you worked very hard on this project."

Manuel seems uncomfortable under so much formalism and dryness. "I can play the guitars for you if you want," he says. "You should listen before paying."

"You are very kind, Manuel, but it's not necessary," she replies.

I can't continue with this hypocrisy. It is absurd to keep faking being so distant. My feelings are hurt very much. I stand up, take the check from the table, and make a signal to Manuel to follow me to the exit. "Thank you, Laura, and good bye," I say and leave.

Outside the restaurant, Manuel looks at me perplexed for what he just saw. "That was too rude, Walker. I thought she was your friend."

"I know," I say, "but you don't know many other things that have happened between us that I can't tell you. But don't worry; it's over now. We have our big check, and she got her guitars."

Before we get a taxi, Laura steps out of the restaurant with another envelop in her hand, "Walker, please take this. Inside you'll find two tickets for Frederik's guitar concert in the Royal Theater tomorrow," she says. "I was planning to use them but I have a trip to London. I thought you and Manuel could go together to watch and listen Frederik playing your guitar."

Manuel, with wide open eyes and happy, looks at me, expecting a positive answer. I feel so bad now. I can see she is trying to keep our friendship despite our impasse. I approach her, take the envelope, kiss her cheek, and whisper: "I am sorry. It was my mistake. Thank you for this. Manuel and I will never forget this gesture of yours."

39

The Aranjuez Dream

EXT MORNING, I AM STILL IN BED, WITH eyes open, staring at the ceiling of the room, when I hear the phone ringing. Who could it be so early? "Hello?"

"Walker?"

It sounds like Emily, but she should be sleeping by now. It's 2:00 AM in Michigan. "Emily?"

"Yes, honey, it's me."

"What happened? Are you okay?"

"I am okay, and I am here in Copenhagen, in the lobby of your hotel," she replies.

It must be another of my dreams. She can't be here. "What did you say?"

"I said I was here in the hotel. Please come downstairs and I'll explain it to you."

"What are you doing here? Where are the kids?"

"They are also with me."

She passes me to the hotel's clerk and I ask him to let them come to my room. This is crazy. How could this be? Besides, she is with Gabriel and Christina, who should be in school today. I don't understand.

Manuel is still sleeping, but I won't bother him until I know what's going on. Someone knocks at the door. I'm still skeptical, but walk to the door. I open it, and there they are, all three of them. I hug Gabriel, Christina, and kiss Emily. "I can't believe you are here. What is this?" I ask Emily.

Gabriel jumps to the bed, and turns on the television. Christina keeps hugging me while Emily explains, "Two days ago I got a call from Kwame. He told me he had four airline tickets to go to Copenhagen provided by a friend of yours, a famous Danish guitarist. Then he told me that he had tickets for a guitar concert tonight, and that we would be there with you. Now *you* tell me, what is this all about? Who is this friend?"

"Well," I say, "my friend is Frederik Jacobsen. He is the classical guitarist we are going to listen to in the concert. But I didn't know anything about his plans of inviting you guys to his concert. This is a crazy idea of his. But where is Kwame?"

"Kwame had to meet with another friend of his. He said he will be at the concert," Emily says.

With all this commotion, plus the noisy TV, Manuel wakes up, greets the newcomers, and perplexed, listens to Emily's story. "This is incredible," he exclaim.

I sit on the bed, while Christina is still glued to me. "It is incredible, but a dream come true. Can you imagine? All who I love, together in one place: my wife, my kids, my friends, and a professional guitarist playing one of my guitars. I can't believe it."

"You deserve it, dad. It is happening because you worked hard all these years," Christina says.

Emily puts her arm on my shoulders, and wipes tears from my face. "I am also happy, honey. I was waiting for this to happen, some day. You know what, I brought your black suit for the concert. I want you to look handsome tonight. And I also brought another one for Manuel."

"Mom, I'm tired," Gabriel complains.

"I'm tired too," Christina repeats.

I understand them. It's a long exhausting overnight trip. "Why don't you guys rest a couple of hours before going to the concert? A ten hour flight is really tiring. Mom and I will go tour the city in the meantime. How about that?"

They both agree and go to bed quickly. Emily, Manuel and I go out together. As we walk along the cobblestone street, Ströget, I realize how fortunate I've been to get to know about the Danish culture. How responsible they are, how forgiving and how much they value friendship. "Emily, I want you to meet Frederik's sister tonight. I am almost sure she'll be there. She has been my contact with the guitar repairing project and has been very encouraging to me."

"Walker," Manuel interrupts, "she said she had to go to London. I don't think she will be at the concert."

"Yes, I remember that," I reply, "but I have the feeling that they had a plan from the beginning."

"They who?" Emily asks.

"Kwame, Ole, Laura and Frederik. I think that once Ole knew I was coming, he called Laura, and they made the arrangements for this to happen."

We continue walking along the busy street, looking at store windows, watching artists painting and singing. We stop to listen to a guitarist playing on the sidewalk, surrounded by many people. The crowd around him is so dense that it is difficult to get close to him. We manage to penetrate the crowd and stand in the first row. He is playing a beautiful piece that I can't recognize. "Do you know that piece," I whisper to Manuel.

"Of course. It's *Natalia*, from Antonio Lauro," he replies quite proud of his knowledge.

"Hey, Walker," Manuel whispers to me. "Did you see the rosette of his guitar?"

I walk closer to the guitarist to have a better view of the guitar's rosette, and to my great surprise, I notice it is one of my guitars. I can't believe it. I step back and say to Manuel and Emily, "Yes, this guitar was made by me, a long time ago."

We wait until he finishes the Lauro's piece. When the crowd is gone, and the guitarist begins packing his instrument, I approach him. "Hi, I am Walker McBride, and this is my wife Emily, and my friend Manuel."

He replies with a good New York accent: "Hi, I am Mike Anderson, from Brooklyn, New York. Did you say McBride?"

"Yes, McBride. m-c-b-r-i-d-e." I quickly reply, hoping that he recognizes my last name.

"What a coincidence, my guitar was made by a guy with the same name, Walker McBride. Look here, inside."

"You don't have to show me. I know very well. I am the same Walker McBride that signed inside your guitar. When I saw the rosette on your guitar I knew it was one of my guitars."

"Oh boy, I've got to tell you this well kept secret among bohemian guitarists like me. Your guitars are high quality, awesome looking, and affordable. You can't imagine how much more you could charge for your guitars. Big guitar companies dominate the market, but these are the guitars preferred by us. We get the most for our bucks."

"I am glad to hear that. I never thought there was a special market for bohemian guitars," I reply.

"Oh, yeah," he continues, "If you play in the streets, you've got to have a sturdy guitar, and yours are the best. Can I ask you for an autograph? Right here on the sound box."

"Oh, I am flattered. Sure, I have a marker here with me." As I sign the guitar, he tells me he bought it about three years ago, from another guitarist who had quit playing because of some premature arthritis. I sign the guitar, and shake hands with the guy.

He looks at my left arm and asks, "Excuse me for asking, but how can you make such good guitars with only one hand?"

I've never been asked such a question so direct, but I don't see why I should care about being handicapped. I've proved to myself that I can do it better than anybody. "Mental toughness can always

surpass any physical disability. And good assistants also helps," I
reply to him as I pat Manuel, and hug Emily.

We keep walking in this marvelous day when everything seems
to fit in place in my life. I've never thought I could be so happy as
today. When we reach the end of Ströget, at the moment I see the
big statue at the center of the Kongens Nytorv plaza —Christian
V on his horse— I remember what the street guitarist said: high
quality, awesome looking, and affordable. These are the three Bs
Kwame always talks about. It means that my guitars have always
been BBB guitars, at least for these type of guitarists.

We cross the street, and get to the plaza from where we can see
the Royal Theater, the location of the upcoming concert. We keep
walking and stop in the Nyhavn area to have a good European
cappuccino in one of the cafés. From the table where we sit, I can
see the white boat where Laura and I met two nights ago. We finish
our coffees and then decide to go back to the hotel to get dressed
for the big event.

W hen we are in the hotel, with all of us ready and impeccably
dressed, the hotel clerk calls and says, "Mr. McBride, you have
two taxis waiting for you to take you to the Royal Theater. It is a
courtesy of Ms. Jacobsen."

I hang up and say, "Well guys, we are being treated like kings
of Denmark. Two taxis are waiting for us downstairs."

"Yes!" Gabriel says, as he lifts his hands up and runs around
the bed.

When we arrive at the theater, the valet opens the doors for us
and guides us to the entrance. I have the tickets, and when I show
them to the attendant, she says, "This way, please." We go through
the *Special Guests* door. The lady guides us to an elevator, and to
the balcony seats. When we get there, I see Laura already seated
along with a tall guy who is resting his arm over her shoulders. I
knew she was going to be here. We get to our seats, next to Laura's.

"Hi, Laura."

C.A. Soto Aguirre

She smiles with elation and says, "Hi, Walker, I am glad to see you again."

"Laura, first of all, thank you very, very much for this. You can't imagine how much happiness you have brought me with this treat. Please thank Frederik for this too. You both now have a special place in my heart. I'll never forget this moment."

"It is a pleasure for me and Frederik to treat you well. My brother is delighted with the guitar you made for him."

I look at her companion, and smile to him. She notices the exchange of glances and says, "Let me introduce you to my husband, Viggo."

I am surprised, but also happy for this. I feel closure of this episode of our impossible relationship. Now I can proceed with my life, and she with hers. "Nice to meet you," I say. "This is my family: my wife Emily, my daughter Christina, my son Gabriel and my friend and future star in the art of guitarmaking, Manuel."

We shake hands and sit. Seconds after, Emily whispers to my ear, "She is so beautiful...but not your type." I say nothing, but a smile of relief shows in the corner of my mouth as I sigh inside myself.

We read the concert program which includes the concerto *Aranjuez* from Joaquín Rodrigo, a lovely concerto that can't be more appropriate for my guitar. It is the purest Spanish piece along with *Recuerdos de la Alhambra* by Francisco Tárrega.

As we wait for the orchestra to be ready, we are mesmerized by the beauty of this place. We look around the majestic theater and admire the architecture and art all around us. There are four big balconies, plus two small ones on each side, very close to the stage. We are in one of these. There is a huge chandelier with what seems like millions of light bulbs. The golden ceiling is fully decorated creating an atmosphere of grandiosity. I haven't seen anything like this before.

The musicians from the orchestra are tuning their instruments when I hear, "Hello, hello!" It is Kwame with Ole. I knew they both were coming together. "Hi, Kwame, nice to see you here. Ole! Nice to see you too; you look great. Let me introduce you to my wife, Emily, my kids, Gabriel and Christina, and my friend Manuel."

"Nice to meet you all," Ole, replies. "I understand that we are going to listen to the fruit of his work today, aren't we?" He says while pointing to me and smiling to the kids.

"Yes, we are. Frederik is going to use a guitar that my dad made just for him," Christina replies. Nice support from my daughter. It is good for children to admire their parents. They are the closest role models they have when they are growing. It is much easier to influence their character if they admire you.

We get comfortable, and wait for the concert to begin. I'm feeling nervous. Frederik enters the stage, and we all applaud. He bows to the audience and sits. The director raises the baton, and a sepulchral silence fills the theater. He nods to Frederik who nods back. A brisk movement of the director's baton and the concert starts. Frederik, while waiting for the time of his entrance, looks at us in the balcony, and squint at us. I take a look at Laura. She has her head resting on Viggo' shoulder.

I turn to Emily and ask her, "Is this a dream?"

"No, honey, this is real. This is a dream come true for you." She grabs my right hand and gives me a tender kiss on the cheek.

After the last note of the concert the audience rises and claps with fervor. *Bravo! Bravo!* The audience yells. Frederik bows to them and leaves the stage. The public keeps clapping and cheering for him. He returns once, twice, and the third time, he decides to perform a solo to calm the audience. The silence comes back as he sits down. This time, before he begins, he grabs the microphone and says, "This goes to my very good friend, the internationally famous and superb luthier, who made this marvelous guitar I am playing with tonight, Walker McBride who is in the left balcony."

I stand up, wave, and the audience goes crazy. This is the best moment of my career, and my family is with me. I will remember this for the rest of my life.

Frederik plays the solo piece and the concert ends with more applause. We decide to accompany Laura behind stage to meet

Frederik. When I see him, I can't control myself and hug him with gratitude. "Thank you Frederik. You made me the happiest person tonight."

"Thank *you*, instead. Your guitars are the best guitars I've ever played. I am in debt to your artistic qualities and your professionalism as luthier."

I introduce my family to him, and stay in the theater for a while talking about the concert, the guitars, his schedule of recitals, and most importantly, about his intentions of promoting my guitars among his friends. I can't ask for a better friendship with him and Laura. I love these Danes.

We go back to our hotel in the same taxis we came in. The kids go to bed. Manuel will take care of them while Emily and I go out to have a glass of wine to celebrate. We go back to Nyhavn and when I see the boat restaurant, I say, "I want you to know this place." We enter the white, fully lit boat. I ask for the table in the stern of the boat. This is the most private place in the boat. Only one table fits in here, and the waiter has to climb stairs each time he comes. We ask for two glasses of red wine and watch the moon in a clear Danish night. For the first five minutes there are no words between us, just gazes and caresses.

"What are you thinking," Emily asks.

"I can't even think. I am just feeling the moment. I feel I was born again today. That is all that counts for me. I have the energy to grow as much as I want, with no limits, no impairment, nothing that restrains me."

"That is the Walker I fell in love with many years ago," she says.

"I am me again. I can feel it. You'll see what I will do when I come back to Michigan."

"We leave tomorrow," she reminds me. "Are you still going to Spain?"

"Manuel and I are leaving tomorrow to visit a master luthier in Spain, at the same place where I took the training class. I want Manuel to meet the teachers."

The Guitar Maker

We finish our wine, pay and leave this special boat which is now part of my history, my very personal history.

40

Life's Three Phases

ANUEL AND I ARE DRIVING FROM MADRID to Sigüenza in a car we rented in the airport after our flight from Copenhagen. The sky has been clear the entire trip, with a cool breeze that we are enjoying with the windows down. We pass by the exits to *Torrejón*, *Alcalá* and *Guadalajara* along the highway A-2/E-90. With a smile of happiness, Manuel faces me and says, "It's nice to see city names in Spanish. In Michigan I feel so foreign surrounded by unfamiliar names. Did you see that we passed the exit to *Guadalajara?* That's a Mexican city too; I've been there."

I say nothing, as I see him enjoying a conversation with himself. We keep driving along the highway until we take the exit to the road 'CM-1101' which should take us to Sigüenza. We get to the famous *Parador* where I stayed last time I came. We unload the suitcases and go to our rooms for a quick rest from the trip.

I then make a call to the master luthier Don Rodrigo, who I met when I was here for my training, and who is expecting us today.

I arrange the time for the visit —half an hour from now. Manuel and I get set and leave the hotel heading to the monastery. When we get there, we pass the internal gardens, nicely done as always, and go directly to the workshop where Don Rodrigo should be waiting. I open the door and see the group of students working on their guitars. Don Rodrigo is sitting in a rocking chair, watching his apprentices from afar, but very attentive to any mistake.

"Don Rodrigo!" I say.

"Walker, I am glad to see you again," he replies. He pats my shoulder and extends his arm to shake Manuel's hand. "And this young man is ..."

"Manuel. This is a real pleasure to meet you personally," Manuel replies.

"Manuel? *Hablas Español?*

"Yes, I mean, *perdón, si, sí hablo Español. Mi familia es de Nicaragua.*

Don Rodrigo keeps talking to Manuel in Spanish, sets his arm around the young fellow's shoulders, and guides him to the other room where I suppose he will teach Manuel some tricks of guitar-making.

I leave the shop and head towards the kitchen, where Father Mauricio should be. I need to talk to him. As I walk through the dark hallways of the monastery a shadow appears in front of me.

"How are you, my dear son?" It's him, with a smiley face and, as the first time we met, with that aura of wisdom and serenity that all monks have.

"Father Mauricio! It is so nice to see you again. I was looking for you," I say as I hug him as one hugs old friends.

"A good friend always brings happiness to an old heart like mine," he replies.

We walk to a bench at the end of the hallway, and sit. I say nothing for a moment, trying to put my thoughts in order. He waits patiently, inside his maroon monastic habit, as if he knew what I am going to say. I begin telling him about how fortunate I am. "I came to tell you that I am a happy person that has found good friends to support me, and an excellent wife to encourage me. When I met you the first time, Father, I was having many personal problems, which were consuming my life from inside. I remember I told you about how to solve problems between two people by being in the shoes of each other, and it worked in my case. It did. Now, my wife and I have entered a happy period and I feel energized to construct an even happier life for both of us."

He smiles and says, "I am glad to hear that. God has given you a second chance to build your life."

"I thought that my wife and I were on opposite sides, but suddenly we came to be so close now."

He plays with his long white beard and says, "There is a principle that you should learn today. It is the concept of *opposites being the same*. It is hard to understand sometimes. Let's talk about hot and cold. You may think they are opposite, but in reality, they are the same. They are two degrees of expression of the same physical quantity —temperature. In other words, hot is less cold, and cold is less hot. There is no absolute definition of cold or hot. They are just relative to each other, and next to each other."

I listen with attention, but can't find the reason he is telling me this. "And what is the connection with my life?"

He smiles and says, "The connection is that your wife and you were never in opposite sides, but next to each other. That explains why you 'suddenly' are so close to her, because you were actually together, touching each other, all the time."

This is a difficult concept. How could opposite sides be together? I'll have to think more about this. He notices how puzzled I am, and says, "I think you need to think about this concept. It is a hard one to understand the first time around."

I nod and say, "Father, there is something more I want to talk about."

"Wait, I have another thing to teach you. This may also explain your new proximity to your wife. How old are you?"

"Forty nine."

"Then let me tell you about the three phases in life. Each phase has its period at different ages, but all three are present during your entire life. The first one is the phase of acquiring knowledge. In this phase you spend most of your time learning from others —parents and teachers, and from your own experiences. If you are clever enough, your create your own wisdom as years pass." He pauses, waiting for a reaction from me. I simply nod.

"The second phase of life is the building phase. Once you feel confident with your knowledge, once you think you know what it takes to survive, you start building a family, a home, a career, wealth." He pauses again, and I am beginning to see myself in his descriptions. I nod again.

"Finally, there is the third phase of life —the phase of giving. When you feel you've built enough in your life you start feeling the need for giving of what you have accumulated. You need to give back to your family, friends, even strangers, what you cannot take with you beyond this life. It is in the third phase that love flourishes in a different way. You begin loving all who are around you every day. Then your spouse becomes the person you feel most attached to, and the person who understand your feelings, your needs, your habits."

"Okay, Father, are you telling me that I am in the third face of life?"

"Right. Each phase lasts about twenty five to thirty years, so you are at about the beginning of the third phase. But remember, you keep learning all your life, you keep building all your life, and you keep loving all your life. It is that each phase has its 'dominant' period in the life of every person."

"You know what," I say, "now that you explain this to me, I realize that I've been a knowledge getter all my life, a guitar maker —a builder— since my mid twenties, and now I feel this urgency to teach, to give back, to love my friends, my family."

"So, you agree with me. But now tell me, what is it that you want to tell me?"

I take a deep breath, pause for a moment, and say, "It's about death." He opens his eyes with surprise, lean forwards, and listens with attention.

"I think, I am sick, very sick," I seriously say. "It may be my brain. I lose consciousness sometimes."

"Did you go to your doctor?" He asks.

"No, I haven't had the time."

"Time? What is more important than health? He asks with a tone that mixes anger and surprise. "Your life is a gift from God that you have been required to live and take care of with the highest diligence. You *must not* treat this lightly."

"This is precisely the point I wanted to talk about. Since I don't believe in life after death, nor in resurrection, I want to hear from you about this subject."

He plays with his beard again and says, "Death is a transition stage, and my belief is that you go to heaven or hell depending on your deeds in this world."

"This is too simplistic, Father. I need a more logical and practical answer. What should I tell my kids, my wife? Should they even know what is going on?"

"I've been living in this monastery for more than forty years, and it is hard for me to be as practical as you want me to be. My answers are based on faith. Remember, God cannot be explained logically, and faith is illogical by definition, hence, it is nonsense to debate God's will, or even God's existence. I told you before, you either believe, or don't believe. Being practical is a matter beyond my wisdom. But common sense tells me that the best you can do is go to the doctor and tell your family the situation as best as you can explain it. If you don't say anything, their ignorance will backfire on you, and it will be worse then."

"But I am afraid they may not take it easily," I say. "This news would be heart breaking. I don't think they are prepared for this yet."

"Preparation is a big, big word, Walker. We spend our lives preparing ourselves for everything. We prepare for adulthood, for marriage, for competitions. We prepare for jobs, for children, for everything, Walker. Life is just a series of *'being prepared for'* tasks. However, few understand the type of preparation we need, especially, the preparation we need to die."

I sit back on the wooden bench, an old bench that has been here for decades I guess. After thinking about what he just said,

I respond. "I do understand, I think. Lately, I've been thinking a lot, talking to a wise friend I met recently, and I've come to some conclusions about this subject. This is probably not new for you, and it is sort of common sense now that I know it, but sometimes common sense is not commonly found. In life we need to be prepared in three ways —physically, mentally and emotionally."

He grabs one flower from a pot next to the bench, smells it, and says, "You missed one aspect. This explains why you came to ask me about death, because you are missing one important part of the preparation of life, that I think you've been ignoring for years. I agree with the three aspects you mentioned. You need to prepare yourself physically, with exercise, good sleep, and good eating habits. You need to be prepared mentally, acquiring knowledge and exercising creativity in your daily life. You need to be prepared emotionally, with the right combination of laughs and tears, and expressing your love to your friends and family. However, all that preparation is not enough for the supreme experience of all. I am talking about the experience of dying. We need to prepare ourselves *spiritually* in order to fill the fourth quadrant of life. Spirituality ties all other aspects together, giving a coherent understanding of contradictory and adversary events in life, like misfortune and fortune, illness and health, sadness and happiness, hatred and love and, or course, death and birth."

We both stay quiet as if we were talking in silence, trying to understand each other's comments. I break the silence with a question that has been dancing in my mind for a long time. "I have another question for you, if I may. What is the purpose of life? Why are we here?"

He scratches his bald head, smiles, and says, "Only God knows, but if you read the ten commandments, you'll find the answer."

I don't like his answer. It is too evasive and with a tone of resignation. "I am more pragmatic, Father, I'm going to give you my answer to that question. I think there is only one purpose in life."

With a smile in his face, he says, "I don't think that any human being can answer that question, but I am curious to know your opinion?"

"In my opinion, the purpose of life is to change yourself from what you are today, to what you can be, in a better way, tomorrow. And this also apply to the people you encounter in life. The purpose is to change their lives —with your words, your acts, how you treat them— in order to make them happier so that they, in turn, change another person and onward through an endless chain of improvement."

He poses his hand on my shoulder and says, "*sapere aude.*"

"What is that?"

"It's Latin for *dare to reason by yourself.* You have a lot of that; I like it. You are a man of the world, Walker, and I am a monk of the monastery. You may be right, but how do you achieve that, if you don't have the spiritual foundation?"

"We need," I reply, "not only the spiritual foundation, but the knowledge foundation combined with love to share our knowledge, our time, our feelings, honestly, and sincerely."

Time has passed quickly, and the stone walls of the monastery have this reddish cast from the setting sun. Father Mauricio closes his eyes, meditates for about a minute while I stay silent, observing, respecting his ritual. When he opens his eyes, I smile, and he mirrors my smile. "I think," he says, "we are talking about the same thing, but with different perspectives. You are right, knowledge provides ability to create changes to achieve happiness. And love allows each of us to share that knowledge to change this world to a better one."

I wish I could talk to him more often. I grab the flower from his hand, smell it, and give it back to him. "Thank you, Father, it was a nice conversation. I needed to talk to some one like you. I'll visit my doctor soon, after I get back home." We hug and go back to our places.

I walk back to the guitar shop to see what Manuel is doing. I knock on the door, open it, and see him and Don Rodrigo working on a side bending, using the heat machine. "Hello guys, how is it going?"

"Walker, you need to see how easy this method of making the side curvature is," Manuel replies enthusiastically.

I am glad to see he learning something new today. As Father Mauricio said, he is just getting prepared in life. "Manuel, I'll go back to the hotel to take a shower."

"I'll be there in an hour or so," he replies. "Take the car, because I am planning to walk along the river Henares that passes close to town.

"Don Rodrigo, thank you for your time," I say, "We'll stay in contact."

"You are welcome any time. Manuel is a pleasure to work with, too. Have a good trip back home."

I leave the monastery and drive to the hotel. Tomorrow I will be flying back to Michigan to continue my journey, my renovated journey of life.

41

Hard Rocks

I HEAR CHRISTINA YELLING FROM AFAR. "Dad, Dad, wake up. It's eleven!" I hear steps running to my bed. "Dad, I am glad you made it," and she poses her head on my chest.

"Hi, honey."

"Dad, do you remember what day is today?" She asks me without lifting her head.

"Saturday," I say with a tired voice. "Honey, I am really exhausted. I just came home three hours ago, after a long flight from Madrid. I want to sleep a bit more."

"But Dad, today is the day," she insists.

"What day?"

"Duh! Tennis! The state tennis tournament. I thought you made plans for this. You promised to be here by today because of this."

I finally open my eyes, grab her by an arm, and say, "Okay, help me to stand." She has been practicing for three months already, trying to get ready for this big day. I can't let her down. "Where is mom?" I ask.

"She is in the mall with Gabriel. They should be back soon."

She leaves the room; I get dressed and go downstairs. Christina is wearing a new pair of red shoes with black and yellow stripes in each side. "I like your shoes, Christina."

"Thank you, Dad. You know what, you have changed. Last time I had new shoes you didn't even care about the color of whatever I was wearing. Now you notice it right away."

"We change as we age, honey. We are always changing. I hope you understand how important is to adapt and welcome changes." I hear the horn of the Emily's car. "Okay, let's go. Mom is waiting," I say.

I kiss Emily as soon as I enter the car. "Hi, Gabriel."

"Hi, Dad. Mom and I bought new lawn chairs to watch Christina's games. The old ones were falling apart. We are ready for a long day under the sun."

I look at Christina and ask her, "Chris, are you prepared?"

She smiles at me and says, "Of course, Dad. I've been preparing for this tournament since we started the school year."

Wisely, Father Mauricio was right. We spend our lives preparing for something, all the time. We spend more time in the preparation than in the final event. Sometimes we are distracted by the importance of the event, when in reality we should pay more attention to the preparation phase. Christina is prepared; Gabriel is prepared; Emily is prepared, and I am prepared. "Let's go and play, then!" What is going to happen today is simply the result of all the preparation we made before today, more than her performance during the game.

As we drive to the tennis courts I am pensive, introverted, thinking about how my family would cope if I were suddenly to die. I can't even imagine the situation. I realize that this is a lack of preparation on my part, and that, maybe, Father Mauricio was trying to make me aware of. What should I do, then? How can one prepare for passing away and leave the family ready to accept and manage the new situation?

We get to the high school where the games are taking place. The kids run fast to the courts, and leave us behind. Emily and I walk to the courts and sit under a shady tree, on a ground covered by large stones. The sun is merciless, but the shade is dense and large. Gabriel helps Christina with the tennis gear —racket, balls, towels, all that. Emily looks at me and says, "What were you thinking in the car? You were all distracted. What happened in Spain?"

"Nothing, nothing happened in Spain that you should be concerned about. But you are right, I was thinking about a difficult subject."

"Like what?"

"Like death," I say at the same time that I stare at her eyes.

A silence penetrates the air between us. "Why are you thinking about that?" She asks.

I don't want to tell her about my dizziness and passing outs yet. "Nothing. It was just a thought." Then I realize that I am not preparing her for the possibility of being without me. "Well, actually there is something I need to tell you," and I glance down.

"What is it?" She asks with a soft voice, almost whispering, to avoid other parents hearing our conversation.

I swallow big, and say, "I think I am ill."

"Ill?" And she laughs loudly. "You are a horse, Walker. You must be kidding."

"But I am, Emily. I pass out once in a while, for no reason."

She opens her eyes wide as two moons. "Why didn't you tell me before?"

"I don't know. I was thinking that I could go to the doctor without you knowing, and resolve the problem by myself. I didn't want to scare you, or scare the kids."

She shrugs her shoulders and say "You have to go to the doctor. Monday morning we go together. We are not talking about a tennis game, we are talking about your life."

"I know. I was planning to go, but then the trip to Denmark was in the middle, and I postponed the appointment."

"Blah blah blah ... excuses. How could you be so, so, ..."

"*Stupid*, I know," I complete her sentence.

"I didn't say that. I meant to say that these things are taken care of first, then other responsibilities come after that."

I gaze away from her, with the saddest face I've ever had in many years. She says nothing for a moment, but tries to cheer me up. "Walker, being sick doesn't mean you are going to die. It's not the end of the world, but we have to take care of this as soon as possible."

"Yes, we need to be prepared for the worst, don't we," I say.

She shakes her head and says, "You sound like the bad Walker; not like the good Walker I want you to be."

No more words about this are said, and we sit quiet, waiting for the first tennis game. Her words resonate in my head, *—it doesn't mean you are going to die.*

We hear the parents cheering for their children as they enter the court. Gabriel is back, and sits on his new chair. "Why did you pick this spot over here," he complains, "there are too many rocks; the floor is not flat here. I can't sit without rocking."

"Don't whine and watch. Your sister is about to start her game," I say.

Christina looks calm, and her eyes tell me how focused and poised she is. As the match goes, the superior athleticism and strategy of Christina is evident. In less than an hour the match ends with a score 6-2, 6-0 in favor of the girl with the red shoes, my daughter.

"Dad," Christina says after finishing the game, while hanging on my neck, "I couldn't loose today. I was so well prepared!"

We all hug her for a moment, and feel joy because of her victory. We pack our stuff, the bags, and the new chairs. We walk over the rocky ground, back to our car. The sun is shining strong and the humidity is high. I stare at the sun, and before I notice, my sight goes blind, I lose my balance, and I feel as if I were suddenly hit on my forehead........

Coma

weeks of nothingness...

nothingness...

    nothingness...

      nothingness...

Awakening

IFT HERE, CHRISTINA. Dad likes to be comfortable, and this position is twisting his neck. Right here."

"Mom, we have turned him around three times in less than twenty minutes, already. I can't do it so often."

"Don't do it then! Gabriel, please help me to lift your dad's head."

I feel cold hands around the back of my head. It hurts. My chest hurts too, and my muscles feel weird, weak.

"Thank you, Gabriel. Your sister has no feeling for her father, today."

"Mom, it's not that, you know how much I love Dad, but ...

"Mom, mom, he is moving! I swear. He moved his eyes!"

"Are you sure, Gabriel?"

I am trying to talk, but my jaw is heavy and my lips are like glued to each other. I hear Gabriel, and Christina, and Emily, too. What is happening to me?

"Yes, mom, he moved again. Watch his mouth... You see? He is moving."

Yes, I am here. Don't you hear me?

"Christina, call the doctor."

"Yes, mom."

I'm trying to talk, but still, why is it so difficult? Is it a dream again? "Emmmm ... Em Em"

"Oh God! He is talking! Doctor! Quick!

"Honey-ney-ney, it's me-e-e-e. I can't talk-k-k-k."

"Yes, Walker. Say my name —Emily, Emily. I am here with you. Say my name honey, please, say my name."

"Em ... Emmmm ... Emil-lll ... Emily-ly-ly. What ... happened to me-e-e-e?" I utter.

"Oh God! You are back! You are back!"

I feel an embrace, strong and warm. I feel tears on my chest too.

"You were in coma for three months, honey, but you are back, now. Oh God, thank you."

I still can't see anything. My eyelids are also heavy. I feel so strange and disoriented. I barely open my left eye, trembling, but my right eye is still immovable. I see a white blurred figure coming to me.

"Excuse me, Ms. McBride, let me examine him."

"Thank you, Doctor. Thank you for coming so fast," I hear Emily saying.

I feel a finger on my eyelids and a light shining on my eyes.

"Do you hear me?" the doctor asks.

I nod my head, but can't talk at the same time.

"Good, very good. Could you tell me your full name?" He asks.

"Walker-r-r-r McBride-d-d-d," I barely say.

"Do you know who is here with me in the room?" He asks.

I nod. "Emily-ly-ly, Christina-na-na-na, Gabriel-l-l-l."

"Okay, take it easy. Don't talk any more. Just nod or shake your head to answer my questions." He keeps examining my body.

Now I feel a cold object on my chest. It must be a stethoscope. Then something pinches my left leg.

"Do you feel anything?"

I nod. I see the white blurred figure moving from the left of the bed, to the right.

"Do you feel anything?"

I shake my head.

"Do you feel anything now?"

I shake my head.

"Okay," he says, "I'll call the nurse to take care of you for a second, Walker. I'll be back as soon as I can. We are glad you are back with us. Congratulations. Ms. McBride, could you come with me, please?"

Something is wrong. Why am I here in this bed? What happened to me? The last thing I remember is my trip to Denmark with Manuel to deliver the replicas to Laura.

I look around, and see Gabriel and Christina sitting on a bench. What are these monitors around me?

"Where-r-r-r am I?"

"Dad, don't talk. You are in the hospital," Christina says, as she approaches the bed.

Hospital? Why? I must be dreaming.

"You went through a brain operation a week after you fell head first on the stony ground the day of my tennis tournament. You lost consciousness, then you had convulsions, and we had to call an ambulance to bring you here. You have been here since, for three months, in a coma."

"Gabriel-l-l-l, come please-ss-ss-ss," I say.

He walks to the bed, hugs me, and starts crying. "Dad, dad, I thought you were going to die."

My tears roll down my cheek, too. "Don't cry-ih-ih-ih."

"You should not talk, dad. Your brain is still swollen, and you need to rest to get well," Christina says.

I see the blurry image of Emily entering the room. "Emily-ly-ly-ly ... come-m-m-m," I say.

"Yes, honey, I am here. What do you want?"

"I need-d-d-d you-u-u-u. Don't leave-ev-ev-ev."

"I won't leave you. I've been sleeping in this room since the first day, praying for you to wake up. Now you are alive and I won't leave you alone."

I feel tired already; I feel confused.

"Okay, kids, let your Dad rest," I hear Emily saying, and at a distance, I also hear Gabriel's voice saying "Why is he talking like that?"

"Gabriel, please, let's talk outside," Emily responds.

I can't hear anything else, but I am so tired mentally, that ....

Five days have passed since I woke from the coma, and I am feeling better each hour. I can talk normally, without drooling and in long sentences. However, the doctor told me that I had a paralysis of the right side of my body. Yesterday I started physical therapy. It was painful, physically and spiritually, since I could barely do anything the therapist asked me to do. The doctor said that in six months, and if I focus my mind on this, I could fully recover my mobility again. The sooner the better, he said. I am not going to let my only hand be paralyzed for the rest of my life. I'll work on this therapy like nobody else.

Emily enters the room with my breakfast in a tray. "Hi, honey. How did you sleep last night?" She asks.

"Hi, Emily," —a kiss— I slept well. The therapy left me tired, but look, I can move my hand now. I think I will be able to go back to the shop in few weeks. By the way, I haven't seen Manuel. Did he go back to Texas or is he working in the shop?"

She unpacks the food, takes a spoon, and starts feeding me. "Manuel is in the shop. He's been working like crazy. You can't imagine how many guitars have been ordered since we came back from Denmark. These have been the worst months of my life: you fell head first, lost consciousness, then a tumor in your brain, then the eight-hour operation, then the coma. I didn't know what to do with all that together. But then Kwame called me one morning, here at the hospital. Since then, things have been easier. He helped me a lot in making decisions.

She gives me the last bite of bread and opens a yogurt cup she brought from home. "Then," she continues, "we started to receive orders for new guitars from all over the world. We have gotten at least five, and sometimes ten orders per week while you were here. Manuel decided to take all the orders, promising delivery dates that were impossible to hold. Kwame offered to help in that matter too, and so they both have been building guitars together for a while now. They'll fill you in on the details later, tomorrow actually. They are planning to come tomorrow morning. They will tell you what big changes they have made."

I am so filled of gratitude. Where else could I find such good friends and family? When life gives setbacks one recognizes who the real friends are. "How about Frederik Jacobsen? Does he know I am here?"

"Kwame called him and his sister the very next day of your accident. They both flew to be here with you during the brain operation. They had to go back to Denmark after that, though."

"I see. What a shame for me."

"Don't say that, honey. It's not your fault."

A nurse appears in the room and begins taking readings from the equipment. "Mr. McBride, I am glad you are improving so fast. You are talking as if you never had any problem," she says.

"Honey," Emily says, "I have to go now. Christina has a tennis game in an hour."

"Emily, how are the kids? What did I miss? What do they say of all this?"

"The doctor said that such questions are not good for your recovery; that we should wait until you are home to go over what happened in you absence." She passes her hand on my cheek, kisses me, and say good bye.

Next day on the morning, Kwame and Manuel

Next day on the morning, Kwame and Manuel show up in my room. They look tired, but happy. "Hi guys, I missed you for weeks!" I joke.

They both smile and give me a hug, too. "I am glad to see you talking," Kwame says. "You scared us so much."

"Yes," Manuel seconds, "we thought you would never come back from the coma."

"I heard you are both working on the shop. Is that true?" and I turn my glance to the old man and ask, "Is it really true, Kwame?"

"You bet," Kwame replies, "I couldn't stay home keeping my regular routine, with so much going on in your life, in Emily's life, and in the shop. So, one day I called Manuel and showed up to work, like a good employee."

"That is not fair," Manuel complains. "Kwame has done more than that. The week after your accident, he came to the shop, learned the wood cuts, the French polishing, the heat bending, and then, without my approval by the way, but with my trust, he hired two more apprentices. He also computerized the operation in such a way that we increased our output by five times compared to when we were only two in the shop."

I look Kwame in the eye, "Thank you Kwame, thank you. How can I pay you for this?"

"And that is not all," Manuel continues, "We are now using all his optimization techniques for each guitar. We saved time and materials; our guitars have an improved sound that can't be better. We are consistently producing good guitars for each customer. We finally learned how to produce a lower cost guitar without sacrificing the performance and quality of it."

"Manuel, please don't exaggerate," Kwame interrupts. "You did your part too. You taught me how to make a guitar from scratch, and without that knowledge I would have failed to improve the process."

"You are two saviors, guys," I say. "You have changed my life for better, and you did it during my absence. How lucky I am."

The nurse comes in, as on each morning, to check that everything is all right. "Good morning, Mr. McBride. How are you today?" She reads the monitors, the temperature, the heart rate, the pressure, and after greeting Manuel and Kwame leaves the room.

"Okay, guys, what else did I miss? You, Manuel, have you met your girlfriend from the airport? What was her name?"

"Yes, we've met several times. Her name is Natalia."

"Oh, yes, I remember. How is it going? Any hope?" I ask.

He gets closer to my bed and says, "You won't believe what I am going to tell you. She moved in with me, and we are already talking about getting married."

"I can't believe you. I am glad to hear that," I reply. "You see! I told you. Don't discriminate against yourself."

He gets emotional and says, "We went to Boston to visit her parents. Her mother is from Spain, and boy, how good she cooks! She prepared a *paella* —seafood with rice— that ... well I couldn't stop eating plate after plate. Natalia had to tell me to stop. And her brother, her brother is an older guy, with—"

"But Manuel," I stop him, "what is important is not her family, or the pasta. Tell me, how is she? What does she want in life? Do you guys feel excited with each other? Forget about the carbonara, tell me the substance."

Kwame nods to me and joins the inquiry with, "Yes, I also want to know that."

"Well, she is sometimes a bit rebellious in her answers, but I guess it's because of her immaturity. She loves dancing, especially Spanish dances, something I like in her. She is a great listener and very concerned about children's issues, like abandoned and beaten children. She told me she wants to have one or two children, which is fine with me. When I told her my goals of building a big guitarmaking company, she supported me, and encouraged me to do it, and never stopped dreaming with me about it."

"It sounds good, Manuel. Marriage is a two way street. You give, and she gives, otherwise, it is doomed to fail. Let me ask you one more question. Does she seem a loyal, trustful person?

"Walker, you keep asking difficult questions and giving me advice."

He is right, but it's the way I am. I guess it is my 'giving phase' kicking in. "You are right, Manuel, but you can't deny I always do it for your well being. So, please, answer my question.

He walks around my bed, thinking about the answer, and responds, "I think she is very loyal to me. She has been very strict in our relationship when it comes to that subject. She wanted to be sure I wasn't married, or whether I had another girlfriend, even before we kissed for the first time. She told me that she would be loyal to me as long as I would be the same to her. Fairness is very high on her list of principles."

"Just remember this, Manuel," I say, "We are like mirrors that reflect feelings. If you give love, you'll receive love. If you give dishonesty, you'll receive dishonesty too. It seems to me, from what you just said, that she understands this very well, and I am glad you found a thoughtful, pretty and good hearted woman."

"Thank you, Walker," Manuel says with a gesture of gratitude in his face, but also of boredom caused by my continuing advice.

"Also, remember this: problems will come, some day, sooner or later. When that happens, keep in mind that all of them are at the interface between you and her. Put yourself in her shoes, with compassion and understanding and you'll find the solution."

Kwame, looking at the bored face of Manuel, interrupts: "Well, I think we need to go to the shop. We have thirty-two guitars waiting for us to be finished."

"Thirty-two!?" I loudly say.

"Yes, thirty-two," Manuel replies, "and this is only a third of what we have made already in the last three months."

"I've got to leave this hospital as soon as possible. I can't stay here while you both break your backs for me." They smile, and leave the room soon after.

The doctor comes to make his daily visit. "Well, Walker, I have good news today. I signed the papers to let you go home.

"Yes! Thank you Doctor. I need to work in my shop as soon as possible."

"Not so fast, Walker. You'll need to visit a physical therapist to gain mobility in your right side. It will take you several months to fully recover from this, but your chances are high, don't lose hope. If you follow the therapist's instructions, I am positive you will walk again."

"Doctor, I have a family to maintain, and a couple of friends who I am in debt to. You can count on me. I'll be walking soon."

"Good luck, Walker."

44

Will

E, EMILY AND I, LEFT THE HOSPITAL a
few minutes ago, very early on this Saturday
morning. It is the end of Fall; front porches of the neighborhood
still have Halloween decorations. When we arrive home, a beautiful
Cardinal flies over the house and lands on top of the flag pole. I've
seen this Cardinal before, but this time I won't let it forecast my
misfortune again. Kwame and Manuel are at the porch waiting
for me. Emily helps me to get out of the car, and into the wheel
chair. I get closer to the steps, try to stand up, but realizing how
weak I am, I decide to stay seated. Manuel and Kwame help to
carry the wheelchair inside the house, a difficult task with my two
hundred pounds of weight. I feel embarrassed for not being able
to do things by myself. The kids are jumping and applauding as I
enter the house. Emily prepared a special room for me on the first
floor of the house, so I don't have to use the stairs. The therapist is
already in the room, waiting for the first session, as I asked Emily

to arrange. I suspect this is going to be a hard long recovery journey for me.

As I enter the room, I see a special bed that can flex the back, the front, and the middle sections. I see the ropes hanging from the ceiling, to help me stand up by myself.

The therapist, a woman of strong build, is quiet but attentive to my moves. "I am Elaine Williams, your therapist. Let me help you to climb on your new bed." She is a woman with a happy smile and delicate manners. Her accent is sort of different, though.

"Thank you," I say as I try to get into position. Everybody is looking at me like if I am an extraterrestrial. "Okay guys, you can leave the room now. I want the therapy to start right away," I say.

Elaine covers her hair with a special hat, and starts a preliminary assessment of my condition. She asks me to stand, to bend, to walk forward and backward, all of that with her help, since I am still unable to stand up by myself. We spend quite some time on this evaluation, until she asks me to rest back on the bed again. She rubs her hands with a red cream, and begins her massages. She takes my right arm, and massages all its muscles, with strength and determination, almost compassionless.

"Where are you from?" I ask.

"I am from Germany. I came five years ago to visit a friend, fell in love with a man thirteen years older than me, I married him, and here I am, living in Michigan since then."

She pulls my right arm up, holds it for about a minute, and then releases it with care. Then she grabs a one pound weight and asks me to lift it and hold it high. This is hard. I can't lift it as high as she wants me to.

"Okay, that is enough," she says. "Let's do it this way instead." She holds my arm, and helps me to push the weight up. "Better, much better," she says.

I am getting tired already, but she keeps working on me. "How is it to be married to a person thirteen years your senior?"

"Well, I was thirty-three when I met him. He was such a good lover, physically strong and mentally active. You know, I look for just that, energy and ideas. You know what I mean by energy, do you. If a man gives me these two things, I can take care of the rest by myself. Besides, he had such charm and passion that I couldn't resist. Age difference is not a problem in our relationship. Actually, I never think about it."

I sense the clarity in her objectives. "What is the problem then?"

"I didn't say we had a problem."

"But the first thing you said was that he is thirteen years older than you. So, you *do* think about it.

"Well, I said it because you are about his age, not because it bothers me. We keep a humorous relationship, with care for each other, attention to our children and looking forward for our retirement, aging together. I am a happy woman, with a happy family, sir."

I noticed her happiness where I entered the room. Humor is clearly an important aspect of a relationship.

She gives me a tennis ball, and makes me squeeze it as hard as I can. I do it once, twice, but no more. My right hand is weak, very weak. She grabs my left arm, and asks gently, "Were you born like this?"

This is a woman with straight questions. I've never been asked that way. "No, it was an accident, a car accident."

"I see. Well, I think we are done for today. The first day is the longest because I have to do an assessment of your mobility and strength, but the rest of the sessions will be quicker, just exercises. I'll be back tomorrow at the same time. It was nice to meet you Mr. McBride."

I rest for a little while before calling Emily and the kids. I am desperate to share time with them.

Gabriel comes running from the backyard. "What does she do to you, dad?"

"She helps me to get better faster. My right arm and leg are not responding well, so she helps me with that," I respond.

"Does it hurt?" Christina asks.

"I little, but when you know that the pain is for a good cause, you take it."

Manuel and Kwame enter the room as well. "How is she?" Kwame asks.

"Very good, I think. I have to wait some weeks to have a more definite opinion."

Manuel approaches me and shows me one of the latest guitars they have made. "Look at this, Walker. I called it the Sigüenza model. What do you think?"

It is a gorgeous guitar, sleek, romantic, finely made. "I like it very much," I say while I feel the shape with my hand. "Play it for me, please."

As he plays it, I get comfortable in the bed, and fall asleep without realizing it.

I have undergone four weeks of therapy by now, but I can't lift my right arm fully, yet. It is 3:00 AM and all are sleeping upstairs while I am trying to get some rest. This illness has deprived me of a good sleep for a long time. I've got to do something to get better, quicker. This therapy is not working fast enough for me. I turn around, grab the crutches and try to stand up. Oh, this hurts so much. I put one crutch down and one foot down, then the other crutch and the other foot. I lift myself from the bed, and try to keep balance for a moment, but then I fall back on the bed. The night is cold and the floor is also cold. I take a big breath and try again. This time I focus my mind on my muscles and I am able to stay straight, with more balance than before. I do one step at a time, dragging my right foot a little, and get to the door that goes to the basement. I haven't been in my basement in months.

I have to release my right hand from the crutch to open the door. This is almost like a circus trick for me. I hold the crutch with my arm pit, and stretch my arm to open the door. It works. I open the door wide, and count the steps before going down. There are thirteen steps. They look like thirteen thousand to me. I rest the crutches on the first step, and swing myself forward to jump to it. It works! I am on the second step now. I keep doing the same, step by step, and after ten minutes, with a couple of rest periods, I get to the basement floor, still standing, without a single fall.

It is even colder here, but the effort has heated me up, so I feel okay. I take a seat and breathe the smell of the wood. This is so nice. I then grab a guitar and start working on it. I must do this if I want my hand to work again. I take the sandpaper, and rub the guitar as hard as I can, back and forth, back and forth. I start sweating so much that my shirt soaks through, but I keep sanding faster and faster.

This is working fine for my hand, but my right foot is not having enough exercise yet. What should I do? I look around, and see Gabriel's soccer ball in a corner near me. I stretch my right foot, so much that I almost fall from the chair. I get to the ball, roll it to me, and start shooting it against the wall, one, two, three times. After some time, I stop because my leg is too tired.

I keep polishing the guitar, now with another new and finer paper. I look at the window, and notice that the sun is starting to shine. I prepare myself to go upstairs, because I don't want Emily to find out that I am here working in the basement again.

Coming down was difficult, but going up seems easy now as I feel stronger and more skillful. When I get to the room, the clock marks 6:15 AM, a good time to go to sleep. I get on the bed, put the crutches on the side, and rest my head on the pillow. I feel really tired but strong at the same time. I close my eyes for a moment, but after a short while I feel the warm hands of Emily touching my forehead. I keep my eyes closed, faking being asleep.

"I know you are not sleeping, young man," she whispers to my ear.

I smile and grab her by her waist. She kisses me with such passion, that everything in me is elevated. I caress her breast, and her pupils start dilating like flowers in Spring. We haven't been together in a long, long while and we can't contain our eagerness. She touches me where only she knows I like it most, and I do the same to her. She undresses me, slowly and sensually, touching and kissing every inch on my body. I can't resist it much longer. I try to open the buttons of her blouse, but I can't do it quick enough.

She does it herself, and goes on top of me with a calm smile that tells me how much she wants to do it too. No words come out of our mouths for the next fifteen minutes, only chuckles, giggles and sounds of pleasure are heard. At the end, when all the love has been expressed with our bodies, after all the staring glances that tell millions of words per second, after all sweat that passes from one body to the other, after the caresses that arouse each hair in our beings, she dresses me, and dresses herself gently which I adore watching her doing. She leaves the room, and I go to sleep before it is time for the therapist.

Two hours later, Elaine arrives. "Good morning Mr. McBride. How are you today?"

"I am fine, thank you. Let me show you something, Elaine." I grab the six pound weight, and lift it to the highest point.

She looks surprised and happy as well. "How can this be? Yesterday you couldn't lift two pounds, and today ..."

"You are right. Miracles happen, Elaine," I interrupt.

"But what did you do?" She insists.

"Simple, Elaine," I reply. "It is the will to improve, to be better, to be useful in life, and the will to love and be loved.

She smiles, shakes her head and says, "I think I know what happened to you last night, but I won't tell." As she starts the therapy, she asks, "What are your plans once the therapy is over, Mr. McBride?"

"Plans? Oh, that's a very good question, Elaine. You know, there is only one life, and I don't believe in life after death. So, my plans are easier now. You see, one day you are watching your daughter playing tennis, and the next day you are in coma for weeks and weeks, with no senses, no thoughts, flirting with death. That was the biggest experience of my life. I have learned how to face life now. I plan for the future, but live each minute as if life were going to end tomorrow. That gives me the urgency and the enthusiasm of today, plus the focus and hope for the future."

"I don't like that," she complains. "You are telling me that we should live the moment and forget the rest?"

"No, it is not like that," I insist. "I meant we live for the moment to enjoy the music from the masters and the birds; to smell the flowers from our gardens and the perfume from our lovers; to watch the color of the rainbow and the sunset on the beach; to enjoy the taste of good meals and good wines; and to experience the caresses of our lovers and the hugs of our children. *But besides,* we also need to plan for a future where you may not be present, and where your descendants will live their present as you are doing today. It is that hypothetical future that we must take care of today. The future of a better life for those who will come after us where justice and fairness, honesty and equality prevail in order to get closer to the happiness that we all dream of."

She stays quiet and nods with her big eyes. When she finishes the therapy, after the regular half hour workout, I walk with her to the front door, without using the crutches. I extend my arm, shake her hand, and say goodbye.

She looks at me, meets my eyes, firmly, happy, and says, "Your spirit has recovered already. I am happy to see a complete man in you again, Mr. McBride."

"Thank you, Elaine."

45

The Final Plan

HAVE BEEN GOING TO THE BASEMENT to work on my guitars and also to kick the soccer ball against the wall for about a month now. This is still a secret for everybody in the family, but this has been the best remedy of all. My right arm is as strong as Hercules', and my right leg can kick the soccer ball better than Pelé. There is no substitution for perseverance and discipline to overcome tragedy in life. We all can succeed with the right motivation, the right goals, and much discipline.

The door bell rings. It must be Kwame. He is coming to take me to the shop for the first time since my accident. It's going to be a weird feeling to see a bigger factory producing so many guitars each day. I open the door. "Kwame! What a great day is today, isn't it."

"Yes, indeed. This is going to be an eye opener for you," he says.

We get into his car, and as we pull out of the drive way, I see a dead Cardinal on the pavement. I smirk at it as we leave the house, with a conquering feeling that only I understand. Five minutes later we arrive at the shop. The sign with the name of the shop has been changed to a more modern one. It's a solid black granite rock with the shape of a guitar with the name of the company carved in it, *The Professional Guitarist Shop*. It looks impressive to me. As we enter the main door, which now is made of a beautiful dark oak, I get a huge reception with applause from the workers. There are at least fifteen, working in different stations, like in a mass production car assembly line. I can see Kwame's influence in all this.

"Here it is, Walker. Few people can be so proud of their own success as you," Kwame says.

"Please Kwame," I reply, "all these was in my absence. You did it all."

"That is partially true," he insists, "because your fame helped to find investors to revamp this factory. Without that, we would still have the same two-man guitar shop you had before. Now, enjoy it. You can do whatever you want to, now."

What do I do with this? It's more than I ever dreamed of having. It is a challenge, but a pleasure as well. Manuel approaches us and takes us to my office. I can't believe what they did with the office too. It has all brand new furniture, new ceiling, new carpet, a computer on my desk, and professional photographs of famous guitarists hanging on the walls. This looks like a lawyer's office.

"But, how much did you spend on this? Who paid for this?" I ask.

"Your friends from Denmark and I," Kwame interrupts, "thought that you deserved to have a better factory because your talent was not being utilized to the maximum with the small shop you used to have. So, when Frederik and Laura came during your brain operation, we sat together and came up with this idea of an international caliber guitar shop."

"But how can I repay all this? How much are we talking about?"

Manuel, who is listening carefully to our conversation, looks at me, smiles and says, "I was also concerned about it, until we got the big one."

"What big one? What are you talking about?" I ask.

They look at each other, ask me to sit down, and then they sit too. Manuel can't contain himself and says, "Three days ago I took a phone call, here in this same office. It was from Spain. It was from the Dominguez's guitar factory.

"And ..."

"It was the president of the company calling. He wanted to talk to you."

"What did you say?"

"I said you were coming back in a week, but that I could handle any business. Then he told me the good news."

"Which was..."

"They want us to be a division of their company," he replies. They want to double our production because they have enough clients to sell our guitars around the world. They have the largest network of retailers, from Asia to Europe to America that can absorb up to three times our production."

And then Manuel stands up and says aloud, "We hit the jack pot Walker, we did it!"

I can't believe this news. I am very surprised with the renovation of the shop, but this deal with Dominguez is almost a fantasy. I put my hand on my head, and think, think. What can we do with all this money that is coming? What can we do?

Kwame smiles and says, "I know what you are thinking, my friend."

"I know you know. I could do so much," I reply.

We've been sitting in the office for about an hour, figuring out how much cash we can generate each month if the promise from Dominguez's president is certain. Kwame just finished his calculations and says, "According to my numbers, for the first three months we'll make no profit at all. We'll have to pay the debt for the renovation, but after that we will be able to grow from zero profit to a level equivalent to the price of a house like yours, Walker, each month."

"That is a lot!" Manuel says with surprise.

"This is great, guys," I say. "I am in debt to both of you for ever. Well then, let's do what I think we should do with all this money. Manuel, what is your take on this?"

"Whatever you say, Walker."

"How about you, Kwame."

"Your are in charge, Walker. I am with you."

I learned when I was a young adolescent that the best gifts were the ones that I gave to my sister and friends, rather than the ones I received from them. I still want to feel that joy of giving what I have in surplus. It can be knowledge, money, love, or simply company, but there is nothing like seeing the face of that person telling you 'thank you' with real sincerity that comes deep from the heart. I feel blessed with this group of friends and with my family who believed in me, even when I was almost dead in a hospital bed. I cannot come and take it all for my own benefit alone. I need to give back, as Father Mauricio said.

"Okay, let's do it. We'll transform this company to create three branches. The educational branch, where people will learn how to make guitars using Kwame's methods of design. The guitarmaking branch, where we will make the guitars for Dominguez and all other clients. And the charity branch that will use our surplus for good causes. We'll work under a new motto: *Learn, Grow and Give Back.*

Kwame smiles, takes his glasses off, and says, "Well said."

I grab the phone, and make the call to Dominguez headquarters. I ask to talk to the president directly and we arrange a meeting for next July in their headquarters. The deal is a reality.

46

Problem Solved

I is July 17, the middle of a very hot summer, and the airport is crowded, noisy and humid as never before. My flight to Spain is delayed for two hours. I am glad I decided to keep this book in my carry-on luggage, so I can read it while I wait. This time, however, it's not a book about guitarmaking. It's the new book of my good friend, Kwame. He chose a good title for it. It was my suggestion: "All Design Problems Are at the Interface; Methods of Optimization Solve Them All."

—The End—

Acknowledgment

I want to express my gratitude to the people that helped in the realization of this novel.

Special thanks to Diego and Daniel who inspired me in every dimension of my life and helped me in many occasions correcting the manuscript. This book is for you and your children.

Thanks to Nazaret for all the time we could have been together, but that I decided to spend in front of the computer preparing the manuscript. Thank you for your patience and love.

Thanks to Michele Simms-Burton who did a fine editing job at the beginning of this endeavor.

Thanks to my friend Niel who read the first full version of the manuscript and provided so much advice and corrections. You were a great help.

Thanks to my good friends John and Marlene who not only read and corrected my mistakes, but also inspired me in several chapters of the novel with the way you conduct your life.

Thanks to my parents Wilmer and Hilda who taught me their values and principles, something that I will keep forever in my heart.